PRAISE FOR

Little Fish

WINNER, Amazon Canada First Novel Award

WINNER, Lambda Literary Award

WINNER, Firecracker Award for Fiction

Shortlisted for the Carol Shields Winnipeg Book Award

***A Globe and Mail* Best Book of the Year**

"*Little Fish* is a powerful and important debut. Plett has masterfully painted her characters as both deeply complex and relatable."

—*National Post*

"*Little Fish* is ultimately not about the past but about the present—and looking forward to trans futures ... A friend recently told me that one of the things she appreciates about Plett's work is how she so clearly writes for trans women. But the novel also deserves a wide audience. Every reader can get this part: being a trans woman is exhausting."

—*The Globe and Mail*

While [Plett] acknowledges the absolute uniqueness of individual experience, she also honours a loosely held trans culture, a shared palette of pain and loss, and a collective heroism (though the author herself might be reticent to call it that). For those of us outside this experience, we can only count ourselves lucky to have Plett's novel, a book that invites us to witness something so important, so complex, and so tender."

—*Quill and Quire* (starred review)

Little Fish

CASEY PLETT

ARSENAL PULP PRESS
VANCOUVER

LITTLE FISH

THIRD PRINTING: 2019

ARSENAL PULP PRESS
Suite 202 – 211 East Georgia St.
Vancouver, BC V6A 1Z6
Canada
arsenalpulp.com

The publisher gratefully acknowledges the support of the Canada Council for the Arts and the British Columbia Arts Council for its publishing program, and the Government of Canada, and the Government of British Columbia (through the Book Publishing Tax Credit Program), for its publishing activities.

Arsenal Pulp Press acknowledges the xʷməθkʷəy̓əm (Musqueam), Sḵwx̱wú7mesh (Squamish), and səl̓ilwətaʔɬ (Tsleil-Waututh) Nations, speakers of Hul'q'umi'num'/Halq'eméylem/hən̓q̓əmin̓əm̓ and custodians of the traditional, ancestral, and unceded territories where our office is located. We pay respect to their histories, traditions, and continuous living cultures and commit to accountability, respectful relations, and friendship.

This is a work of fiction. Any resemblance of characters to persons either living or deceased is purely coincidental.

Chapter 1 of this book previously appeared in a slightly modified form in *Plenitude*.

Cover and text design by Oliver McPartlin
Cover illustration by Sybil Lamb
Edited by Susan Safyan

Printed and bound in Canada

Library and Archives Canada Cataloguing in Publication:
Plett, Casey, author
Little fish / Casey Plett.
Issued in print and electronic formats.
ISBN 978-1-55152-720-8 (softcover).—ISBN 978-1-55152-721-5 (HTML)
I. Title.
PS8631.L48L58 2018 C813'.6 C2017-907216-1
C2017-907217-X

For Doug (who else)

Praying was much like doing housework: it was too easy to think that nothing had been accomplished unless you kept a record. And like housework, where you repeated the same chores over and over, you had to keep praying for the same things over and over.

—Sandra Birdsell, *The Missing Child*

I don't think anyone really knows how they look.

—Lexi Sanfino

November

0

The night before her Oma died, Wendy was in a booth at the bar with Lila, Raina, and Sophie. It was eleven p.m., and they were all tipsy. Sophie was saying, "Age is completely different for trans people. The way we talk about age is not how cis people talk about age."

"You mean that thing," said Wendy, "where our age is also how long we've been out or on hormones or whatever?"

"Or do you mean that thing," said Lila, "where we don't age as much. Because we die sooner."

"Both those things, yes!" Sophie said. "But there's more! There's much more. Think of how hormones preserve you. Look—we could all pass for twenty-one if we wanted to. Fuck, I met a lady in New York who was *sixty* and been on hormones for decades; I swear she barely looks older than us. One sec," she said as she flagged down the waitress and they all ordered another.

"For the guys too, hey?" said Lila. "My boyfriend gets carded all the time ... He's thirty-four, man. *I'm* younger than him."

"Exactly," said Sophie. "And yet not just that!"

"Are you giving us the latest from Twitter, Sophie?" said Raina.

"Fuck off," Sophie snorted into her empty bottle. Wendy couldn't tell if she'd laughed or was actually upset.

"You are kinda our link to the Trans Girl Internet," said Wendy.

Sophie made an exasperated *aachh* sound. "This is something I've thought of for a while. Can I go on? Is that okay with you?"

"Apologies," said Raina. "Please."

"Okay," she went on. "I don't just mean the difference in how long trans people live. And I don't just mean in the sense that we have two kinds of age.

But the difference with transsexual age is what can be expected from you. Cis people have so many benchmarks for a good life that go by age."

"You're talking about the wife, the kids, the dog," Wendy said.

"More than that. And also yes, that. It didn't stop being important," said Sophie. "Cis people always have timelines. I mean, I know not every cis person has that life, but—what are the cis people in my life doing? What are they doing in your life? Versus what the trans people in your life are doing? On a macro level. Ask yourself that."

"Is that just cis people or is it straight people?" said Lila.

"Yeah, maybe," said Sophie. "I just mean: How mainstream society conceives of age doesn't apply to us. I swear it doesn't."

The waitress came back with the round. "Thanks, ladies," she said.

"I wonder if cis people think about their past in the same way we do," Raina said suddenly.

"How do we think about our past?" said Wendy.

And Raina said, "Hmm."

"Well," said Sophie, "if you want news from the Trans Girl Internet—" but then another waitress dropped a tray and some jokers in the bar cheered and Wendy got up to pee anyway and sat sipping from a mickey of whiskey in the bathroom, calmly thinking.

1

The night Wendy's Oma died, she had sex dreams. Only sometimes did she have sex dreams—usually Wendy had nightmares, and usually she was being chased or hurt. But this morning in her dreams, when her grandmother died, a girl was fucking her over an old television in an abandoned gym. She woke up with her phone dinging. Her dad. *Call me when you get up it's important.*

Wendy put her face back in the pillow with her hair piled around her like a hill. She trailed a long arm down the side of the bed and skittered her phone across the floor. Her bladder was pulsing; sunlight through a crack in the curtain hurt her eyes. She was still drunk, and every part of her hurt.

Wendy lay there curled into herself in the half-light, her head softly beating, not sleeping. She lay like that for a full hour. Her pee swelled, and the light grew brighter.

When the phone rang, she made her body get up and scrabble for her phone. It was her father.

"Jesus shitstick Dad, what," Wendy said. Her voice was deep and raspy, a smoker's voice though she rarely smoked anymore. Her words felt as chunky in her mouth as a potato. She was still drunk. She'd feel fuzz behind her eyes the whole day.

Her dad was crying.

"Ben?" said Wendy, putting a hand to her mottled face, ruddy-cheeked and pale.

"Ben? Dad?" It was chilly and the first snows were sticking. She tied up the curtain and shut the window to let light and warmth into her room. Her legs were shivering.

The funeral was quiet and simple, at the EMC Church out in the country. Wendy wore a simple black dress. She cried exactly once, during a hymn, silently and horribly, like a little girl told to shut up. But for the rest of the day she felt warm and blessed. She felt a lot of love for her grandmother. She felt grateful she'd had so much time with her Oma. She felt grateful her Oma'd been given a long life. In that way, Wendy had a beautiful, strange synergy with all the old Mennonites in the room, the ones who ignored Wendy or spoke to her in microseconds and hushes. The ones who truly believed the old woman was in heaven. They and Wendy both were sad that she was gone. But they were happy to think about her too.

That's the difference, Wendy thought, between her grandma and everybody else who'd died.

She turned away when she saw people she didn't want to recognize her. It was stupid. It would be hard to mistake her around here—her hair was black and went down to her waist, and she was tall by anyone's standard.

And what, what was the point in fighting? Sacrifice wasn't meaningless. It'd been eight years since she said to them, "I'm a girl," and some things you couldn't fight that long. She was angry about it, but she didn't start anymore. She did not appear in the obituary or funeral program, and her dad had warned her about it ("It's out of my hands, I'm sorry") and it pissed her off, but she didn't say a word. Her family had gotten kinder over the years. It wasn't that hard.

Back at her Oma's house, neighbours brought hot dishes and a Superstore bag of buns, then left. Her aunts began to prepare the table. Wendy came into the room with a beer, looming over them like a tree.

"Can I help with anything?"

"Oh, well, thank you, Wendy, but we're very set here! You just go ahead and enjoy yourself. You go visit."

Wendy sat and drank her beer in the living room as her uncles and cousins played on their phones.

She listened to her aunts gossip about their kids, about their kids' sports teams. One of them fetched her daughter to run to the van. When they ate, nobody cried. It was like a normal family gathering and no one was crying and did Wendy care every time she heard the cut-off first syllable of her old name and sudden third-person *he*s and *his*es? It used to be worse. It didn't matter. Her grandma was dead.

Long after everyone else went to bed, Wendy was on the back porch staying up with the men.

"You remember how Mum would pack us homemade tomato juice?" yelled her dad.

"Oh! *Najo.*"

"Hahahahaha." He was blitzed. "Complete with fuckin' tomaaaaato *chunks!* You'd be trying to be all fuckin' cool for some girl and take a swig and your whole mind's on how you're ever gonna get your hand up her shirt SPLOOSH," and Wendy and her uncles all laughed and drank and laughed.

There were cigars. Wendy smoked one. She enjoyed the rich ugliness of cigars. Someone took a picture that she later loved and put on her wall, back in the city: She's sitting dazed and drunk on the bench next to her dad, cigar in her mouth, her hair streaming down her sides like onyx waterfalls and light snow coming down, American postcard-style snow. Ben was laughing and leaning back with his mouth tilted against the sky, grey hair flowing to the ground.

"There's probably tomato juice still in there."

"Is anybody else frightened to look in the fridge."

"Need the morgue more for the fridge than we did for her."

"*Najo.*"

"Jesus Christ," Ben said. "So when Wendy's mum—God rest her soul—when she first ever came to the house. She's this big city girl from university, right. Here at our fuckin' backwater-ass—"

"—and you're still trying to get your hand up her shirt."

"Probably on this bench."

Wendy laughed and hacked something up.

"You okay, girl?" said Ben.

Wendy coughed. "I'm fuckin' grand." She loved hearing stories about her mom. She had no memories of her.

"So here she is," he continued. "This smart and sophisticated city girl, she thinks she's coming to the farm for some hearty country meal, right? And Mom comes out with a big fuckin' vat of soup, *slams* it down, and there's a fuckin' *chicken leg* sticking right out of it!"

"Chicken's probably still there too."

"Your mother said grace on that one, God bless her."

Wendy hadn't brought her winter coat. She was so sleepy, and almost went in to bed, but instead got a blanket and wrapped it over herself and sipped her dad's vodka and listened. Wendy liked being quiet around her family. And being quiet wasn't usual for her. It was nice. She didn't remember going inside.

Two mornings later in her dreams, Wendy was being chased down a long hallway with carpet. And white wallpaper with the patterns of cherries and locked wooden doors. Her hair was short in this dream. She was running fast, but they were faster.

When she woke, it was morning but not daylight. Her long muscles creaked and uncreased as she stood up from the living room fold-out in her nightgown, lacy and shimmering and moon-blue.

She went to start the coffee and stood by the kitchen window where outside, slivers of purple were breaking through the dark. The coffee burbled, and rays of orange and magenta and violet spread out over the snow. Everyone else was gone, and Wendy and Ben were going back today. It was always sad leaving here. And how many more times would she be coming back now. Realistically.

"Dad."

"Yeah."

"When are we leaving?"

"I thought we'd head out at one."

"You're kidding me! That's so early."

"I know, I got this guy to meet."

"Whatever. It's fine."

"Good."

"Who do you—"

"*Ssssh sssh ssssh*—this part's important!"

They were watching cartoons. Wendy rolled her eyes and got up for more cereal; her grandparents' old house was the kind of space it was hard not to eat in.

Then, in the kitchen, the phone on the wall rang.

"Hello?" Wendy said into the receiver.

"Hello!" The voice was unfamiliar and female and old. "Aganetha?"

"Aganetha?" said Wendy, confused at first. "No, there's no Aga—." Wendy put her hand on her forehead. "I'm sorry," she said. "No, this isn't her. We called her Nettie. I'm so sorry. She's dead."

Silence.

"Five days ago. It was sudden," she added.

More silence, then the woman said, "Oh my word." A long time passed, then she added, "My condolences. I knew. She had not. Been well." Wendy thought the woman might be crying, but then she said, in a heavier tone, "She's with the Lord now."

"Yes."

"No one told me."

"I'm sorry," Wendy said genuinely. "I—I am. Someone should have."

"Am I speaking to family?" said the woman.

"Yes."

"And who am I speaking to?"

Wendy's reflexes kicked in. "I'm more like a close friend. Friend of the family." Her voice became higher, more melodious. "Would you like to speak to Ben? He's just over in the living room. I'll get him."

"No!" said the woman. "No. No, I don't think Ben—well." More silence. "Is someone else at home?"

"No."

"Ah." This puzzled Wendy. Most people calling on Nettie liked speaking to Ben. They got a bang out of him.

"May I ask who you are?" said Wendy.

"Anna C. Penner," the woman said. "From Morweena. Morweena, Manitoba."

Wendy waited for her to say more.

"That's north of Arborg," Anna continued. "In the Interlake."

"There are Mennonites up there?" Wendy said before she could stop herself.

"Oh, yup. Quite a few," said Anna. "Doesn't surprise me some people may not know that, but. Aganetha and I. We went to school together." The woman was clipping her individual words but her sentences were slow, rushing through some parts and leaving gaps of quiet in others. And the accent in her voice was coming out clearly now, the kind that paradoxically turned *school* into *skul* and Pepsi into *Pahpsi*. She continued: "I just called to—so, you're a friend of the family. Your name?"

"Wendy."

"Don't know of a Wendy," said Anna. Then she made a slight titter. "Oh! I suppose you're. Seeing Ben. Forgive me, I didn't mean—"

"Bless me!" Wendy said acidly. "You know, perhaps I would rather not have this conversation over the phone."

"Of, of course, forgive me, rude of me—well. I'll just tell you. I wanted to tell Aganetha something that concerns her husband. As well as her grandson. Ben's son. You know Ben's son."

Wendy was silent.

"You must," clipped Anna definitively. "Goes by Tulip now. Or some such name. To my understanding."

Tulip had been Wendy's first name for about a year.

"I know about Tulip," said Wendy. More silence then: "Anna, why are you calling?"

"Is another family member coming later in the day? One of Aganetha's sisters, I wonder I should speak with them."

"No!" Wendy said. Suddenly she was done with this conversation. "Look," she said, summoning up old codes, what'd pass with this woman for angry. "I do not mean to be rude. However, we are sorting out quite a lot right now. Our grandmother is dead and there is a house and there are—cats, and ... There is so much to do!" she concluded. "So, if you would like to tell me your business, I would be happy to assist you, but if not, perhaps you could simply send condolences, I am sure you know our address."

"You said you were a friend," Anna said quietly.

"*I'm a—*" she said loudly and cut herself off, but a surge of anger that'd stayed down in Wendy for days suddenly raged through her blood, like she'd breathed it in with the air. She clenched her fist and bit down on her knuckles—

"Who are you talking to?" Ben called.

Gently, she calmed herself and put her body back down on the ground. She was about to excuse herself and say goodbye and hang up when Anna said something in Low German she couldn't understand. Then she said, "You must have heard stories about Henry. Aganetha's husband."

"Yes." Her Opa had died when Wendy was nine. He had been a quiet, stable, and gentle man. The opposite of her dad. Wendy had loved him deeply. For a short time in Wendy's adolescence, his memory had provided her with the kind of man she'd hoped she might be.

"Yes," Wendy said. "I remember Henry very well." Then she shut her eyes. *Shit.* This was coming apart. *How's she supposed to not know me if—*

"He was like Ben's son. So there you go."

"*WHAT?*"

"So there you go!" repeated Anna, slightly more high-pitched. "And there are some letters and things. I thought she'd want to see. I ... sat on them for a long time. A long time. But lately I have been. Remembering things, Aganetha would say. About Henry many years ago. I realized ... perhaps it was not good to keep this secret. That's what I feel. The Lord was telling me. So I just decided that this morning and now I called and got you."

Wendy opened her mouth, and it was dry as plaster. She touched her fingers to her hair.

"But now she's gone. And I don't know who you are," Anna said rapidly, shakily. "I'm talking to a stranger. About all this. I better go—no, I'll ask a favour. I'll ask you to tell one of Aganetha's sisters. I assume they're still alive."

"Yes."

"Would you tell one of them what I told you, and ask them to telephone me? I'm going to trust in the Lord now that if you say yes, you will do it."

"Perhaps I can, indeed," Wendy said dumbly.

"Good," said Anna. "They can look me up in the phone book if they don't have the number. My address is right there too. They can come visit too, long as they call first."

"Okay."

More silence.

"I'm going to be going now," said Anna.

"Have a good day," Wendy said faintly.

"My condolences about Aganetha. I thought about her often. She is finally with the Lord. Hallelujah."

"Hallelujah."

So many Mennonites these days, it seemed to Wendy, were rich. The humble old desperate towns of Rudy Wiebe and Sandra Birdsell books were gone, or at least shrunk, or fast on their way to existing only in traces, photos, myth, and books, and in the bedrooms of old people. In their stead were McMansions and Liquor Marts and gourmet coffee shops. The Liquor Marts closed at ten, and the coffee shops at midnight. There were big boxes and subdivisions and construction for new high schools and stores that sold fireplaces. The high schools had raffle prizes that gave trips to Vegas. They were the fastest growing towns in the province. Most rural municipalities were bleeding people, but Hanover and Stanley and Rhineland and La Broquerie were growing in double-digits—it had been a long time since Wendy had talked, really talked, to someone like Anna at all.

And in the city. The ones in the city. Wendy worked at a gift store close to Polo Park, and every other wallet with five credit cards belonged to a Friesen or a Penner. They could spend seventy dollars on a scarf and ask if there was a charge for a plastic bag. They would buy books on mindfulness and Taoism. She would see Hutterites driving Hummers.

Wendy stood in her nightgown, ratty skids of hair down her back, holding the phone receiver. She heard the alarm-drone noise of it being off the hook. Ben came into the kitchen and refilled his bowl with cereal. He took the receiver from Wendy's hand and hung it up. "You miss that sound?"

"No!" she said, high-pitched and startled.

"What's going on? Who was that?"

"I—I—"

"Tell me," said Ben.

"Someone called about Opa," she said, the first thing that came to her mind.

"No way."

"Yeah," she said, returning to her normal rasp. "They were behind the times."

"Who was it?"

"I forget," she said.

The best lies always come to you as you're saying them, she'd been reflecting lately. It was planned untruths that didn't end well.

"Something Hildebrand," she added. "It wasn't important. The guy was an asshole—oh, *and* he kept asking me if I was a man or a woman. Wouldn't let it go."

"What a dickwad," said her dad.

"Whatever," she mumbled. "Is there more coffee?"

"No. Make more," Ben suggested. He poured his milk and went back into the living room.

Wendy's head was imploding. She made another pot and then went into her room and poured raspberry vodka into her coffee mug. She rarely drank in the mornings—but. Well.

Downstairs, in her grandmother's sewing room, there was a bookcase of photo albums labelled by year. Wendy put her hand on the earliest, 1961.

Pictures of her dad as a baby.

A lot with her dad and her Opa, wearing a grey shirt and huge owl glasses. *Cute.* Wendy'd always remembered her grandfather with bifocals.

An adorable picture of her dad on a stool, filling a cup with water.

Her grandpa in a field, wearing the same grey shirt.

She sat on the floor, sipping coffee and flipping through more pages. He was always wearing a variation of the same big grey men's shirt—*That fits, though*, she thought. *Wear the same outfit day after day, your brain gets numb to how it looks or feels*—Wendy shut the album. No. She hated going down that road. She hated analyzing the whys of trans girls. She had always hated it, and she hated how easy it had become; the bottomless hole of egg mode. It made her burn with anger, thinking of all that lost energy. You could do it forever, and she'd played that fuckin' game years ago when she'd needed to, but she knew where that led and she was done with that game. She'd had a boy life. It was shitty and murky. So her grandfather probably had too and just never got out. So her Opa'd been a woman. Fine. Closed. She would keep the memory of her two grandmothers in her heart and that'd be that. Whatever. She drank the rest of her coffee in a slug and put the photo album back in the bookcase. Good enough.

"Hey, we gotta go," said her dad. "Get your stuff." He refilled her coffee without asking.

She put an ice cube in her mug and opened the fridge and her dad closed it and said, "Go go go, we gotta move!"

"Jesus, relax!"

"We have to go!"

Wendy closed and opened her fists, letting anger flow out of her.

She packed her things and added more vodka to her coffee. She lifted her moon-blue nightgown over her head and put on a white T-shirt with black jeans and a pink belt. She washed off her crusted day-old eyeliner, put it back on and added wings.

She shouldered her purse and bag. Her dad was still packing.

Wendy looked out on the yard again, sunny and bright and clear. It hit her—this might be one of the last times she'd stay in this house.

Ben yelled to warm up the car. She went out and started the engine and put her shit in the back.

It really was nice out—no wind, serene, sheltered by the poplars on the side of the driveway that her Opa had planted decades ago.

Aw, hell.

She grabbed her bag, took off her boots, and ran inside. Her dad shouted something again.

"I'm coming, Christ!" She padded downstairs and put the album from 1961 in her bag. She hesitated, then picked another from the year her Opa had died and another from the early eighties.

⁂

They drove into town where an old pasty woman with a kerchief sold perogies and gravy out of her mini-van beside the Walmart.

"Twelve cottage cheese, frozen," said Ben.

"I'll have three, fresh," said Wendy.

The woman turned to pack their containers.

"I want a cigarette," Ben mumbled.

They drove back into the city. Her dad didn't speak. Wendy hadn't registered any emotion from him, that his mother had died. They had been on good terms—but he didn't seem any different. Wendy'd wanted to learn to make those perogies herself some day, but her dad had forgotten how. She'd meant to ask her grandma, but she was dead.

2

Back home, the snow was mush and dirt. Wendy dropped her bags on the bed.

She idly tapped her phone. She found herself typing on Facebook, "So maybe my grandfather was trans? Uh fucking what?" then deleted it.

She didn't want to look at the photo albums.

Her clothes were all dirty.

Crossing Portage and hip-checking the laundromat door open, she saw a new boy manning the desk. Hunched and stubbly with a grey V-necked shirt. Brown skin and thick black hair like the owners. Young and tall, unlike them. He smiled at her.

Wendy went to the washers and took off her coat. She wondered how she looked to him. Her hair was in a long ponytail that rose up and curved down her back. She thought about her hair bobbing up and down and the pink belt around her pants as she bent over the machine.

Sometimes Wendy tried to remember what she looked for in girls before transition. She could never summon anything clear. She could remember how boys talked about girls when they thought girls weren't around. She could replay, as if in third-person, those handfuls of penis-in-vagina sex. But never any inner thoughts or feelings. When she tried to zoom in on the emotions of those moments, they became diffracted, lost, in a way other memories didn't. Wendy remembered a lot about being a boy. But she couldn't remember that.

She thought again about her body from the back. She'd always felt like more of a girl, imagining her body from the back.

When she got quarters from the boy she said, "How's your afternoon?"

"Fine. I'm drunk."

She did a double-take. "Really?"

"Just kidding. But who can tell?" he said.

She laughed at that. Wendy had a deep, guttural, and unmistakably feminine laugh; it was something she actually loved about herself. She disliked her voice—low and unsexily raspy, passing like a female Tom Waits—but she liked her laugh. And it always showed. A smile tugged at the boy's cheeks.

"Can I help you?"

Wendy gave him a five. "Did you just start working here?"

"Yeah. My dad runs the place," he said. "But I go to school," he added quickly. "I'm a musician."

"Mmm. Well, I guess I should use these quarters."

"Give me a shout if you have trouble."

After loading the dryer, she came back.

"I'm not actually drunk," he said.

"I know. What's your name?"

"Taj."

"I'm Wendy."

"Nice name."

"I like it."

"Your mom or your dad pick that?"

"My dad," Wendy said instantly, though she'd never been asked that question before. "He had a teacher named Wendy? Who he liked? I think. It's funny—I don't actually know the whole story behind it."

A clear thing Wendy did remember from boy life: She'd been a terrible liar. *Maybe there is something to trans women being deceivers*, she thought.

She pulled a finger through her ponytail and sat back down. She watched Taj at his station, tapping his phone, washing rags, fixing a jammed machine. He didn't see Wendy watch him, and she knew it. He had that obliviousness of men that she envied, even missed. The permission of it, anyway.

After folding her clothes, she went back to him. "Still not drunk?" she said.

"It's a pretty hard job here."

"Would you like to be drunk? I live right around the corner. I have vodka."

She didn't know why she said things like this.

"Seriously?" he said.

"Sure. It'll be great."

He looked startled and turned to the clock. "I'm—I'm off in half an hour."

Wendy poured them drinks, then sat on her bed. "So, what did you do before you began your career in laundromancy?"

"I was a poker player."

"Really."

"Online poker. For, like, five years."

"You can make money doing that?"

"I did."

Eventually, he kissed her. That was nice. He kissed her hard, and he drew her close; his body felt electric. He smelled like lotion and soap. She could tell he was trying to be gentle as he touched her cheeks and the sides of her torso.

They were on their knees on the bed with their pants pressing into each other and she kissed him deeply as she took off his shirt and put her hand on his back. He took off her shirt and put his mouth on her tits and kind of sucked and licked them. She whispered, "Bite, for fuck's sake," and he did and she felt lightning. She dug her hands into his hair and pressed him hard into her chest and he bit harder and wrapped his legs and arms around her and they fell over on the bed. They kissed totally and furiously. She didn't see herself do any of this, like she had in the laundromat—she saw his shoulder blades and felt his skin; her body mapped the dip of his chest and the suppleness of his arms. She didn't see herself at all. He kissed her for a long, beautiful time.

Eventually, she ducked her head, and her hands went to his belt buckle. He shifted his torso to let her—then he went still.

Wendy looked up. His eyes widened and narrowed all at once. "Wait," he said.

She looked at him placidly, her heart drowning.

"Oh my God," he said. "Are you a man?"

"I am not a man."

"Like ..." he trailed off. "But you were. You were born a girl, right?"

"I'm not—" she cut herself off, about to yell.

"No?" he said quietly.

"No," she said, resigned.

Then he was standing, and his shirt was back on.

"Oh, come *on*!"

"Sorry," he said. "Sorry! I don't know how I feel about—I can't—Jesus Christ. I have to go."

⁂

He left and started down the stairs. Then he came back. "Give a man some warning next time!" he said. "You don't know what could happen! That's not smart! Jesus Christ!"

Wendy listened to him pull on his boots and coat and leave the house. Then she drank the rest of his vodka.

Was it bad she wasn't scared during any of this, she wondered. There was a time in her life she would've been.

She felt sad. And pissed off. But it also felt nice to think about pressing him into her chest. And the way he'd kissed and wrapped himself around her. Wendy lay on the bed, watching the room rotate, fixing that feeling of his body in her memory.

The clouds outside were swirling grey, like crystal balls. Everything was still and quiet. She lay there for a long time, putting off doing her laundry.

She heard the mailman *thunk* envelopes into their mailbox and crunch away in the snow. *Anna*, she thought.

Raina came home, and Wendy didn't tell her about the guy from the laundromat. She did tell her about her grandfather.

"That's a discovery," Raina said. "You must be somewhat shaken up."

"I am and I'm not."

"No?"

Wendy curtly shook her head. "What's the point? He was probably trans. It must have been terrible. What more is there?"

Raina nodded. "I see."

"And I can't tell my fuckin' dad," she added. "He couldn't handle it."

"Of course not." Raina opened cabinets and took out glasses. "The letters, though," she said. "Does that not intrigue you?"

"It does," said Wendy. "But that feels different. I don't know how I feel about it. That feels—"

"Like disrespecting the dead?" Raina's voice was calm.

"Maybe," Wendy said idly. "Have you eaten?"

"Yes. But I have not had a beer. Would you like a beer?"

"I *would* like a beer, thank you. And thanks for texting me at the funeral, I appreciated that."

"Of course," said Raina. "And your family was—okay?"

"Ah." Wendy flicked the beer open and poured. "They were fine. They all believe my Oma went to heaven, and she was old and didn't suffer. My family was the same as they always are. It's fine."

Raina nodded. "I understand."

Wendy picked at her hands and steadily emptied her glass.

They both sat in silence as flecks of foam dripped down Raina's sepia-coloured chin.

Then: "Are you going to call this woman?"

"I should," muttered Wendy. "Do I want to? Probably not. I don't think I want to talk about it anymore. How are you? How was work?"

"Hard," Raina said. "I had to go to the hospital and advocate for one of the women."

"Boyfriend?"

"Father."

"Motherfucker."

"Yes."

⁂

"I was going to watch some TV," said Raina.

"I'll join you."

They went up to the living room on the third floor, and Raina put on a British TV show that she loved. Wendy sank into a cushion on the couch and let the accents wash over her, blue light flickering on their bodies. Wendy finished another beer, then ran to the corner store for Fresca to pour into her vodka. Back upstairs, she heard frantic knocking on the back door of the downstairs unit. Eventually she looked through the window, but there was no one, only other buildings and the back lane, fresh with the first caked-on layer of ice and snow.

Their two cis roommates came home, said hello, and as usual, went into their rooms. Wendy settled back into the couch and drifted in and out, fog and words sailing by her, until eventually Raina laid a small, gentle hand on her shoulder and said, "Wendy, Wendy, I'm going to sleep, you should probably get to bed."

Down in her bedroom, falling onto her blankets, she was reaching for the light when she saw on her chair the bag for the hormones she'd picked up the week before. Lying open with the info pamphlet sticking out, the one she usually threw away. At the top: READ IF YOU HAVE NEVER TAKEN HORMONE REPLACEMENT THERAPY BEFORE. Some deceiver.

3

"Can I see the pictures?" asked Sophie.

Sophie paged through the first photo album as they sat on Wendy's bed.

"He was pretty," Sophie said.

"I liked his hair," said Wendy. Her Opa's hair had been soft, wavy, and black. Wendy swished her fingers back and forth over the sheets. The sun was almost down, and dark pink streamed into the room.

"My aunt's place was like this," Sophie said. "In Kleefeld. I liked it there."

"Mmm," Wendy said, her eyes closed. "Your whole family's EMC too, right?"

"My Mom is. God knows how many ways we're related."

"Six," Wendy said, not opening her eyes. "I'll guess six ways."

"Har har."

Sophie flipped through more of the album, her short dyed-red hair falling into her face.

"Will you call her?"

"I don't fuckin' know, man!" Wendy said. "Probably. Where do you even find a phone book anymore? The library?"

"Wouldn't it be online?"

They checked. Canada411 didn't know where Morweena was. They searched for any Anna Penners in Manitoba, but that didn't help either.

Wendy lay back on the bed. "Oh well."

"Someone in your family probably knows."

"Maybe."

They heard a knock on the door. "May I come in?" came Raina's voice.

"We're having butt sex!" Sophie hollered. Wendy rolled her eyes.

Raina opened the door wearing a chiffon blouse and a shiny purple skirt. Smooth foundation on her chin.

"Your butt sex is very tantric," she said. "I—I'm going on a date—do I look okay?"

"You look beautiful," said Sophie.

Wendy squinted. "Not one of your work outfits, is it?"

"I'd never wear this skirt to work. Does it look okay?"

"Shut up, you always look classy," said Wendy. "You and your—big-city-America powers."

"That's very kind," said Raina. "But yes, this lady and I have been messaging on OKCupid for some days now. I think I'm fond of her. We were both raised Catholic, which is a first for me. It *will* be unusual, though. It's been a while since I dated a cis lady."

"That's because you've dated every trans dyke in the province, honey," said Wendy.

"And a lengthy list that was," Raina said dryly. Sophie laughed. Raina smiled mischievously. "Hm. Never would've thought of myself that way."

"Have fun, sweets," said Wendy. "Text us if you need rescuing."

"Doubtful," said Raina. "Thank you, though."

"Tell us what the cis are like!" said Sophie. "What do they want?" Raina gave a short bark and went out the door.

Raina was the only one of Wendy's friends from out-of-province, and had grown up in a Puerto Rican family that moved all over the States. She'd gone to York and tunnelled through social work school and married a Toronto girl young. Then she transitioned, and one day came home to find that the

Toronto girl had neatly packed Raina's things in boxes. The first job she could find elsewhere was here.

Wendy changed into pyjama pants and threaded out of her bra, her boobs poking through the camisole like flaccid balloons.

Sophie shut the album, and a side of her hair flicked up in a poof. "So why don't you want to call her?"

"Is there a point?" said Wendy. "Look, *you* know. He was probably a girl; it probably sucked. I'll bet a million fuckin' Mennonites were trans. They probably all killed themselves or they lived stoically and added it to their triumphant burdens to bear for God. Maybe it wasn't even that bad in that light, who knows."

She lifted her drink to her lips, and the ice clinked. "Anna probably thinks he went to hell, anyway. Like, what's the point?"

"But Wendy! What about the lost history of the Blumenort drag circuit."

"Sure," Wendy said. "Right. You're a real fuckin' scream."

Sophie looked hurt at that.

"Whatever. You know what? Here's how I feel. I don't think tracking down dirt about my Opa is going to result in anyone feeling better about their lives. *Or* his, for that matter."

"Anna might," Sophie said. "Not that you ... necessarily need to care about her well-being, I suppose."

"No," said Wendy. "I don't."

Sophie lay down next to Wendy, her skirt against Wendy's pajamas. Their heads touched, and Sophie curved her hand around Wendy's fingers.

"Doing anything tomorrow night?" Sophie said.

"No."

"Would you want to come to this costume party at Frame? There's a guy I want you to meet."

"Is there."

"Yeah, you'd like each other. He's hot. He's smart. He's a social worker. At—shit, I forget where. I mean, you certainly don't have to, I don't want to pressure you."

"You're not," said Wendy. "Is he weird about shit?"

"I fucked him," said Sophie. "And *you* have a vagina."

"Bring Lila and Raina, eh? Trans girls' night out?"

"Hell, yeah."

The sun had set, and Sophie reached over and turned on a lamp, her skirt making a rasp against Wendy's clothes. For a second, Wendy felt an overwhelming sense of peace, like the two of them were suddenly younger—much, much younger.

Sophie tucked her head under Wendy's chin. Wendy stroked Sophie's hair, which looked and felt and sounded like straw.

"I've thought a lot about old Mennonites being trans before," Sophie mumbled into Wendy's neck.

"Mmm."

"Especially when I think about my mom."

"WHAT?"

"No!" Sophie giggled in her high-pitched girly way. "Not that way. At least I'm pretty sure my mom's not a guy."

"Explain," said Wendy.

"Well, lapsed Mennonites like her, they had to learn to negotiate a larger world. I don't mean the simpler stuff, like learning how you take a bus. I mean socially—but maybe not even that."

"What then," Wendy said, irritated. "What not-simpler stuff."

"I just mean, you can learn to look normal very quickly," Sophie said softly. "Think about how fast people adopt certain words after a few months on the Internet. You can go from being clueless to yelling at someone almost right away. It's so fast. It takes longer to register a car. But you can't learn to talk about real wants, hates, desires as quickly. You can't figure out when to care that your actions will hurt someone and when to figure that person can go fuck themselves. Their culture never built any of those skills. They didn't need them in the first place. It must be hard escaping that. And people like your Opa, like my mom, they grew up where everybody was supposed to feel the same about everything."

Wendy was silent. "My dad's not like that."

"That's because your dad's fucking bonkers," Sophie replied. Wendy blew a raspberry on her head.

"You said, 'They didn't need those skills in the first place,'" Wendy said. "What do you mean?"

"I used to think," Sophie said, "in the old days, it must've been beyond suffocating, how no one said what they thought. And I'm sure it was. But maybe, in that world, you didn't need to as much. If you were a parent, and your kid got wasted or snuck home a record player or whatever, it was ordained how unhappy you were supposed to be and how they would be punished. So who needed to talk about what you felt? Ever been called a faggot when you're with another trans woman?"

"Yes," Wendy said instantly.

"Did you need to talk about it?"

"No. What's your point."

"I know it's not the same thing," said Sophie. "I just get what it's like when something needles you, but talking isn't necessary. Maybe living through it isn't the only hard part. Maybe being in the world afterward is also the hard part. You know?"

"Where does my possibly trans grandfather come into this."

"Just that I see what you're saying—I *think* I see what you're saying. I don't want to put words in your mouth," Sophie said hastily. "It was probably just another earthly burden to bear for him. And God would be proud of him for resisting. Done. He could've left for the city, he could've found a way, but how hard would that have been? On top of how awful it was for any trans lady back then."

"It wasn't even a choice," Wendy said sharply. "There was no option for him at any point in his life, and you know it."

Sophie was silent, her skirt shifting on the bed.

Wendy had a very deep memory of her Opa praying for guidance on how to be of service. That same day, he'd said, "I wish people would just ask God for something more when they prayed than, 'Protect my wife, my children, protect me.' I don't think enough people pray in hopes of learning what they might *give*."

They were by the gravel pits that his brother owned, and he was throwing fish food into the water and it made the sound of rain. Her Opa was the least opinionated of people. But he'd sounded frustrated when he told her this.

"Well, anyway," Wendy added bitterly, "I hope that's how he thought of it,"

"Oh?"

"He was always really sweet. He was so gentle and kind. If he never had a hope of being a girl—and he didn't—I hate to think he believed with all his soul that he was going to hell for it too."

Sophie rubbed her eyes. "That'd be rough."

"I used to sing to you," Ben said that night on the phone, drunk out of his mind, before Wendy drifted off around one in the morning. "I used to sing to you every night."

"I remember that," replied Wendy, snuggled in her blankets layered three-deep, warm as fur.

"You were always such a good kid," Ben continued. "You never got in anyone's way, you would tuck yourself in and then I would come into your bedroom and turn off your light."

She heard car horns and police sirens through the phone. "Dad, where are you?"

"Corydon. I'm almost at my place. I went to the King's Head."

"You've been walking a while."

"Don't worry about me, kid."

They hung up. A key skittered in the lock downstairs, then the sounds of laughing. Raina. And her date. The sound of a body shoved against a wall and gasping and wet kisses.

That's nice, Wendy thought. The streetlight was making a triangle on the outline of her legs. The sound of the wind was soft.

4

Sophie dressed up as Audrey from *Little Shop of Horrors*, and Wendy went as a raccoon.

Raina rapped on the door. “Can I come in?”

“Come in!”

She entered shyly. Wendy’s mouth dropped. “Is that latex?”

“Yes.”

“You’re beautiful.”

“You’re beautiful!”

“You’re going to have girls hanging off you.”

“Oh, am I,” said Raina.

“Unless—is your girl from last night coming?”

“She doesn’t do well with crowds, unfortunately. But she doesn’t mind me going.”

“Ah.”

“Your boobs are so shiny,” said Sophie.

“I thought so.”

“Who are you? Batgirl?”

“Lord, no,” Raina said. “I’m just a bat.”

“Ah.”

“Is Lila still coming?”

“We’ll get her on the way.”

“Who are you?”

“Audrey from *Little Shop*.”

“I love that movie!”

“‘Oh, Seymour, you’ve been getting hurt so much lately!’”

"You girls," said Raina. "You keep me young in this town."

"Aren't we older than you?" said Sophie.

"I thought age didn't matter for us," teased Raina.

"Yeah, you're in bat years now!" (Wendy said this louder than she meant, already a little drunk.)

Raina smirked. "Saucy raccoon you are."

Wendy raised a brown-gloved hand to her face. "Thanks, sugar."

"Gin anyone?"

Wendy raised a glass. "Two steps ahead of you."

"I'm okay, thanks," Sophie said uneasily.

"No?"

"I'm takin' it easy tonight," she said. "Just takin' it easy."

"Alright," Wendy said. Then there was an awkward beat. "I can put this away."

"No, it's fine."

"I should have asked you, I guess."

"It's fine."

"Would you be uncomfortable if I made rickeys?" said Raina.

"It's all good!" said Sophie. "I just want to take it easy tonight. Please don't worry about me, please!"

"*Un moment, je te faiserais les meilleurs boissons.*" Raina sashayed out.

"How is it the American knows French and we don't?"

"Because the American works for the government and we don't."

"*Je vous entends!*"

"Well, I understand that!"

"*Je saissssss!*"

"Better her than us," said Sophie.

"Yup."

"American," Raina said bitterly moments later, returning with drinks. "A gentleman at the bus stop today demanded to know why I didn't go back to the rez. He was very passionate about this."

"What'd you say?"

"I said nothing. Do you want to get a cab when we go?"

"Let's walk," said Wendy. "It's not that cold."

The three of them walked down to Lila's building. She answered the door of her basement apartment in dark red and white face paint, carrying a sceptre with a heart on it, and her long jet-black hair up in curls. "You're kidding!" said Sophie.

"Off with your head!" said Lila. Someone down the hall poked their head out the door, shook it, and went back inside. "Okay, so we're taking shots," said Lila.

"Where's your boy?" Wendy craned her neck in.

"Being a fucking pussy," Lila snapped. "Bottoming for the kind of lesbo who'll top him! I don't fucking know, I broke up with him."

"*Whoa!* Lady!" said Wendy.

"I'm sorry," said Raina. "Are you alright?"

"*No!*" Lila shrieked in a funny, relieving way, in a way that made the other three relax. "If I wanted to sleep with gay men, I would have stayed a fucking man! I want someone who'll take off my panties with his teeth and fuck me, not some *Everyday Feminism*-reading tenderboy who treats me like a fucking baby deer! Probably the worst part of this for him is now at parties he doesn't get to say: 'As the partner of an Indigenous trans woman ...' I'm going to get drunk—can we go?"

"Cheers?" said Wendy, offering a flask.

Lila sipped. "We're still taking shots."

"Your majesty," Sophie curtsied.

Outside, it was mild and cool; dusty snow flitted through their hair. Raina reached into her bag and unfolded a pair of black wings on the doorstep. She strapped them to her back, long stretches of fabric that were layered with feathers, like an angel's. They walked with cars honking, Raina stumbling, the four of them gulping from Coke that was two-thirds rye. They were a sight; Wendy and Sophie and Lila, the three looming transsexuals of variously tall heights, with Raina at least half a foot shorter than the others. A lone huge man in an idling car said, "You're not fooling anyone, boys!" and Wendy shouted, "Fuck you!" and the rest of them grab-dragged her down the street and Sophie pleaded for Wendy to apologize as the guy yelled, then sped away, and Lila flipped him off as he went.

At Frame, Sophie paid the fifteen-dollar cover for Wendy, and they walked up three flights of old stairs and buzzing lights with Lila's sceptre raised like a lance. Sophie got blistering drunk the fastest, and rather than waiting for the washroom, she peed standing off the fire escape; Wendy was out there bumming a blue-moon cigarette and Sophie looked beautiful and wild as a flaming star, her straw hair and long dress whirling in the wind and the last drops of piss blending with the falling snow. Sophie's guy showed up, and his name was Ernie: Tall, bearded, dressed like a Blues Brother, kind of looked like Dan Aykroyd. They talked and danced and Wendy kept saying, "We're on a mission from God" enough that it quickly went from annoying to background noise, and Ernie started to laugh and soon they'd emptied his plastic bottle of half water, half gin. Lila was ranting to Raina in the corner, Sophie was running around with a dead flower she had brought in a can.

When they danced (it was a swing band), Ernie knew how to lead, and

Wendy danced for—well, really, the first time. Real dancing, anyway. At thirty years old and eight years post-transition, it'd still been one of those things that'd just never happened. She tripped once or twice, falling against his body, laughing. "I can't help it, it's the Mennonite blood," a silly lovely joke that wasn't true (of course that wasn't why she couldn't dance), and he steadied her gloved hands and bare arms and whispered in her ear, "You're fuckin' pretty, you know that?"

He touched her face and then kissed her, and Wendy melted into him, her flesh telling her something deep and natural at the same time that she stupidly thought, *His beard's thicker than it looks.* She asked how tall he was and they stood back to back. They were exactly the same height. He laughed and said "That's cute!"

He had a ruddy-red face with pale patches. He drew his fingers through the gleaming black wall of her hair.

She learned some general things. He had to work the next day at the detox unit—somewhere, she didn't catch the name—and had to be up at seven ("Booooo!" she said). He claimed he had no hobbies ("I don't want you to think I'm interesting," he said without deadpan or performativity). He grew up in Western Manitoba, around Killarney, and when he said, "And you?" Wendy said, "No, no, no, I've been here all my life"—gesturing toward an open window and the shuttered lights of the frozen city—"I've never lived anywhere else."

Then Sophie accidentally dropped and crushed the dead flower from the can she was carrying and shrieked raw and loud enough to disturb the crowded dance floor where the swing music had inexplicably given way to house. "*God fucking damn it! Fuck fuck piece of shit cunt God fucking—*"

As Sophie progressed to screaming vowels instead of words, and before Raina and Lila could get to her, she began to make dents in the plaster wall. It was a sight. Two girls, one dressed as a bat and the other as the Queen of

Hearts, holding down a screaming giantess in a leopard-print dress. They talked to her soothingly while Sophie hyperventilated snot. The small crowd staring at them filtered back to the floor.

Wendy realized she'd seen that flower pinned to the wall above Sophie's night table.

You are so fucking stupid, Wendy thought. *Why the fuck would you bring something important here.*

Ernie wanted to talk to Sophie too, and Wendy put a hand on his cheek. "They're looking after her," she said brightly.

They made out in the abandoned front room, and then Wendy sucked him off behind the blanketed table where earlier, the venue'd collected the cover charge. He didn't touch her head or grind into her, and she liked that. When they got up and found a full open can of beer on a shelf, they drank it. But that set Ernie's stomach off. He tried to go downstairs but instead painted thirteen steps in a row a splotchy yellow. Wendy hustled him to the fire escape and put a finger to his lips when he yammered how embarrassed he was and how he was never this screwed up ...

"Trust me," Wendy whispered, pressing a stick of gum in his fingers. "Trust me. I don't care," and he said, "Okay okay okay," with wind and flakes swirling around him as he breathed heavily and shuddered on the black iron grate and Wendy loved his horror and vulnerability in that moment; she loved that this was his standard of embarrassment; she loved the broken concern on his face when Sophie was punching stupid fucking holes into this beautiful old building; if he suggested right now that they get on a plane, she'd say yes.

They began to say goodbyes to everyone they knew, but it was catching up to them that they were drunk, they were so so so drunk, drunk enough to have trouble walking or finding each other after Ernie cleaned up in the washroom.

He slurred out that his place was close, and she said, "Great great great," and while getting their shit, they tripped in the corner on a pile of cans as thick as a ball pit. Wendy whacked her head on a counter. They carried-held each other over to the front room and found: Sophie. Sitting on the blanket-covered table with flushed eye-shadow-stained skin.

"You're beautiful!" Sophie said to a girl coming up the stairs in a leather jacket and polka-dotted blouse. She said goodbye to Wendy and Ernie, then broke off when another strange girl came through. "You're gorgeous!" Sophie said to her. "Your shirt is so pretty! I love your shoes! You are so gorgeous, and I want you to know how amazing you are!" They heard Sophie's voice trailing all the way down the stairs: "You are beautiful you are beautiful you are beautiful you are always beautiful and you always will be!"

Ernie hailed a cab they sat in for five minutes, then they took an elevator far up, and Wendy said, "Ernie, do you have something to *drink*," and he opened a beer in front of her and she tipped it straight up like a glass sword, and after that her memory shut down.

5

Her body was roiling when she woke up. She felt ruined. Like when jumpy innocent teenagers in desolate weakness wake up from a first bender in misguided horror of what they'd done to themselves. But Wendy was very attuned to the signals of her body. She only had to experience something once or twice to know exactly what her body was telling her.

Wendy turned very slowly from one side to another. Ernie's comforter was huge and felt like moonlight. She opened her eyes. He wasn't in the bed. She turned her head to see the room—bare white walls, grey carpet, no furniture except the bed, a closed door on one side and a washroom on the other.

Kitchen noises from behind the door, streetlight filtering in the blinds with the first signs of dawn.

She had to pee incredibly badly. She stood up very, very slowly. As she walked she was as shaky as a surgery patient.

On the toilet Wendy realized: She was wearing his clothes—a bright blue tank top and white cotton shorts. She laughed, seeing herself in the mirror. She looked like an oversized version of herself from grade school. There was something deeply satisfying and funny about it, being here, in his washroom, and seeing herself like this. She rested her beating head on her hands and smiled.

She could say goodbye to Ernie before he went to work. *Maybe he made coffee.* She creaked herself up. She moved to the closed door. Then she fell on the bed and slept for two more hours.

When she woke, a spring was blooming in her insides. She scrambled out of the cloud-sea of covers and ran to the toilet and threw up everything in her body.

She felt worse than she had a couple hours before—actually, she felt sicker than she'd been in a while. *I never puke anymore*, Wendy thought. *I don't remember the last time I puked.*

Drinking a sip of water then lying on the cool linoleum, she took long slow mouthfuls of air and forced her body to breathe. Half of her hair was bunched between her head and the floor, but it hurt too much to move it. Her hair hurt. The cabinets under the sink were pinwheeling and clicking back into place at the same time.

Wendy had a thought. She moved a hand to her pussy and pressed. It was tender, hurt different than the rest of her.

So they had had sex.

Her ass?

She wondered whose idea that'd been.

Eventually she forced her body up, commanding it like a robot. Ernie's alarm clock read 9:37.

The rest of the apartment was an ageless bright room with a kitchen and a couch and a TV. There was no Ernie and no coffee and a half-full carton of Five Alive in the fridge. She sat against the fridge door and drank it down, its light flowing into her like flowers.

Blacking out used to devastate Wendy. She used to obsess about what she might have done, messaged friends: *Did I do anything shitty?* But she learned eventually. Annoying people with drink-related guilt just annoyed them more—and anyway, Wendy rarely did anything bad. Drunk guilt was childish, and worrying about it didn't make things better. So she didn't worry about it anymore.

Her phone. Of course! Of course Ernie wouldn't leave a note! She stood up, feeling stronger, and went back to the bedroom. Six texts:

Lila: *I had fun tonight. Love you. (4:01 a.m.)*

Raina: *You aboot? (7:36 a.m.)*

Raina: **pokes you* Wendy-burger I had the best time last night now wake up and come home! (7:52 a.m.)*

Sophie: *I'm sorry about last night. Thank you for putting up with me. Come to breakfast with me and my mom? (8:32 a.m.)*

Sophie: *She has a shift at 10 so it has to be soon (8:34 a.m.)*

Sophie: *Oh did you end up at Ernies? Raina said you left with a guy. Haha nm ;D get that d (8:35 a.m.)*

Lila: *I hurt everywhere and I hate you and I want you to die. You better have got that d. (8:40 a.m.)*

Lila: *P.S. If you didn't get laid we're not friends anymore. (8:41 a.m.)*

Lila: *Love you. (8:42 a.m.)*

No new contacts and no texts that Wendy had sent herself. (In the past, this had sometimes clarified things.)

She searched for Ernies in Facebook but found nothing. Sophie had posted: *I'm sorry I'm sorry I'm sorry*, and a bunch of people had liked it and some said, *You have nothing to be sorry for* with a heart, and others had said, *Sorry for what?*

Wendy thought momentarily of typing: *Anyone in social work world know a hot guy named Ernie? Who was at Frame last night?* but she hadn't posted in months—and besides, what if he was uncomfortable with that?

Oh, for fuck's sake! She could just ask Sophie—who actually knew him. Duh.

And then, arrestingly, heart-droppingly, she thought, *You know, guys who fuck you then want to hang out again usually have a way of making sure that'll happen ...*

She wrapped her arms around herself, fit her fingers into the back of the blue tank top.

Where were her clothes?

Her clothes were a raccoon costume.

Next to the bed, a shiny brown polyester lump lay against the colourless blanket and wall.

Wendy changed, put on her coat, found her bag, and went back to the kitchen.

Well, she would write *him* a note. Regardless. Nothing to be gained by not writing a note. She looked around for paper. Then the Five Alive revolted and she threw up in the sink.

"Okay," she panted. She leaned over the sink, weak again, her skin shuddering and warming beneath her heavy clothes. "Okay."

Wendy washed out the splash of puke, drank a small slosh of water, and shuffled to a side table to look for paper and pens.

She would write something like, "You're sweet, if you'd like to hang out again I'd like that." Simple and honest. Nothing cutesy. She was getting too old for cutesy.

The side table was brown and old and had beautiful moulding, standing out from the sterile room. In a drawer she found pens and a notepad along with loose push pins and an iPod cord and both a city and a provincial phone book.

She blinked.

She took the provincial phone book and sat on the couch and checked the directory.

Anna Penner—10425 Hwy 329—Morweena—498-0925

Wendy tore out the page and put it in her bag, drank more water, and zipped up her coat. She wrote "Ernie" elegantly at the top of the notepad and glanced around idly.

There really was almost nothing here—an Ikea bookcase with more shelf space than books. The sad little couch. A quad-photo frame on the wall she hadn't noticed before. She could make out the top one. It was Ernie with someone smaller, a kid—

Wendy stood up and moved to the frame.

A small girl, maybe eight or nine, with brown hair, who looked like Ernie. She was standing in front of a brick building with steps. She looked scared.

In the next frame, the same girl in a classroom at a small desk, looking startled and snuck-up on. There was butcher paper in front of her.

Next, she was in an old, empty stand of bleachers, with a canola field on one side in the background and big new-looking houses on the other. In that one she was smiling.

Next, she and Ernie, sitting in the fellowship hall of a church. He was in a suit and smiling at the person with the camera, and the small girl was open-mouthed and reaching for his coffee cup. And Ernie had glasses.

Wendy put her hands to her face. She pressed her temples, calmed herself.

In her raccoon suit and winter coat, Wendy stood back, levelled her phone at the frame, and took a picture. Then she moved back and took a close-up of all four.

She checked they came out clear, scrunched up the paper with "Ernie" on it, put it in her pocket, put away the blank notepad, and slipped out the door.

Going down in the elevator, her heart fried.

Don't be stupid, she thought. *Nothing means a future. Nothing.*

She pushed the button to go back up, scribbled "Call Me!—Wendy

775-2410" on the back of a receipt and pushed it under his door. *Okay, there*, she thought.

6

Remembering her promise to Anna, Wendy called her great-aunt first.

"That's certainly an interesting theory!" she said when Wendy finished the story.

"I don't think I have an opinion," Wendy said delicately. "She just wanted me to pass the message along so I did."

"And I do appreciate that," said the great-aunt. "Well, Anna's an interesting one, and I'm sure she has lots of things of my brother's."

"Oh?"

The older woman was silent. Then: "Well, we could talk about that forever. Wendy, I think it best if you don't mention this call to anyone else in the family. I think if we leave it be in this time of grieving—yes, that's for the best. Are we understood?"

"Sure," Wendy said in a tiny voice.

"Blessings," her great-aunt said warmly. "How are you? How is your job?"

"It's great."

"Good! How's your dad?"

"He's great."

"Oh, that's excellent, that's excellent."

Then Wendy called Anna and got an answering machine. It'd only been a few days since Wendy'd talked to her, but it was startling to hear her voice.

Among other things, the stuff with Ernie had got her thinking again about how she came to like guys. Wendy was one of those women who'd only turned onto men when the lady pills started. There was a guy she had worked with, a tall boy from Portage La Prairie with blond-red curls. It hadn't been slow. They'd had one conversation the first week he started and that night her head went, *Bing! You are in love.* Something about it embarrassed her now.

On her lunch break, her dad called.

"Hey, girl! I got some good news. We're getting rich!"

"We are?" said Wendy. She'd left to get food and had to shout over the wind.

"A deal's coming up. I heard about it through the office. I'm gonna be one of the first investors, and you're never gonna *believe* what it is."

"A building? Real estate?"

"No, it's got nothing to do with work," Ben said quietly. "But it *is* a local thing. It's all gonna be right here in the city."

"What is it?"

"Rickshaws," said Ben.

"Rickshaws!" Wendy screamed. Her hair whipped around and covered her eyes.

"You know what those are, then."

"I know what those are, Dad," she said, pawing her hair out of her face, her head and eyes still fuzzy from her hangover. "Are you fucking kidding me? You're putting money in a rickshaw company? Here? Fucking *here*?"

"Well, they're not going out tomorrow, dummy! It's when the summer gets going. Think about it—it's perfect! Get around the Village, the Exchange—everyone's out, they're drunk, they're a mile away from their car or their apartment or whatever. Get some rickshaws rolling around, get some good-looking kids to pull 'em—"

"*Please* don't put a lot of money into this."

"Aw, don't worry, kid, I know the guys, they're friends with my boss, they know what they're doing. It's going to be good. *And* I'm putting half the shares in your name."

"Oh," Wendy said. "Oh, wow."

"Yeah," her dad said. "Well, your grandma was always a saver and us kids are getting a cut from selling the house, so I thought, what the hell, I haven't looked after you the best that way."

"Well—Jesus."

Wendy actually didn't know how to respond. Ben had made money promises since she was little, but something this concrete was new.

"Um," she said. "What do I have to do—do I have to do something?"

"Cash in when we're rich and get a boob job!"

"Okay," Wendy said flatly.

"I mean, your boobs are plenty nice, don't get me wrong, I just always thought if you had the dough, you'd want to—"

"*Ben*."

"Look, I overheard the boys talking, and they clued me in. It's gonna be good, kid. Listen, you should be excited!"

Her dad wanted to move up at his job, a real estate office where he was an admin assistant. He got the work five years ago after his last stint on welfare. Wendy hated the men in his building. She didn't think they respected him.

Wendy woke up the next morning feeling like she'd barely slept, shaking and achy again. Some mornings—not all, not even most—she'd go, *I shouldn't drink tonight.* An hour later, she'd be feeling fine. Coffeed up and running, teeth brushed, hair brushed, eyeliner and foundation, and out the door. And often, later in the day, she would remember, *Oh, right, I wasn't going to drink today*. But by then, the notion seemed silly. Like, right, that was a thing she'd planned—but was it truly necessary?

Wendy liked that feeling of giving in. It felt gentle and soft and sleepy and weak. Like within was rest. She knew that wasn't good, but when she tried to hold it all in her head and really think about it, it would evaporate. It would slip out of sight like something pulled from a cat's paws.

The next day before work Lila called. They didn't talk about Ernie or the night at Frame. It turned out a friend of Lila's had gotten some medroxyprogesterone.

"Holy shit," Wendy said matter-of-factly. "Who?"

"I don't think you know them."

"Just tell me."

"Her name's Tora."

"I don't know any Toras."

"Told you," said Lila. "You want medroxy, right?"

"I told you my doctor wouldn't give it to me," said Wendy, loading her coffeemaker. "I don't know."

"She has lots. She got a case from the States. I just thought—"

"I think so?" said Wendy. "I don't know. Has she taken it? Does she know anything about medroxy?"

"No, she's cis, and I don't know anything about it either. I just thought you wanted it."

"Oh," Wendy said. "Probably? I wish I knew someone who's taken it. I've heard it can be more dangerous, like, with strokes and blood clots and stuff."

"You ever take regular progesterone?"

"Yeah, it was fuckin' bullshit, didn't do anything. I had to plead with my doc for, like, a year too. I've heard medroxy can be worse for depression, like suicidal depressed. But maybe it's just like cis women and birth control? I don't know."

"Okay, look, man, I can't decide for you," Lila said.

Wendy stood up and drummed her fingers on her dresser. Her coffee-maker was steaming. "I'm sorry. Thank you. Probably. Right now I'm going to say probably. You ever known *any* trans woman who got a blood clot? Who's taken HRT, like, this century?"

"No."

"Yeah, exactly," said Wendy, brushing her hair. "Doctors hold that shit over our heads like we're falling over by the hundreds. Like *this* is what's fuckin' killing us. I know I'm being indecisive. Can I text you tomorrow? I'll probably get it, I just need to think it over. I do appreciate it."

"Sure. So tell me about Ernie."

"Ernie?" she said, strangely confused for a second. "Oh—right, Ernie. Haven't heard from him yet." Wendy filled Lila in about the whole night, leaving out the part about the pictures of Ernie's kid.

"Bummer, girl."

"Yeah. Well. Thanks for asking."

They were silent for a second, then Lila offered, "There'll be more d."

"Ain't that the truth."

Sometimes Wendy liked to imagine herself in a red dress on a grassy hill in the summer, and she liked to imagine arms both rough and soft surrounding her and lips kissing her hair. She liked to think of wind blowing. She liked to think of him as about her height because even in her dreams, she couldn't conceive of him taller. She liked to imagine being at home and him doing things for her. She would sit in the kitchen while he cooked and he would make her laugh and show her movies and she would drink in the bed, drink on the couch, loving him, waking up mornings to pills and coffee he would put beside her bed. She did want to live, she did, she just didn't want to live *that* long, and she didn't want to take care of anybody, anybody anybody anybody.

That night, she walked to the Vendome to meet her dad—there'd been arguments about her Oma's will. "I ain't trying to involve you," he'd said. "This is stuff between me and my brothers. I just kinda need your opinion if'n you don't mind."

On her walk, two guys began to follow her. They were old and small.

One said, "Hey, beautiful! Do you like cats?"

Without turning around, she said yeah.

The other asked, "Are you a cat lady?" They were drunk and cheery and their coats looked like mushed olives.

"No!" Wendy laughed, her hair whipping around in a gust of wind. "I'm not a cat lady."

"Why not? Why aren't you a cat lady?"

"I dunno!" she said over her shoulder. They were still following her, but they weren't keeping up well.

"I'll get straight to the point," one shouted. "I'm into anal!"

She turned around without stopping and gave them a thumbs up. Then they went away.

Some days, Wendy thought she'd programmed herself to deal with sketchy guys by just trying to be nice and sweet. One day she realized: That's what she'd been doing. She'd freeze her anger and play the big, dumb, innocent-faced, long-haired white prairie girl. And apart from any strategy or mechanism, she did believe in being nice and sweet. She wanted so desperately and genuinely to believe in sweetness. She wanted to be kind. She missed the idea that she could be kind to everyone.

Wendy had always been irritable and snipey by nature, and as a teenager especially had tried to tame her brusqueness. She had tried hard, really hard, to be a Quiet Nice Boy back then. She had thought of Henry, actually, as her guide in memory. She would never be as gentle as him, but she tried. And in a lot of ways, playing Nice Boy had worked, and some days she wanted that world back.

Hanging outside the Vendome later, dreamy-drunk and bumming a cigarette and looking in the empty windows of a building across the way, a baby-faced young guy came up and put his arms around her. He was beefy and sallow and wearing only a black T-shirt and black jeans despite the cold. He wordlessly put his arms around her and touched her like an old lover. And she let him because she was drunk too, and his touch felt nice and warm and she liked his face and she was already feeling calm and pleasant, at peace.

Then he jumped back like he'd been burned. "Are you a guy!?" he said.

She exhaled, an old and broken autopilot kicking in. "*No!*" she said. Then, snap decision—"What you're asking is if I'm trans," she said. "I'm not a guy. I'm trans."

And suddenly she *was* speaking kindly. She wanted to be kind to him, like her role had suddenly warped and now she was an aunt with a bratty child. "Just remember that, okay?" she said sweetly. "That's the word. I'm not a guy. I'm just trans."

And she put a sweet look on her face and made to go in.

"Fuck you."

"Hey! I'm not a fucking guy!"

"Fuck you!"

"*Fuck you, I'm not a fucking guy!*" And now Wendy was mad again, fully blind-mad, sudden and raging as the wind.

"Fuck you!"

"Fuck you!"

"Fuck you!!"

"*Fuck you!*" she screamed. "*Fuck! You! Mother! Fucker! Do you wanna fucking go! What do you fucking think, huh?! With me? Huh!? Fuck you fuck you fuck you—*"

A friend of the guy's appeared and quietly led him away. She went back in. And then she calmed down quickly. She laughed and chatted with her dad like nothing had happened. Ben was playing VLTs and Wendy said keep the twos and he got a full house.

"Nice job, girl!" He reached up with his enormous hands and tousled her hair. "You're always such good luck. I should get you in more with our rickshaw business, you're so fucking smart. Shit, I'm in a great fucking mood!" he said.

And in that moment, so was she. She really was. She didn't feel mad at all. All that despair and anger died like an unplugged screen. Minutes after the fact, she'd almost forgot it happened. It made her wonder in a bad way.

7

Wendy texted Lila: *so yesterday? I'm in*. Lila called Wendy five minutes later.

"I just texted her," Lila said. "You can go over tomorrow. She lives close to you. I'll text you the address. And, uh, girl?"

"What."

"She's a drug dealer."

"Obviously she's a fucking drug dealer," said Wendy.

"Yeah, but that's like what she *does*," Lila said impatiently.

"Okay. So what's the problem?"

"Her main thing is jib."

Wendy shuddered. "I don't like that stuff."

"I know, man. That's why I told you."

"I *really* don't like that stuff."

"Do you still want to go?" said Lila. "I could go for you. If it's too—"

"You're breaking up. Wait, where are you?"

"My mom and I are going to see my auntie. We just stopped for gas. I can go for you when I come back, it's only a few days," said Lila. There was a murmur in the background, then Lila faintly saying, "I'm talking to Wendy."

A scuffling sound on the phone. "Hi, Wendy!"

"Hi, Renata," Wendy yelled.

Lila's mom worked at the sexual health clinic on Broadway. She was a tall Métis woman who wore long, flowing dresses. Once, Wendy was at the clinic for condoms, and Renata came round the corner as Wendy was stuffing a paper bag full to the top. After an awkward beat, Renata'd gestured deadpan to the vending machine across the hall and said, "All that and a bag of chips," then laughed her head off. Wendy liked her. Lila liked her more now than she used to.

"So," Lila said as she got back on the phone. "Am I getting you weirdo cowboy hormones or not?"

"I'll suck it up. Go big or go home, right?"

"Your boobs agree," Lila's voice crackled. Wendy laughed at that.

That night in her dreams she had a dick again. She was running through a field with an erection and there was a girl trailing behind her. Suddenly they slammed through a door, and they were safe from the men chasing them. Then Wendy took the girl's head and she fucked her face, she fucked her face hard and fast and hard and fast and harderfasterharderfasterharderfasterharderfaster and the girl loved it and was begging for more and then people began to notice and watch. They screamed at Wendy to fuck her even harder and when she did her soft hairless cock felt drugs-electric pleasure in the girl's mouth and the girl gripped Wendy like murder, left bloodlines on her ass.

She woke up with a jerk of her feet and the sound of wind, tree branches skittering at the sides of the house. Instantly she felt for the hole in her crotch, pressed at the little bundle of muscle and nerves on her pelvis where they put the head of her dick. She flipped around and pressed her face and crotch into the bedding as hard as she could.

Then she sat up, scratching her hands. She reached for the bottle beside her bed and drank from it deeply, breathed out, let her muscles relax and loosen. It only occurred to Wendy then, randomly and eerily, that she still hadn't looked at the other photo albums she'd taken from her grandmother's house. *Not now*, she thought.

❧

The dealer responded to Wendy's text in the afternoon. *Go to back of building*, she said. *Tell me when ur here.* Wendy'd already forgotten her damn name.

She walked over and peered up at the wooden back stairs. She hadn't bought drugs in a long time.

Wendy tapped on her phone, and a door on the third floor opened instantly. A woman in a sweater and jeans waved. She left the door open as Wendy walked up even though it was one of the first days of real, serious cold.

The dealer was small with waxy-pale skin, in her mid-thirties with curly hair. The door opened to a living room. There was a big blue carpet and pink and red velvet-flocked wallpaper and two ashtrays on the counter. And a small mini-blowtorch on a coffee table. There was a mix of cigarette smoke and an awful, metallic, Windex-y tang.

Wendy sat and took out a bottle of cucumber-scented lotion and rubbed it on her arms and face and took a breath from her hands. The woman was digging in a drawer.

"You know Lila well?" said Wendy.

"No. My girlfriend does," said the woman. "She's the one told me you were looking for stuff. I don't like having people over," she added. "I usually make people wait in the back lane. But this is a different kind of call. And I like trannies."

"Me too," said Wendy.

The woman let out a huge, shaking laugh. "'*Me too!*' Christ."

She sat down with a plastic bag that clacked and pulled out a big bottle of Walmart brand vitamin D. She opened it up and offered it to Wendy.

Inside were small sheets of pills in foil. There were ten pills each and the sheet was clearly labelled in tiny font.

Medroxyprogesterone Acetate Tablets IP
MEPRATE ®
Each uncoated tablet contains:
Medroxyprogesterone Acetate IP 10 mg
(Micronized)
SCHEDULE 'H' DRUG
WARNING: To be sold by retail on the
prescription of a Registered Medical
Practitioner only
MFD 02/2014
EXP. 01/2017
Dosage: As directed by the physician.
Store in a cool, dry and dark place.
Colour: Lake Brilliant Blue

"This might be a one-time thing," said the woman. "I'm not gonna get more soon." She coughed. "It'd be cool if you bought a lot of it. I don't know who else will want it."

Wendy looked up. "No," she said. "I'm not sure either." She looked through the other sheets in the bottle. "How much do you have?"

"Shit, let's see ..."

The woman screwed up her eyes and let out airy breaths as she counted. "I have sixty of those sheets and I'm pricing them at ten dollars each."

Wendy smiled to herself. She had random but genuinely fond memories of drug dealers doing math. "A dollar a pill," she said.

"That's so cheap, don't even try."

"And if I bought a lot a lot?" said Wendy. She could probably unload it on other girls if it didn't work for her.

A door opened and closed behind them. Wendy shifted to see the silhouette of a man cross to a washroom in the dark. The woman tossed her head. "Depends."

Wendy had four hundred dollars in her pocket, most of her savings. "What if I took half of everything you have."

"Then we'll make it two hundred and fifty," she said, distractedly tapping on her phone.

Wendy paid her and received three of the vitamin bottles. "If you still got them in a month, I might buy more."

"Mmm."

Wendy swallowed one of the pills, then checked that the sheets were all the same in each bottle before leaving the apartment to a blast of deliciously clean freezing air. It was a strange feeling to get new hormones again, eight years after the first ones. *Got em.* she texted Lila. *Am I starting transition plus?*

Wendy went straight home, changed, threw her dirty clothes and underwear in a garbage bag, and barrelled through sudden horizontal snow to the laundromat. That guy she'd tried to sleep with was at the counter again—

Taj? His name was Taj.

Wendy chuckled. "Hey, friend," she said, breezing past him. He startled behind her and mumbled something back. She threw in her clothes and coat and put the water on hot.

Then suddenly she remembered: Ernie. He hadn't called. It'd been a few days, yet she'd forgotten there might have been another possibility. It was like she'd expected it.

Lila responded to her text: *you are super trans now congratulations!!* Wendy decided to text Ernie, then re-remembered she also never got his number.

Right.

She moodily wiped a finger over her blank phone.

Taj came over. "Hi there," he said nervously.

The buzz of a text again. Lila: *Fag.*

"Oh, I'm sorry," Wendy said icily, "do I know you?"

8

Two days later, as Wendy clocked out of work, there was a voicemail from Anna on her phone. She apologized for missing Wendy's call.

She'd been in hospital. But feeling much better. Wendy could call back tomorrow. If Wendy liked. Anytime.

When Wendy got home, she found out she only had a shot of rye left. And the LC was already closed.

The vendor was open, but she didn't want beer—she usually didn't like drinking beer alone—and tonight especially for some reason, it sounded gross. She liked the clean, utilitarian immediacy of hard liquor and water.

Also she was broke. Payday was tomorrow.

Wendy put her hands to her face. Could she pilfer some of Raina's? Just ask her? Borrow some money? But how pathetic was that, how—

"Fucking dummy," she whispered to herself.

She changed into her nightgown and moisturized up and down her body, giving her skin fragrance and light. She massaged her nipples. They were tender, pleasantly so, already fragile and hurting again. She hadn't expected the new hormones to work so quickly. It felt nice. Her chest felt healthy, something organic with life. Wendy closed her eyes and held her breasts, breathed in the scent of her soft, lush-smelling skin.

It's okay, she thought to herself. *You could use a night without, you know.*

She turned on an episode of *Angel* and settled into bed, arms above the covers, her hair rivulets down her sides.

Wendy was afraid at first, but soon she just felt sleepy all on her own. Calm. Not restless. The surge of anger she'd expected fizzled and dissipated before it began. She felt peaceful. She wondered if she'd feel more rested in the morning.

Halfway into the episode she remembered—she actually had some Feeney's. She used it in her coffee some mornings and kept it in the kitchen, so she'd forgotten about it. She got it and lay back down in bed, but the cap was stuck and her fingers were smooth from the lotion.

She wrapped the bottom of her nightgown around the cap and then a Kleenex on top of it, but it was still stuck. "Damn it," she said to no one.

Wendy sat up with her feet on the floor and put the bottle between her legs, doubled over like she was driving a fist into her stomach.

When she eventually got it open, it instantly tasted creamy and sweet and her head felt drunk with an immediate fullness, a fullness-drunk she hadn't known for—how long? It felt childlike; the decadence was obliterating. It was different than any other night of drinking Wendy'd had in recent memory. It was wonderful. She fell asleep feeling hazy and warm, cuddled and soft and beautiful.

"Did you speak to Henry's sister?" Anna said the next morning. Her clipped, accented *you* sounded more like a *yuh*.

"Sort of," Wendy said, her head full of static and her stomach achy (she rarely drank anything sweet). "She didn't want to talk to me. But she didn't seem surprised either."

"Hm."

"Did she call you?" asked Wendy.

"No."

"What do you think that means?"

"Heh. Many things," Anna said.

"I see."

Wendy twisted a piece of hair around a finger. She sat on the edge of the bed in her nightgown, sliding her feet in and out of her slippers.

"You talked about letters the other day," she said after a silence.

"Yes, I did."

"What do they say?"

"Various. Desires. And things."

"Oh?"

"Yup."

There was a longer silence.

"Hard to talk about over the phone," Anna said.

Not a straight answer to save their fuckin' life. An old rant of her dad's bubbled into Wendy's mind. But she felt calm. It had only recently occurred to her—the burden this woman was carrying. Sophie'd been right. And Wendy felt a little ashamed about it.

"Well," she said, "I don't mean to press you."

"Oh. Well," Anna said instantly. Then she added, "Wendy, I have forgotten. what's your—surname?"

"Reimer."

"So you married in."

"No, I'm just another Reimer."

"But you also said. You were a grandchild." Silence. "I think I'm mixed up."

Wendy had planned this out beforehand. "My mother is not around any-more. And Ben's family didn't like her. But Ben took to me. He's more a father to me than anyone else has been and always was as I grew up. It's complicated. But Ben's the only real family I have, and I did know Henry briefly, when I was a child. Aganetha and I did not get along, but I was at her funeral. It *is* complicated. I'm sorry I couldn't say this when we first spoke, Anna. My own past is strange and not a very completely happy tale. I hope you know I thought the world of Henry, and I want to hear what you have to say."

"Well!" Anna let out a long sigh. Wendy wasn't sure if she'd buy it or if it was all too weird and sinful for a woman like her in the first place, but she just said, "I'm old."

"I'd like to know more about Henry," said Wendy gently. "Maybe other people in the family wouldn't. But I cared about him very much, and I would like to know."

"Oh," Anna said, as if surprised. "Well. I suppose I ... Nice that someone wants to know more about him. Henry."

"Perhaps I could come up and have a coffee with you sometime?" Wendy said. "I'm happy to talk on the phone, certainly, but it would be nice to meet you and hear more about the family." This she hadn't planned on saying and she suddenly thought, *Premeditated lies*. "I don't mean to impose."

"No, no," said Anna. "Sure. Couldn't. See why not. I don't have a husband anymore. So I'm very free."

"Oh, I'm sorry," said Wendy.

"That was a joke."

"Ah."

"He's dead," Anna added.

"Ah. Well, that's funny," said Wendy. She clapped a hand over her forehead. *Jesus Christ, Wendy*. There was more silence. "Anna, can I ask you something?" she said. "Did Henry have a name he preferred?"

"Beg pardon?"

"Did my Opa have a name. Like a gir—"

The word caught on her insides in a way it hadn't for a long time.

"An—alternative name," she said. "Maybe not a masculine name."

"No," said Anna, sounding confused. "He liked Henry. To my understanding. Thought it was a healthy name. Strong sounding. Wanted Ben to have his name, you know. Aganetha. Objected."

"Now *that's* interesting," Wendy said, more to herself than to Anna.

"I'm sorry?"

"Interesting he'd want to pass on his name. Or just not even choose a different name."

"Why? He was old."

"Well, wouldn't he want a girl's name if he wanted to be a girl?"

"*Good heavens!*"

"Huh?"

"Ohmyword. Oh. My *word*. That is." A long silence. "Where would you get that idea?"

"*What*? Well, *you*!" Wendy said. A sob of frustration came out of nowhere. "You *told* me! You *told* me he was like—" *Shit.* "Like Tulip," said Wendy. "You told me he was like Tulip."

"I know Marvin—uh, Tulip, I know he has a—a—a—a taste for men. All I meant. But that. What you say. No, never. No."

Wendy sat with the phone in her hand. "You know what, never mind," she said. "Forget it. Sorry I called back. Never mind any of this."

"Hm, but just a second. I—" said Anna.

"I have to go," said Wendy. Her body was vibrating. "You know how to get—you can call me. You know, good luck with everything."

"Well, but."

Wendy waited.

"Be nice to talk about him," Anna said desperately. "With someone."

"Okay," Wendy said flatly. "I have to go to work now."

"Perhaps I'll call you another time."

"Goodbye."

"God's blessings."

"Later."

The next day Wendy woke up at noon, but it was one-thirty when she got out of bed. It was her half-shift day; nothing to do until five. She made a big pot of coffee and got into a good mood. She turned her phone off and turned up loud poppy music and began to clean her room. She was singing and sweeping and tossing clothes and bottles into piles.

Looking out the window, she saw a guy sitting in his sunroom in the building across the lane. He sat on a couch wearing his coat, surrounded by stacks of blue plastic school chairs. It didn't seem like he was doing anything. It looked to Wendy like the funniest thing. An ache of something happy welled up in her chest, and she stared at him, grinning like a moron.

Eventually he saw Wendy and waved. She waved back. She got more coffee and added whisky this time. It was three o'clock. She realized she was still in her nightgown. Why on earth *was* someone out in their sunroom in the winter?

She had the next day off and woke to sounds of Raina and her girlfriend in the living room.

"Hey, sports fans." Wendy lumbered up with a coffee, rubbing her face.

"Good morning," said Raina. "I'm afraid Genevieve and I didn't know if you were waking soon, so we ate all the breakfast already." They were both wearing pyjamas and loose-fitting T-shirts.

"No one's getting hurt," said Wendy. She waved jauntily at the girlfriend. "We haven't met yet? I'm Wendy."

"Hello."

Raina began to clear the dishes.

"You home tonight?" said Wendy.

"Not sure," said Raina. "If I am, we should have a rickey. Or two."

"Or three," said Wendy. "You kid. You make those real drinks, you keep me young."

"Yes, well," demurred Raina, "the one woman who did not partake the other night went on to punch holes in the wall, so I suppose that says something, doesn't it."

The girlfriend snorted involuntarily, with eyes wide.

"You haven't met Sophie yet, have you, my love?" said Raina.

"No."

"Well, that must change."

"Yeah," said Wendy, pulling her ponytail tight. "Does that ever." The girlfriend tried to look happy about this.

Sophie herself called as Wendy was getting dressed. "I need to drive to the shop to get wipers. Mine broke. So could you possibly come with me?"

Her voice was so fucking sweet and melodious.

"Why do you need me to come, Sophie?"

"I can't see."

"What do you mean, you can't see?" said Wendy, zipping up her skirt. "It's not snowing."

"Yeah, but when I drive, all the water gets kicked up. I need someone to look out the window and reach out and wipe the windshield."

"It got that warm?"

"Look outside, dude."

Wendy opened her curtain to a lake of melting crystal. A car sped through the lane and washed the building across the way. "Jesus," she said.

"Yeah, it's like ten degrees out. It's nuts."

"Sophie, that's—why don't you take the bus?"

"I don't like buses."

"Kinda inconvenient."

Silence. Wendy put a hand to her face. "Sorry. Yeah, I'll come with you."

"I'm cat sitting for Lila, I'm not far."

She walked south to Lila's place and got in Sophie's car. Sophie was right—the melt kicked up on her windshield the second she moved.

The parts store was at the other end of downtown. At every intersection they reached out to wipe off the windshield. A middle-aged guy in a sedan laughed his head off. They waved and laughed back. It wasn't unfriendly.

Wendy'd thought she'd tell Sophie the new stuff about Anna and her grandpa. But every time she opened her mouth, she said something else.

They went for pizza across the street, and a guy said, "*Damn*, ladies!" A boy Wendy knew from high school rollerbladed past the window.

"Heard from Lila you're taking medroxyprogesterone," said Sophie.

"Yep."

"How is it?"

"Making me less depressed, I think. I didn't expect that."

"No kidding."

It was true. "Yup."

"Never heard that before about progesterone."

Wendy shrugged. "Hormones are weird. No one really knows what they do anyway."

"Okay, but you said *less depressed*. Do you mean happier?"

Wendy was sometimes annoyed by questions like this. But she sucked on her pop and thought about it. "I think so," she said finally. "I've been calmer, I guess. Does calmer count?"

"I suppose. What about your boobs, what'd they do?"

"Bigger. Rounder."

"That's great. I wouldn't have guessed."

"Fuck you."

"Aw, that's not what I meant—I'm just saying, I couldn't know."

"Fuck you."

"You're wearing a fucking coat, dude!"

Sophie swiped at her phone as they finished eating. She said, "There's that trans march meeting next month. I guess they're gonna try to have one in Pride this year."

"What's the trans march like?" said Wendy. "We've never had one. Well, I guess you know that."

"You just show up and go," said Sophie. "It's not like the parade. I've been in a couple; they're fun. It's nice to see us all together."

They finished their food, and Sophie morosely stared out the window. "I wish I'd known you," she said, "back in the day. I didn't know any trans women growing up here. Not a single one."

"It would've been nice to know you too," said Wendy.

"You wouldn't have liked me," Sophie blurted out. "I was so different. I was such a timid thing. I was so quiet and proper. Naïve."

Wendy nodded. "Babe," she said, "go back a decade, we were probably all different."

Sophie's eyes were still vacant. "You've done sex work, right? Do I remember that right?"

"Yeah," said Wendy. "You?"

"Yes."

"Mmm."

"Why do you ask?" Wendy said. Her eyes darted from Sophie's to outside. "Did you work the street?"

"No," Sophie said. "Well, once. But no."

"I only did incalls myself," said Wendy. "My old place on Spence. Couple houses from where I lived as a kid—that was kinda weird." She was silent. "Why, what's going on?"

"Thinking on the fuckin' *therapy* I had to do," Sophie said. "Oh-my-god-does-this-make-me-gay—all that."

"Sure."

"I was all *Whipping Girl* about it for a bit," Sophie said. "You know: 'Of course you're not gay.' No guy who likes trans girls is gay. You don't want hairy dudes; you want us as girly as possible."

"Heels and lipstick and cock."

"Yep. And that's all true, there's no question," she went on. "Of course, those guys are straight; of course, even the liberal ones are homophobic in ways they don't understand. Of course, there's something ugly in their brains that won't let them be. That's still what most of me wants to say now: 'Boy, listen, you love girls. You just like girls with clitties big enough to fuck you. You love girls.' If only they would be good to us as girls. You know what I'm talking about."

"That I do," Wendy said.

"I used to be gung ho about that. Now, that's about what ninety-five percent of me thinks."

"And the other five percent?"

"'I don't fuckin' know, man. You tell me—you're the one with my dick up your ass.'"

Later, Wendy went to a benefit concert in the old United Church of Christ. Two young women and one young man played music in front of the choir loft. One had a guitar face-up in her lap, one had a keyboard, the other had some kind of stringed thing. Sometimes the music sounded beautiful and sometimes it sounded awful. It would be gorgeous and haunting, then tinny and weird.

The church was so huge and empty even though fifty people had shown up. Wendy sat up in the balcony at the back, hugging her knees to her chest with her boots off and coat and scarves piled next to her.

Her grandparents' church was maybe a quarter this size. Henry'd told her how it used to be that men sat on one side, women on the other. That had stopped not too long before. "For the better, I should make clear," he'd wheezed. "Don't want to give the wrong idea."

"Why would I get the wrong idea?" little Wendy had said. "Men and women should sit together. Men and women are the same, aren't they?" And he responded with something about how he and Wendy and her Oma all got to sit in church together now, and wasn't that a treat. This memory came to Wendy suddenly; she hadn't thought about it in years.

Home tonight? she texted Raina on the way out.

Am over at Genevieve's. She is upset with me I'm afraid. I said something very admittedly insensitive and unacceptable. I miss you though.

She stared coldly at her phone, then typed, *Yeah. Miss you too. Love you.*

When she got home, shuddering and watery from freezing rain, she went right up to her room and opened the second photo album she'd taken from her Oma's house, the one from the early eighties. But Henry wasn't in it. Not in a single picture. Everything else was in place—Ben in his early twenties, Ben and his brothers with various degrees of moustache in front of a Christmas tree, Oma baking with a sardonic look at the camera. But no Henry.

Wendy stayed up long into the night looking through every picture again and again, in her bed, in her nightgown, with a glass of whisky by her side. But she hadn't missed anything. And her grandma loved taking pictures. Barring some truly weird explanation, her grandfather just hadn't been around.

The only clue was one picture where a large blue men's shirt was barely visible to the side, hanging on the doorknob of her grandparents' bedroom. Unusual in itself; her Oma was the kind of housewife up at eight every morning, tidying and vacuuming.

She looked through the third album, which dated from 1993, the year before he died. Henry was in that one. But Wendy knew that; she was in it too. She'd been eight. She spent a lot of time at the house that year; they'd almost transferred her to a country school. It'd been one of her dad's less stable periods. Her grandpa'd been weak and on his way out even then, but very, very sweet to her. He took her to the gravel pits a lot. He said he liked the quiet. Wendy liked being with him. He would say to Wendy, "Your father loves you. He is imperfect, and he has done many wrong things."

He would say: "His love is greater than his faults."

He would say: "Love is not attached to our human foibles because if we are truly loving, it comes from God. Love withstands our sins; love is higher than all the ... crud we might inflict on those we love. Your father needs to beg forgiveness for his sins to you and to the Lord. But that is a separate thing from the fact that he loves you. And he will always love you. That is how love works." He repeated variations of this a lot.

To many kids—many adults too, she supposed—it'd all be total bullshit. But in Wendy's case, it was true. Those were the right words for her father's love, and when she was younger she believed them with all her heart. This got her into trouble later on.

She liked those old boy pictures of her too. She'd made a cute kid, lanky with a bowl cut and a stupid huge grin.

Wendy'd been devastated when her Opa died. But when she came out as an adult—*Thank God*, she'd thought, *thank God he's not around for this. Who knows how he would've dealt?* Wendy treasured that she could keep his memory clean and undisturbed.

Which, she reflected now, was maybe a stupid thought in the end. Considering.

I'm going to find out about you, she thought, closing the album and going to sleep. *I'm sorry I didn't take you more seriously. I'll find you, I promise.*

9

You want to go for dinner tonight? she texted Ben the next day.

Why wouldn't I, he said. *Let's go to Saffron's.*

She went home after work and got lost in a stupid Facebook argument—Sophie had gotten into it over some cis lesbian posting about vaginas.

Wendy typed a thought then deleted it. Lila showed up on the thread and started getting into it too. Wendy sat so long thinking about what to say, then saying nothing, that she was late to meet her dad.

"So this stuff with my brothers is getting tough," her dad said as they sat down.

"What's going on?"

"Eh. My mum left me a bigger share of the dough than they got, and they—don't like that."

"They make so much more money than you! Can they do anything about it? Wills are law, aren't they?"

"They can contest it," Ben said grimly. He shook his head and his toque went crooked on his grey nest of hair. "Which would drag it out. And I'm kinda counting on that money. I signed the papers on this rickshaw investment."

"You're kidding."

"Wish I was kidding. Not about the investment, that's gonna be just baller."

"*Baller*," said Wendy.

A waitress came by. "Can I get you folks some drinks?"

"Two Kokanees," said her dad, then turned to Wendy. "Yeah?"

"I don't always like beer by myself, but I always like beer with you."

He nodded at the waitress. "Two Kokanees." The waitress looked confused. "It's my daughter, I'm being a good influence," he said. She laughed and left.

"Dad," said Wendy, taking off her toque and running her hands all the way through her hair. "Who's doing this to you?"

"Bah! Mostly Al. He's just hurting. He was pretty close to Mum. It's not just about money. It never is."

"But that's terrible," Wendy said. "Like, that's shitty, fuck-you-forever territory. It's fuck-you-forever territory as far as *I'm* concerned. Like, *I* don't want to ever talk to him again, Father!"

Her dad put his hand out and said, "People need your love the most when they deserve it the least."

"Oh, bullshit!" snarled Wendy.

"Nope, I'm absolutely serious. People need your love the most when they deserve it the least."

Wendy turned her head and put a hand through her hair again. "'Kay."

"You're gonna figure that out more as you get older, you know." Her dad nodded.

"Sure," she said calmly.

She had to ask about her grandpa but she didn't know how.

After they ordered she said, "Hey, Dad, what was *your* grandfather like?"

"My grandpa! My Opa!" said Ben.

"Yeah. Like my Opa's dad. Or Henry's dad. My great-grandfather. Or whatever."

"Aw, he was a hoot," he said. He took a long pull on his beer and leaned back in his chair.

Yes, Wendy thought.

"Kinda jealous when it came to his wife, which was weird."

"Why weird?"

He shrugged. "People didn't really bone each other's wives in those days. Well, people did, but it wasn't even something you'd imply. I dunno if that makes any sense. You know, it would just be improper to even joke about any flavour of it. Maybe like—" he gestured up and down his daughter's body, "your shit. I'm trying to say it wouldn't be on people's radar. Plus there's Biblical connotations with jealousy. Anyway, it was always a little awkward. Why?"

"Don't know much about the guy. Grandpa never talked about his dad."

Ben scratched his stubble. Her father had such a leathery face. "He was very religious," he finally said. "The jealousy thing was more a quirk. He was humble for the most part. I guess like most men around there, that time. He was quiet. Funny when you didn't expect it. Smart, but—couldn't do anything about it. By the time the church okay'd doing shit besides farming, he was just too old. I think he always wanted to go to school." He remembered something and raised a finger. "He was afraid of money. He couldn't deal with having the stuff. Some'd argue there's something to be said for that, though I disagree. He died in '83. And *my* dad and him got close just before then. Your Opa was always next door."

Ben remembered something else and nodded up and down. "It was a big deal that he gave the land to my uncle Peter. Should have seen my mum blow her lid about it. Because the gravel companies got interested in our land—oh, probably '80, '81. You know my grandpa made over a million dollars in those last few years before he died? And he gave it all, and I mean *all*, to fuckin' MCC. He kept like a fraction, barely anything. There was almost nothing for us when he kicked it. A *lot* of people didn't like that. Self included, honestly. I think he figured my uncle Peter would split it up. Though that's definitely not how it ended up working out. Who knows. He died, the will said what it said, my grandma didn't know anything. Like I said, Grandpa was afraid of money. He didn't want to have to deal with it."

"I had no idea."

"My dad wasn't miffed about it," said Ben. "*He* was in the thick of this weird religious period around that time." His brow went dark. "Sometimes I wonder if maybe he was egging my grandpa on, saying leave him out of it, don't give anything to his family, not him. Wouldn't have been out of character."

"What do you mean?"

"*You* probably would've had a better childhood if my dad thought to fight for his piece, for one. I hold something against him for that." He finished his beer. "I gotta go to the bathroom." He got up and Wendy stretched her cheeks with her hands, and for a few minutes her eyes didn't focus on anything.

"I ordered you another beer, pardon the assumption," Wendy said when he returned.

"Hi, have we met? I'm your dad."

"Cheers."

"So, anyway," he sat down again, "as I was saying, before my grandfather died, my dad became very, very religious.. And my parents were always religious, but they were never *fanatics*. You know? That wasn't them. They were just godly. I like to think of them like that," he mused, nodding. "They were just good people. I know you and my mum had issues with your whole transgendering thing—but for the most part, they were just *good*. They never had the heart to be too extreme. They were never like my brothers, y'know? My brothers go to church and they're Christians, but they're not godly. My folks were godly.

"Except, like I said, there was this weird period with my dad. I think he was scared of losing my grandpa. *Losing*-losing him, like he wasn't going to heaven. You know," he said, settling back against his chair, "you were brought up differently, Wendy. When you were a Christian, all you heard was 'Just accept Jesus into your heart,' and that was it—you're a Christian, and you're ready for heaven."

"It wasn't all like that," Wendy said.

"Yes, it was. You have no idea what I grew up with," Ben said sharply. "You got nothing like what we got. Back then, nothing guaranteed you salvation. My grandfather would say that. 'If I am admitted into heaven, it is only through the Grace of God.' He said it a lot before he died. I think that was part of my dad getting all fiery for Christ. No—fiery isn't the right word. Actually, maybe the opposite. He withdrew more. He spent a lot of time at the pits, and he spent a lot of time with his dad. Took him to his appointments in the city. It even bugged my mom. Once I was home for a bit, and she said, 'Well, am I crazy or should Dad be spending more time at the house?' In some ways, he was just being a good son, I guess. I sure wasn't that good to either of my parents."

Ben's eyes got big and sad. He scratched his stubble again. "Anyway. My dad did speak to us less, and when he did it was always about Jesus. Not in an unkind way. Or even a judgmental way. But whatever you said, it came back with God wrapped around it. You know how there are some people like that, right? With anything, not just God. Everything you say to a person comes back with a certain tinge?"

"Yeah," Wendy said. "Yeah, I do."

Ben coughed deeply from his chest. "I wasn't the easiest kid to raise, and

I was kinda fucking off from the church 'round that point, and you know, my dad didn't know how to handle that. He was just never a lay-down-the-hammer kind of guy, he just couldn't do it. Even when he punished us, I don't think he took joy in it. My mom was always the tougher one. You probably figured that out when you lived with them."

"I didn't really live with them ..."

"You basically did," he muttered. "Anyway, it was strange. He became almost ghostly for a few years. Church, work, his dad—that was it. He came back to us more after Grandpa died."

"This is in the early eighties you said."

"Yes. '81, '82. My grandpa died in '83. You came shortly after, of course."

"Did he ever leave for a while?"

"What do you mean?"

"Did he ever skip town or—?"

"Oh, God no!" said Ben. "No, he never stopped providing, never stopped working; he was always there. He was always a good dad." Ben trailed off and picked at the label on a bottle. "He was always around. I didn't appreciate that like I should have."

"It's okay," Wendy said soothingly. "We all have stuff like that. And that's wonderful of him."

"It was."

The waitress came by with their food and they ate. Her dad was lost in thought.

"There was this one weird thing," he said. "I was downtown one night at a bar after classes." He coughed again and made hacking noises. "Just having a beer with my buddies. And then he walked in. Your Opa walked in the door of a bar."

"Oh my God, what bar?" said Wendy.

"The Windsor."

"Oh—"

"Well, every bar was probably all the same to him. I don't think he was a fuckin' closet blues fan or anything. But yeah. And he didn't see me. He talked to the bartender, and then he left."

"Ever find out what happened?"

"Too scared to ask him. All I know? Bartender said he'd been looking for someone who didn't work there anymore."

"Weird."

"It was," said Ben. He hack-coughed again. "Jesus." He hit himself on the chest and a button on his shirt came undone. He was wearing purple flannel.

"Okay, here's a question. Did Opa ever drink at all? Maybe in secret?" Wendy said.

He shook his head. "I never saw him drink in my life. It's not impossible, I guess, but it wouldn't make sense. He didn't have bodily weaknesses. That I saw. Unlike, uh ..." He put on a face that Wendy couldn't decipher. "Unlike other members of his family."

"Well, that's kind of admirable," she said cheerily.

He shook his head. "No idea what you're talking about."

She laughed and pulled again on her beer. Wendy appreciated the soft steady slide of getting drunk on beer. Like slowly clicking down the volume on a TV show.

She checked her phone in the washroom. A text from Raina inviting her out with her girlfriend and—

Ernie: *Sorry it's been a few days. I had a good time with u. I'm busy for a while but let's hang out next week?*

She smiled big and touched her legs together. Cool heat flooded her stomach and through the rest of her body.

You give up too easy, she thought softly to herself. She hadn't opened it and triggered the read receipt yet. So she would wait till tomorrow to text him back. Because—well, because. And in the meantime, oh, did she take delight in knowing, okay, so she'd see him again, she'd see him at least once. She really *did* like him.

Do it right this time, she thought. *Go for dinner. Tuck in big before you have a few. Wear something classy.*

She had a fatalism about this stuff—guys, dating—she had to fight. She fell too easily into fatalism, period. (There was a reason she avoided the Internet as much as she did.) How could men ever love her? She would never be loved, and now she thought, *No*. She thought, *Do it right*. She even set a reminder in her phone. 12:30 p.m.: Ernie. *Do it right, love.*

"It was like," her dad said, a non-sequitur later in the night, both of them drunk and family talk long spiralled away, "when I was living with my mom a few years back—you remember that."

"Yup."

"Yeah, you were living on Spence by our old place. Anyway, I was living with her and she said, 'I think you need to go see a therapist, I think you're depressed.' And I was like, 'Dude, I'm forty-five years old and living with my mother. Of course I'm depressed.' She didn't appreciate that."

He sat back and twisted around to look for the waitress. She wasn't there. Ben looked at Wendy intensely. "You've always had pretty eyes," he said suddenly. "That's the one thing that's never changed about you. I never understood how your mother and I made someone with such pretty grey eyes."

Her dad wasn't up for a night of it, so around ten, feeling pleasant and warm, beer-drunk and hazy, she walked through the Village and bought a mickey of vodka, then headed over the bridge and lazily snaked north and west, sloshing through the ocean of puddles, idly sipping, not wanting to go home, feeling lingering and peaceful. There were apartment buildings and houses and the constant far-off rush of cars and beams of light from Osborne and Portage and Broadway and Sherbrook. It was the time of night when everyone was walking around, people everywhere, night people. It was so strangely warm, she even had her coat open and let the air cool her. Everything was clear. On Furby a hook of flesh wrapped around her arm and suddenly her body was being tugged to the side. The guy said, *Oh shit oh shit oh, you're beautiful, oh I'm gonna fuck you. Oh shit, oh shit, oh shit.* He was carrying a plastic bag with his other hand and talking incredibly fast. He was short, older, bits of grey hair. Wendy didn't feel scared. She said, *No, sweetie, no.* The guy said, *Ohhhh, I'm gonna fuck you.* He pulled on her arm, trying to lead her somewhere, but it didn't feel that hard. He was short enough that she could put her chin on his head. He was wearing a navy blue button-up paisley shirt. She said, *I'm sorry, honey, I'm not going to do that.* She kept walking. He didn't let go. *No no no no. I'm gonna fuck you.* He sounded excited like he couldn't control anything. She wasn't afraid, but she instantly had the perfect lie and said, *No, honey, I'm a working girl! And I charge money, and I'm very expensive.* He steered her to a street behind the building and said *Ohhhhhhhh, okay, I'll pay, I'll pay, okay okay okay.* She said, *I'm hundreds of dollars! I need four hundred dollars to do anything!* He said, *Okay, okay. I'll get the money.* She was drunk. She was so, so drunk. She was guided so easily. She tried to get away from him, but he was stronger than he looked. *Okay.* She would wait until he tried to get the money and then turn him down again and really say no and leave. They were sitting on the back stoop of a building. She didn't realize they'd come here. She wondered if she could just talk to him. Maybe he was nice. The paint on the stoop was thick, globular, like bubbled oil. She acted nice and realized she really could just talk with him. She drank some of his beer. He took her hand and put it on his penis, which was out, she then saw. He put her hand over his dick and kept going. Mechanically she jerked him off, her brain barely catching up to what her body was doing. His face was twitching and convulsing as if electrified, as if he'd seen God. He dove with his hand for her cunt, and she swatted it away even as she was still jerking him off. *Let me ... your pussy,* he moaned. *NO!* she said. She was foggy. Nothing except for that dive with his hand was registering as it was actually happening. She finally said, *Hey, I need money!* Her brain lifted her hand away. Y*ou told me you would give me money. I need my fucking money.* He fumbled into his pocket for his wallet and desperately, while looking away in what strangely and momentarily looked like shame, held out a small fold of blue bills—five, maybe six of them. She snatched it and put it in her pocket. She thought to stand up and walk back to the street, but his hand was pulling her back again. He still seemed harmless. Wendy did not feel like her life was in danger. Everything in her head was swimming and submerged and operating so slowly and confusing, but she did not feel her life was in danger. She should get up. She should leave. He looked fearful and apprehensive, a look she recognized, and she said, *You're nice.* Her hand was sticky. She didn't realize he'd come. It was thinner and clearer than she'd ever seen, like coconut water. He looked down and up. Frightened. She leaned down, put her lips to his cock, and gave it a small, sweet peck. His come tasted like nothing. She sat back up and his face had wonder on it. He said, *That was really nice of you.* Automatically she said, *Well, you're nice.* She took his beer and drank as much of it as she could, and then something steady and animal propelled her to her feet. *I have to go*. He said, *Stay! Stay*, as he pulled his pants up. She walked back to Furby, her nerves exploding, and her brain and skin were evaporating. She was having trouble thinking in words or sentences. She drained the finger of vodka still in the mickey and heard him talking, but he wasn't closer to her, and the lights of Portage were close now. There was the Good Will. She was close to home, but she walked in and ordered a double. She drank it in seconds and ordered another. That one she drank at a regular pace. She saw the bartender and the other customers, kids her age, some younger, looking at her and trying not to look at her. She didn't see anyone she knew, and they all looked so far away, blinking, distant constellations of other humans. She said to no one, *How are you that old?* Then she woke up in her bed with a headache. She was wearing the same dress, and her coat was on the floor. The sun was up.

10

Raina was walking her girlfriend out the door when Wendy went into the kitchen. She was hammered. Not hungover, not still vaguely drunk—hammered.

"*Hey!*" said Wendy.

"Good morning. Or good noon, I suppose," Raina smirked. "And how are you?"

Wendy laughed and put her hand around the coffee pot and leaned into the cabinet. "I ..." She didn't know what to say and she could barely stand. Wendy tried to articulate what'd happened last night to Raina, but half-formed words evaporated inside her.

Raina looked up at Wendy's mouth moving with no sound. A bemused expression came over the shorter girl's face, like, *Oh you.*

Wendy realized the clock said noon.

It was Tuesday, she worked at one.

And Raina had her evening shift.

That was why they were both here.

"Work. We have to go to work," Wendy said.

"I have some leftover coffee upstairs," said Raina. "If you like. Genevieve didn't drink hers."

"Please, yes," she said feebly, sinking to the floor. Raina chuckled and went upstairs.

Raina sat on the lone chair in the kitchen, reaching down to stroke Wendy's hair. "Rough night," said Raina.

Wendy tried words again.

Then she sipped the coffee, shaking her head. She breathed in and out, letting the microwaved liquid warm her. Raina nodded and continued to stroke her hair and said, "Beautiful girl."

Wendy made a noise of gratitude and tried to say something again, but it was very, very difficult to do so.

Raina said, "I get it, my dear," and started another pot in the machine. Wendy drank deeply from her cup and Raina went upstairs as the coffee burbled.

Wendy's worst hangover in months began in her first hour of work, but she chatted and was friendly with customers all day and helped her manager do the schedule. "Do you want an extra shift?" he asked her. "We have someone leaving. I might be able to give one to you."

"I heard someone was leaving," said Wendy. "That hope did cross my mind." He laughed. He said she was funny. Wendy was at thirty-two hours a week. "Anywhere it works," she said. "I'll do it."

Then she asked, "Do you want to come to the mall with me on lunch?" She was so relieved when he said yes. They crossed the street in the dark together to the food court. She laughed when he blew root beer onto her face with a straw. Her phone still patiently bannered the hours-old reminder TXT ERNIE 12:30 P.M.

On her way back to the store, she texted him: *Hello. Yes. I would definitely like to see you again wearing something classier than a raccoon costume. Tell me a day please. Dinner?*

After her shift, she texted Raina: *You home tonight?* and got an instant response: *Covering at work. Home in two hours. Just me tonight Wendy-burger, all yours.*

Okay <3

She put down her phone and stared into the lit void of the parking lot.

Wendy got off the bus at Sherbrook with her phone in her gloved hand and waited for the light to change. A guy and an older woman stood on the curb with her, breath bright with streetlight.

"Hey! You wanna buy some T3s?" said the guy.

(A wave of shock and panic completed its full trip through Wendy with the *Hey*.) "For real?" she asked.

"Yeah."

She paused. "How much?"

The woman broke off and the man moved closer. "A buck each."

"Hm."

Wendy, what are you doing? "Actually, no thanks," she said. "Never mind."

Then the guy tilted his head. "Hey," he said. "Are you a fuckin' man?"

Her vision closed on his face before she could breathe. "No."

"Seriously."

"I'm not! Fuck off!" The light was about to change and she walked backwards into the street.

"Don't *lie* to me, bro!" the guy said angrily. Then he laughed, jolly and breezy, and turned to follow the woman.

Wendy calmly crossed the street looking behind her. She lifted her phone up and called her dad.

"Kid!" said Ben.

"Hey, Dad. How's it going?"

"I'm fuckin' fantastic, how are you? *Where* are you? Are you outside?"

"I'm walking home. Where are *you*?"

"Lying in bed. Watching porn. Eating Cheetos. Wondering why my dick's always orange."

"Eww! Fuck!" Wendy said, swivelling around. "Dad! Jesus!"

"Aw, come on, I'm kidding."

"Eww!"

"What, you've heard me tell that joke."

"Yeah, I know," Wendy said desperately, "but—"

She looked around, realizing how loud she'd been. The only people nearby weren't looking at her. If they had been, they'd only have seen a vibrating, wild-eyed girl twitching her head around.

She swallowed. "Okay. I'm just feeling sensitive right now," she said. "I had a hard day."

"Oh no, what's up?" Ben's voice quivered.

Wendy wished she could tell her dad, *A man made me jerk him off last night*. (Did he make her? Was Wendy making that up?) But what would her dad say to that?

"Well, anyway," he eventually said. "The rickshaw thing's going well. Not that you asked yesterday."

"Sorry."

"I'm already over it. But, yeah! We got the warehouse yesterday. It's on Adelaide. In the Exchange."

"Cool." She thought about when he'd said, "You have such pretty eyes. I don't know how we made someone with such pretty eyes." Then she was on the stoop jerking the guy off again, and her mind and body went blank.

"Now, you know," Ben's voice came back to her, "we could probably set you up as a driver. I'll bet you'd make a lot of money, good-lookin' as you are."

She was in front of her house, and the lights were on, yellow against the night. "There's a thing happening at home, I'll have to let you go."

"Toodle-oo."

"I love you." She whispered it, her voice unrecognizable and wispy, soft and high again as opposed to her usual ex-smoker's rasp, forcibly soft and high where it would stay now, for a few days, for the time she remembered it, for a little while.

In her room, she shut the curtain and dimmed her lamp and opened her laptop. One of the quiet cis roommates was listening to CBC.

Facebook said: *What are you thinking?*

She started to type what happened with the guy on the stoop. Then immediately thought of the people who'd post hearts or say call the police or that they were so sorry or that she shouldn't drink so much and what if she took drinking off the table for a week, maybe two, or every variation on *Ugh, what is wrong with people?!*

Wendy shut her laptop and placed three melatonins under her tongue. While they dissolved she changed into her nightgown, then filled a pint glass, half whisky and half water. She stood by her dresser and methodically drank the whole glass down. Gulp, gulp, gulp, breathe, gulp, gulp, gulp, breathe, gulp. She pulled the blankets over her without turning off the light. Ten hours later, she woke up cold and in a sweat from dreams of—she raised a hand to her head—did she have any dreams?

The next day, Wendy wandered by Value Village on her lunch break and saw a team of Holdeman Mennonites lined up outside the front door. Each of them held a small non-descript box. She stared at them from across the street, perplexed, but none of them moved.

Wendy looked at her phone. Ernie still hadn't read her text from yesterday.

She texted him an emoji of a beer stein and an ice cream cone. This one came back as, "read: 3:56 p.m."

She stood over her phone for another minute, waiting, her hair fluttering in the wind. She walked over to the food court in the slush and purple light, her shadow long as a pickup truck.

Inside the mall, Wendy wondered about her grandfather again. Had he found others like him? Who'd he been looking for when Ben saw him at the bar? Did her grandfather ever think of abandoning his life?

Or maybe he wasn't so silent. That was the kind of thing that could happen, but people just didn't talk about. It wasn't an out-and-out lie—Mennonites had trouble doing that—just an omission. She could even see her Oma admitting it if Wendy had known to question her. Like, *Oh yes, yes, he used to go out to the city for the weekends, and I had ideas about what he did. Not a fun period. But I kept quiet and prayed to the Lord, and soon enough he asked His forgiveness.* Like, that wasn't completely impossible.

The temperature tumbled back to normal that night. Wendy was up for work early the next morning and the footstep-divots from the slush had frozen and the streets looked like the moon. As Wendy waited in the kitchen for her coffee, she saw an old woman on the sidewalk with two canes wobbling on the ice in the early dawn light, inching toward a cab.

11

Wendy had spent her childhood frightened and being hit by boys. Her dad began to teach her how to fight when she came home the first day of grade one with a bloody nose. He thought she ought to fight back. Wendy was big, but there were always more of the others. She never got hurt *that* bad, in the end, but she was afraid of these boys, always. Not that she and her dad lived in the roughest of neighbourhoods but—there were better.

It'd all stopped around high school when they'd moved south of the river (a third floor apartment in a well-kept house off Lilac and Corydon; Wendy'd loved that house), but the memory of that fear bubbling up in her bones was permanent.

She knew trans girls who described fears of suddenly being seen as a faggot, but Wendy'd heard the word since she was old enough to hit a baseball. It wasn't that she was particularly feminine, but she was never exactly *closeted* either. She wanted dolls, sure, but she didn't *pine* after them. She wanted to wear pink—but she liked black and grey too. Hand flips, voice lilts, a love of beautiful, pretty things—she was no more inherently femmy than any average scrappy girl with a weirdo poor single parent, but these clear traits still came out regularly, and no one failed to notice. Ever. Even at the new high school, where kids handled her brand of odd a little better, even when the response wasn't abuse, everyone always noticed.

When she transitioned at twenty-two, that old bodily fear from childhood reawakened. She was living in a shitty room by the U of W and working at the music store up Portage. She was a year on lady pills when she moved in and was passing as cis for the first time. Guys would whistle and slap her ass with their jackets. Before this, she'd always been brave enough to tell boys to fuck off and throw fists when she had to, but passing as cis, she was suddenly demure and weak—how could she say anything back at them without them realizing the girl they were teasing was a man? Her dad had said, *Aw, that's just what guys do. Play along, and they won't bother you. And, hey, look at you—you're attractive!* But the belligerent well of bluster that, for better or worse, Wendy'd always drawn on for strength was—it wasn't the same anymore. She didn't know how to talk about it.

And once, a tall man followed Wendy into her building and said, "You a transsexual? A guy told me you're a transsexual! You a man or a woman?"

"What guy?" she'd said, but he repeated, "Are you a fuckin' man?" He followed her inside, made a grab for her, demanded she let him suck her dick, and spit in her face before he left. He was definitely high on something (bath salts, maybe?). He yelled, "I will never die, bitch!" And she learned right then: You always had to be on your guard. It didn't matter how often you passed, it could always be taken away. Always. She'd never be little, she'd never be fish. It could always be taken away.

The next day, one of the ass-slapping dudes screamed, "Hey! Turns out you're a fuckin' *man,* hey?" That group of guys on her block got meaner then. They never hurt her, per se. They'd mock-scream, "It's a maaaaaaan! You think you fuckin' *fooled* us?" They threw rocks at her, stuff like that. Someone threw a sandwich at her once from the top floor of the building next to hers. One night she was chased to her building and got in just in time. In retrospect, it wasn't too different from escaping from a few torturing kids in grade school who were agnostic about hurting her physically but got deeper pleasure from messing with her brain. If you could freeze-frame the first second she came around the block, some of those boys would've looked glad to see her.

Now, bussing back from work, Wendy did not feel mad. She only felt tired and jumpy. And as she got off the bus and walked home, she called on some internal, gentle well of knowledge that shortly she wouldn't be scared again, that her fear would congeal into scar tissue.

She tramped up the stairs to her house and changed into a nightgown. She made a vodka-diet-soda and drank in the rocking chair beside her bed, the nerves settling, like leaves floating down through her insides.

Wendy felt more normal by the weekend. Look, if she saw that dude again, she'd just sock him. Done. Sealed. He was a loser. Whoever that guy was, he was an evil fucking do-nothing loser who was probably some unloved poor drunk and a fucking dipshit. Whatever. Fuck him. He was a snivelling piece of cowardly shit, and if she saw him again she'd sock him, end of story. Maybe he was stronger than she thought, but she was still fucking bigger. Done. What more was there to think about. It's not like anything really horrible went down in the end!

12

Sipping dreamily from a flask, slip-n-sliding her way down the sidewalk, Wendy walked home from work after eleven. The temp had been dropping for days, and now it was the first night of true inhuman cold, the kind of thirty-below-before-the-wind-chill air that seemed to leech pain straight from the nerves.

The sidewalk was still made of divots and moguls, steam issuing from every building, Pedestrians looked shrunken and soldered into themselves, void blobs of spaceman fabric.

Wendy was drunk and felt great and she was sick of taking the fucking bus.

She cut through Wolseley instead of staying on Portage. Who cared. She had all night. She thought she'd head to Cousin's, but close to Westminster she ran into Eddie and Red.

"Eddie!"

"Heyyyyyy! Wendy!"

"Red!"

Red had asked Wendy on a date once. Eddie'd told her, *Don't even think about it. That big Icelandic fuck—he ain't good to women.* Eddie was in his forties, worked bar fronts and sidewalks for change and usually wasn't here in the winter. Nothing had ever happened with Red; Wendy'd agreed to meet him one night—but then bailed. Another night that summer, she'd been chilling outside in the Village and one random guy's face suddenly contorted and he said, *Wait—are you a boy or a girl!?* Red clapped the guy's shoulder out of nowhere, and said *Hey! Wendy's cool!* Wendy was grateful for that. Another night, she'd wandered down to Osborne and saw Eddie and Red with a bunch of kids, and she sat on the sidewalk, hanging out, and cops pulled up and wordlessly muscled Red into their car. Fifteen minutes later they came back and pushed him out. He was wincing and got up slowly. Someone lifted his shirt up, but the cops hadn't left marks. Wendy'd made to touch Red, just softly, on his knee, to comfort him. Eddie shook his head and put a hand out, like a parent around a stove, and said *No, no.*

Now they were both here at the bus stop.

"What're you doing here?" Wendy asked. "Thought you were in Vancouver."

"I'm getting too old for this shit," replied Eddie.

"You got a toonie?" said Red.

She gave one to him and they shared her flask.

"Let's go to Osborne," said Eddie. "There ain't no fucking money here right now."

"Let's walk on the river," Wendy suggested.

"Alright. Hey, you still driving?"

"I've never had a car," said Wendy.

"I'm starting an auto shop outside of the city."

They went down on the river and emptied her flask. "You wanna build a warming hut?" Eddie said to Red. "I saw it in the paper, they give you five thousand dollars if you come up with a good design and they put you here on the river. We can do something better than any of those fucks. You know how you keep heat in? You don't let it out. It's not fuckin' rocket science."

"I'm no good at that stuff," said Wendy.

"*Shit*," said Eddie, wheeling around as a guy passed them.

"Huh?"

"Ah, I thought that was this one motherfucker. Goes around bragging about little girls. Bullshit, I don't stand for that shit. I ever see that guy, I'm punching his fuckin' lights out."

Her flask was completely empty. "You got kids?" said Eddie.

"I don't."

Eddie waved his hand. "I saw my boy today."

They got off the river and up to Osborne, and Eddie and Red set up shop in front of the Toad. Wendy went in to see who was inside and have one drink before heading home.

She did fuck Eddie once. Coming out of Ozzy's on a cool summer night, she'd made a stop at the vendor, and he was working the crowd outside. They got some king cans and went to drink by the dumpster with Red. Eddie said, *Hey, c'mere, just let me talk to you for a sec.* They walked down the back lane then across Confusion Corner, and he was saying, *You don't want to be with Red, that big fuck, he ain't good to women,* but suddenly Eddie was touching her all over her body. *Man, I don't know why I'm so attracted to you!* he said. *I don't get why I like you, but you're so beautiful!* She'd giggled and lightly touched his arms and slouched into the side of a building. Eddie was a tiny guy. He put his hands on her shoulders then slid them down her acre of a chest and said *Are they real?* and when she said yes, he pressed her tits, not like a forty-year-old man with rawhide skin but with wonder, like a boy. She didn't mind. He fucked her on a picnic table in the park behind Wild Planet, with her orange striped dress up and her dick flopping around in the wind. He said, *Wait, I don't want to come in you!* and pulled out and—came on the grass, she guessed. She walked by there a few days later and looked as if maybe she could tell.

Raina was in the Toad, sitting with a girl Wendy didn't know. They sat under a TV showing football and looked bored. Raina was eating fries.

Wendy sat on a stool, drinking a rum and Coke and watching them. Finally she texted Raina:

I can see uuuuu. You eat those friiiiiiessss

Raina took out her phone and examined it coldly. Wendy laughed. She got a text in a second: *bathroom in* 5

"Are you trying to bang that girl?" Wendy asked her from the stall.

"Lord, no. She's a friend from work. And an uninteresting one, I'm afraid."

"Ditch her!" said Wendy. She hiccupped. "Let's go home and watch movies and cuddle. You're not with—I mean is your lady—?"

"Genevieve is at her parents and just told me she went to bed. So I think that is an excellent idea."

Outside, Eddie and Red were still working the exiting drunks. Wendy waved. Eddie bellowed "Bye, Wendy!" Raina's face tightened. She didn't like men.

"Wendy-burger, how have you been? I feel like it's been some time."

"It has."

"I've been occupied with Genevieve and work. I'm sorry about that. And I do have a morning shift." She rubbed her eyes with mittened hands, then took Wendy's gloved right one, swinging their arms back and forth like schoolgirls.

"Seems like you like her a lot, hey?"

"Genevieve is wonderful," Raina said shyly. "She is very, very good to me. I hope you two can spend some more time together."

"Are you the first trans lady she's dated?"

"No," said Raina. "She dated a sister in uni. She's also dated women on the spectrum. Which has been refreshing."

"I bet," said Wendy. "Well, hey, I'm happy for you. We should all hang out some time."

"I would like that. But, really, how are you? You've seemed out of sorts the last couple days."

Wendy still hadn't told her about the guy on the stoop and didn't want to. She felt pathetic and weak just thinking about it. She didn't want to tell anyone. "I called Anna. The old woman who knew my grandpa."

"Oh?"

"It turns out he was just gay."

"Huh. Are you sure?"

"That's what she said," Wendy said. "My grandpa told her herself, supposedly."

"I'm just thinking," Raina said, "of the fact that many sisters throughout history didn't understand the difference themselves. Particularly back then. I can't imagine it would be different for Mennonites. Unless I'm mistaken."

"You're not," said Wendy. They reached the bridge and were slammed with wind. "Why didn't I think about that? I know that. Of course I know that." But Raina couldn't hear her.

"My surgery date got re-scheduled," Raina said when they reached the other side of the bridge.

Wendy groaned and squeezed Raina's hand. "Oh, not again, sweetie, what happened?"

"No," said Raina. "It got moved up. I'm heading off January fourteenth now."

"Raina! Girl!" said Wendy. Wendy said *girl* at very particular moments. Raina'd stayed in Manitoba for three years to hang onto her place in the surgery pipeline. "That's wonderful!"

"I'm very, very relieved," Raina said shyly.

"I'll have your bed and meals ready when you get back," chirped Wendy. "I'll have movies ready, and I'll wash your fuckin' dilators, don't worry about a thing."

"You're a sweetheart."

"And *you're* about to be inducted into the Vagina-of-the-Month Club!"

Raina laughed. "That doesn't make—oh, stop."

Then Wendy's phone rang. It was Lila.

"Hello?"

"I need you to help me," Lila sobbed.

She stopped and motioned to Raina. "Oh no. Lila, what's up?"

"I was driving a call for Sophie," Lila heaved. "She never said if the call was good. It's been an hour, and her phone's going straight to voicemail. I'm still outside the hotel."

"Oh shit—okay," said Wendy. "Wait, Sophie's working. You mean working-working."

"Yeah."

Wendy shook off the surprise. "Okay. Alright. Wait, you drove her? She has a car ..."

"It's in the shop," Lila said. "Or sometimes her mom needs it. I don't know."

"I—" Wendy was disoriented. "Okay. So did you try the door for the room she went to? You want someone to go with you? I can come there. Where are you?"

"I didn't get the room number."

A dread that Wendy hadn't felt for a long time flushed through her.

"What do you mean, you didn't get the room number?" Wendy said quietly.

"I don't know, man! She was in such a bad mood!" said Lila. "I asked *what's the room number*, like, I said, *what's the room number* but then she was shutting the door and she just left—"

"But why wouldn't you make sure," Wendy's voice rose steadily. "Why wouldn't you make sure you knew what the room number was, Lila?"

"I don't know! I don't fucking know. I'm sorry. I don't know. I'm sorry."

"Fuck," Wendy said. "Okay, let's think."

"I texted her right after, but she didn't respond."

"Stop it."

"I'm sorry, Wendy, I'm a piece of shit."

"We're going to figure this out," said Wendy. She thought of how her dad would speak. "Apologies and worrying won't help, you hear me? They won't do anything. So we'll figure it out. Is the phone going straight to voicemail?"

"I'm sorry I'm a fucking piece of shit!" said Lila.

"Stop it."

"I'm sorry!"

"*Shut! Up!*" said Wendy. She put her hand to her face. "I'm sorry."

Raina'd been silent, watching Wendy, her face stony.

"Where are you?" mumbled Wendy. "You outside the hotel?"

"Yeah, I'm in my car." Lila told them where she was.

"Girl? Listen, we're close to you. We're by the Ledge. Wait there. You can't do anything in the next few minutes anyway. Wait in your car, we'll come there."

"Her phone's going straight to voicemail, man, I don't know."

"It's cold. Why don't you wait in your car? You get warm," said Wendy. She didn't realize she was repeating herself.

"Okay," said Lila. "Who are you with, who else is coming?"

"Lila. You're not stupid, kid," said Wendy.

"I'm not a kid, and I *am* stupid," snapped Lila.

"Girl? Take a breath."

"Just hurry."

Lila was in her car with the heat blasting, looking wrecked and normal as could be.

"You still haven't heard from her," said Raina, getting into the front seat.

"No," said Lila. "Nothing."

"Was she drunk?" Wendy asked.

"She just seemed unhappy. I don't know if she was drunk. She misspelled her text—that was weird."

"I've never seen her misspell anything," said Raina.

"I bet you dollars to fucking donuts she was drunk," said Wendy. "That girl drinks. Like, she *drinks*. She might be sleeping it off in the guy's room. She might be too hammered to call you."

"Maybe," Lila said moodily.

"I know you're scared, girl," Wendy said. "I know you're scared, but nightmares don't happen as often as you think. In this business. I'll bet you her phone's dead, and she's just sleeping in a big bed up there. Or maybe she's in the bar.

She's probably in the fucking bar. Did you check there?"

"Yes. She's not there."

"Hm."

Wendy put her hand to her face. "Hate fuckin' asking this ... has she ever done jib? With calls? Have you seen her doing jib? Like, at all."

"I don't think so."

"You sure?"

"No," said Lila distractedly.

"Uh-huh."

"Could we talk to the hotel people," muttered Raina. "Find out which room she went into? Cameras, maybe."

"They won't do it," said Lila.

"No?"

"I went to the front desk guy. I thought I'd pretend she was on this blind online sex date, right? Like, hey, my friend was gonna text me when she got to the place, but she didn't give me the room number and she never called me and I'm worried about her, and do you have, like, cameras maybe? Could I maybe see if she came in and maybe which room she went into or something? The guy just fuckin' laughed. Ass motherfucker! He told me to go home. He had this big fuckin' smile on his face! He kept saying, *go home*."

"That was a good idea," Wendy said.

Lila didn't respond. "My phone's about to die," she said after a silence.

"Where's your charger?" Raina said.

"At home. I can't plug it in. What if she calls—I can't let my phone die!"

"You should charge your phone," said Raina instantly. "I know you want to stay. But you should charge your phone."

"I'll stay," said Wendy, picking up Raina's signal. "You two go charge your phone and get warmed up."

Lila turned around. "But what if she comes out? I can't have her come out without someone here."

This hotel has other exits, Wendy thought, but said nothing.

"I'll stay outside," she said. "My coat's warm."

"It's cold out," Lila said. "But okay. See you."

Wendy stood outside the front doors. Air was leaking in through her scarf and up her sleeves. She was so, so cold. She looked up and down Portage. She walked into the hotel. Two exits in the back, one of them an emergency exit and one not. She got a text from Raina:

You know that besides police there's nothing we can do anymore.

Wendy clutched her face and leaned into the wall. She paced up and down the block, keeping an eye on the front doors. Then she went through a back alley—had Lila walked around here?

She saw a dumpster.

She swallowed and looked inside.

Garbage.

A street guy was watching her. Wendy nodded hello. The guy looked at her hard. Wendy said, "You see a very tall girl come through here at all tonight?" Described her. The guy looked at her hard again. Shook his head. Wendy stared at him. The guy stared back. Wendy slunk off down the alley, the only sound her boots on the ice. She checked another Dumpster.

Wendy turned down the next street over. A multi-level parking lot on her left. She went in. The light was bright white and yellow. Two neon-jacketed attendants, both male, inside a glass compartment. They turned to look at Wendy, and she nodded and raised a hand. A few cars in the lot—

There was a coat on the ground.

She knelt down. It was faux-fur, beige, with toggles. Wendy'd never seen Sophie wear a coat like this—but it was big, and Sophie's usual winter coat was frumpy and worn, and this was a little sexier, so ...

Wendy took off a glove and pressed her hand to the coat. It wasn't cold.

She put her glove back on, then her hands inside the coat to warm them and think about this.

"What are you after?" said one of the attendants, suddenly towering over her.

"Did you see a girl come through here?"

"No."

"She stole my coat." Wendy adjusted her lopsided toque. "This is my coat."

"You have a coat," said the attendant.

Wendy glared. "This is my friend's," she said slowly, "that I'm wearing. I just borrowed it. I couldn't come out here without a coat on, could I?"

"Okay." He didn't move.

"Neither of you saw anybody?" she said, loud enough for the other attendant to hear. "Neither of you saw a girl come through here? Red hair, pretty tall?"

The other attendant laughed. "She wasn't here."

"So—no?" Wendy was starting to lose it.

"No." They were both snickering. "You got a boyfriend maybe? Native guy? 'Cause he came running through earlier. Boy, he was worried about something. He was having a *bad* night. That your boyfriend?"

It took Wendy a moment to realize they meant Lila.

"You sure it wasn't him?" They looked like they were having the time of their lives saying this to her. "He was tall. He was upset. *Bad* night for him. But it looks like you got your coat. So you can go now."

Wendy stood there for a beat. She wanted to lunge at them. Her brain fused. "'Bye."

Wendy paced for almost an hour in the end. Raina texted periodically:

Lila's phone is charged. I think she is doing better. Be back very soon. We are Facebooking with some other friends.

No one has seen her. Still worried.

Her phone's still going to voicemail.

They returned, and Wendy bundled into Lila's car, shivering herself warm, her cheeks like splattered tomatoes.

At first no one spoke. Then Raina said flatly, "Well, we can call the police and tell them what we know, which is almost nothing, and then they are involved and have her name. And ours. And it could be extremely, extremely bad for every one of us, including her. Or, we can wait till morning and see if she turns up. And I don't want to do that either. I am also not sure either of these choices will do more for Sophie than the other."

"It's been three hours since she went in there," said Wendy. "Right? I have that right?"

"We checked Backpage in case she reposted her ad," said Raina. "But no."

"That wouldn't matter," said Wendy. "You can set that automatically."

"Oh."

Wendy was shaking. "I don't fuckin' know. Is there anywhere else she would have gone? Somewhere around here if she got out with no phone?"

"Club 200?" suggested Raina.

"She met a trick at 200 once," Lila said.

"We'll check there. We can ask. It's a thing we can do," said Wendy.

They drove over, and Wendy ran in. Red and white circles of light hit her face. Dozens of people, boys in undershirts and girls with sidecuts.

Wendy recognized: A straight guy, looking drunk, standing at the VLTs (had he been a client back in the day? maybe); a sweet trans guy couple who, for a while, regularly had Wendy over for dinner; a twink she'd been drunk with a thousand times at bars like this and never seen anywhere else. None of them knew who Sophie was. The bartenders knew Sophie but said she hadn't been in. Maybe they didn't notice, though, they said. It'd been busy.

Through every part of the bar Wendy pushed, wanting to physically turn the back of every head of short red hair. There were so many strangers and old familiar faces, but no Sophie, and so few people who even knew who Sophie was, knew her name—

For fuck's sake.

"Hey!" she poked her dad, spinning on the dance floor.

"Kid!" said Ben. He put an arm around her. He was wearing a suit, his nice one, black and pinstriped in silver. The DJ was playing a sped-up remix of Sia. It was almost last call. He was drunk.

She was speechless. Then she screamed, "What are you doing here!?"

"I love partying with fags!" he bellowed. "You know that! You met my friend Brian? You gotta meet my friend Brian!"

"I gotta go. Sorry!"

They went back to the hotel and sat with the car running. The snow plows would come around soon.

"Maybe there's a different person at the desk now? It's probably the best chance we have," Raina said.

"Yeah," said Lila.

They sat in silence for a minute. Then Lila said, "Wendy, you should go, hey?"

"I should?" said Wendy. "*You'll* know if it's the same guy or not."

"You're a white girl, Wendy," said Raina.

"Right. Sorry. Got it."

Wendy tried the same thing Lila had on the man behind the desk, a tall tanned blond guy who looked like his parents owned the place. She recounted her story, eyes pleading and voice wispy and afraid. The man chuckled. "Yeah. We can't do that. You realize, you understand. We can't do that. I don't even have access to the cameras, okay? Look, I'm sure your friend's fine. If you really think I should call the police, I will, but I'd sure hate to have to do that. Do you want me to call the police?"

Back in the car, Wendy said, "We have to just go in there and start fuckin' banging on doors."

Lila was already getting out of the car. "Raina, wait here."

But the elevator wouldn't open without a room keycard, and the guy at the front desk saw them and kicked them out. "If you come back in here again," he said, looking at Lila, not making eye contact with Wendy, his voice wavering and darting like he was on coke or trying not to look scared, "I'm just going to call the cops! If you come back. Okay? Your choice!"

"What can we do?" said Wendy, back in the car.

Eventually Lila said, "I guess I can take you home."

Raina and Wendy went into the house and up the stairs and stood in the kitchen looking blank.

"Are you going to sleep?" said Wendy.

"Yes," said Raina. "I still have my shift tomorrow. Unfortunately."

"I'll keep my phone on and charged. I'll try to keep calling her."

"Okay, dear," she said. "You know Lila is too, though, yes?"

"Yes, I know she said that."

Raina shuddered and drummed her fingers on the wall. "Is there anything more we—"

"What, what could we have—what?" screeched Wendy.

"Yes. Okay. Let's just—" Raina shook her head violently. "I'm going to pray this is better in the morning." She started up the stairs to the third floor. Her raven-coloured hair shone black against the stair light. "It's three in the morning, Wendy." She went up, and Wendy looked at the wall on the landing.

Only then she realized: *The coat*. She had brought it in without even thinking to ask Lila. She texted her immediately but didn't get a reply.

Wendy curled up on the bed, rounding herself into a husk and clenching her skin.

After half an hour, Lila called.

"She's here. We're at my house."

"*Oh my fucking God thank fuck what happened?*"

Lila whispered into the mouthpiece, "Hold on." Wendy heard her walk into another room.

"It's fucked, man. When she got to his room, he took her phone away. And he was huge and drunk and wouldn't let her leave. So, thank fuck, he eventually fell asleep, then she ran over here. She just got out."

"Oh my God—how's she doing?"

"Scared. She says she'd never been so scared in her whole life. She's fine. Like, physically. I mean, she said he was rough—but, like, she doesn't need to go to the hospital or anything. Is what I'm saying."

"Can I do anything?" Wendy said, dazed.

"We're just having a beer," said Lila. "Girl's probably gonna sleep soon. She's staying over. She's jittery, but I think she wants to sleep."

"Okay. Hey, Lila, was she wearing her coat?"

"What?"

"Was she wearing her coat? Her coat you picked her up in."

"The grey one. Yeah. Why?"

"No reason. Okay. Tell her I love her."

"Okay."

"I—I'll tell Raina all's good when she wakes up."

"I gotta get back to her."

"Okay. 'Bye."

Wendy curled herself into the bed again, tense with the years of doom and helplessness that she kept quarantined belched up through her like a backed-up drain. She thought of her feet soundlessly running up the stairs and past Raina's door through the third-floor living-room window; she could easily and silently open the window, then back up and sail headfirst out into the sky with enough force so that when she landed—*run run run run up the stairs go do it DO IT GO NOW—*

She snaked a hand out from under the covers for her whisky and drank. She drank and drank and drank—though not wildly. Really, she never drank wildly. The gulps hit her stomach with a sludgy thud and flowed out from her centre like lava. Glug, breathe, glug, breathe, and she did this until she stopped, stopped, stopped, stopped, stopped.

13

Wendy woke up at noon. She had a day off. Outside the kitchen window, kids across the street played in red and purple snowsuits looking like multi-coloured stars.

She texted Lila and Sophie. No response.

She made her bed for once. She did all the dishes in the kitchen. She added Feeney's to the coffee. One of the quiet cis girl roommates was listening to CBC again.

Upright at her desk, she scrolled through the Internet on her computer. Nothing from Sophie or Lila there either. Facebook said: *What's on your mind, Wendy?*

Wendy put on her boots and coat and walked south. She went down to the river and sat and stared at the ice. A family in matching orange Michelin-man snow jackets skated down toward the Forks. There were beer cans in the sticks of bushes.

Walking back home, she saw that Sophie and Lila had posted a breakfast picture together on Facebook, at 2:34. They were at Sal's. They both looked happy. Wendy posted a heart.

Wendy'd always been afraid of something like this happening when she was a hooker. She'd had angry guys, threatening guys, *plenty* of disrespectful assholes, in addition to all the timewasters and fuckboys chasing freebies, but never anyone who actually laid hands on her. Or kept her against her will or anything. She'd quit sex work for a few reasons (she'd finished her laser, and her neighbours were threatening to call the cops, to name a couple) but also she figured it'd just be a matter of time until her number for something bad came up.

Wendy posted another heart.

This time Sophie liked it. Then she got a text from her:

Hey I'm okay. Like, I'm not. But I'm okay.

She sipped her coffee then typed back: *I get it. Can I come by later?*

Thanks but I probably need to just sleep for a long time. Lila and I stayed up all night last night.

I love you, she said. *Gunna check in with you later can I do that?*

Sure.

Then Wendy texted Raina: *around tonight?*

Genevieve is getting back from her parents and will need to see me I think.

Wendy threw the phone at her pillow.

Though. If Wendy'd ever actually planned to kill herself, that wasn't how she'd do it. Jump off the fucking roof. Three storeys. How stupid would that be. She had a smarter plan. She'd wait for one of those sunny minus-forty days in winter, then rent a car and drive to the States and get a bottle of Everclear. Then she'd drive back up and get a bottle of whisky. Then go somewhere isolated, near Lake Winnipeg or Lake Manitoba—somewhere eternal, quiet—and drink the whisky in the car. Then walk out in her hoodie with the Everclear and drink it fast and hard by the lake until she fell down. That was her plan, and it comforted her. She never made any action to go through with it. But it comforted her. It was hard to explain. She had her plan, and because she didn't start going through with the plan, then that meant she wasn't actually going to die. As long as she didn't start the plan, she would live, even if she didn't want to. It was a clear task for her not to do. It would start with renting the car—so don't rent the car.

Sophie had talked about an old high school friend of hers who'd kept a bottle of Everclear on her nightstand. *It's my security blanket*, the friend had said.

This story was where Wendy'd got the Everclear idea from. Sophie and the friend had stopped speaking years ago. She was still alive, though. Sophie'd checked into that.

The next night after leaving the store, Ben texted: *Hey let's get beer*. Sophie wasn't answering her texts. Raina was at a work function. *Maybe don't go home till you're ready to sleep*, Wendy thought.

"Rickshaws shaping up great," said her dad. "All the parts are on their way, the boys got a good deal. Next time this year, you wait, kid. Shit, I need you to sign those papers for your half." He fumbled in his bag. "I forgot 'em, shit. That's why I called you in the first place! Hey, you should come over to the house next week."

Sometimes Wendy was so relieved about her father's ability to talk and talk. "Sure," she said. "Hey, what kind of parts are in a rickshaw?"

Hours later, Ben mentioned that his brother was easing off the will-contesting thing. "We had a nice phone call the other night. I said to him, 'Hey, we're blood. We both got smacked by the same father, we don't gotta do this, I wanna work this out. Tell me how we work it out.' I think he got it. We're talking again next week."

"Your dad hit you?!" Wendy said. She had never imagined this, not once.

"Of course!" said Ben. "Mennonites hit their kids like everybody in my generation. My dad wasn't sadistic about it, but sure, he beat us. Specially me, being the little shit disturber I was. I dunno if he hit us more than most parents. Maybe a bit. I dunno. He definitely didn't take pleasure in it. But he did hit us a lot."

He put a bite of poutine in his mouth and read the look on Wendy's face.

"Hey," he pointed a fork at her. "Don't let that change your memory of him. He was a good dad. He genuinely thought it was the right thing to do. He thought that's how you raised a family." He chewed and thought. "But I will say, because of how he hit me is why I resolved to never do that to you."

Wendy touched her hair. "But you did hit me."

"I spanked you exactly five times. I never beat you. When you got to grade one, I vowed to never hit you again. I felt bad about that, you know." His voice went fragile. "I saw what I was doing. How afraid of me you were. I never wanted you to be afraid of me. And I've never hit you since." He drifted off. "I do have those regrets. I wish I hadn't spanked you."

Wendy was silent. "I don't feel raw about that," she said.

"But," he said, lifting a finger, as if he hadn't heard her speak, "you did scream like a little bitch about it." She had.

14

The next day, she had to work early, cranky hungover in a baggy thin shirt and ripped tights and her hair down. Her manager took one look at her and put her on phone calls for holiday orders. "You got it," she said gratefully.

She was mindlessly dialling and daydreaming when someone put a hand on her back.

"*Wha!*" Wendy wheeled around.

"*Aike!*" said the woman who'd touched her.

"I'm sorry," Wendy recovered instantly. "I'm easily ... well anyway, my fault. Can I help you?"

"No—I don't think—" the woman said, still flustered, waving her hands. "No." She walked away.

Wendy shook her head, her hair curtains on her face, and continued with her calls.

Then the woman came back. She was a prototypical customer—middle-aged, white, sensible coat.

"I'm sorry," she said. "You just startled me because from behind I thought you were a girl."

Wendy blinked.

"I am a girl, ma'am," she said.

The woman tilted her head slightly. She raised her eyebrows and smirked.

"I am a girl."

The woman stayed for another five seconds, smirking, then turned and walked away.

Most days, Wendy felt that eight years after transition, she had made her peace with trans stuff. Whatever she hadn't made peace with, she'd made peace with the fact there'd never be peace, so to speak.

Wendy knew how to deal with looking cis and she knew how to deal with looking trans, but she would never, ever figure out how to be both. How the world could treat her so differently—within days or hours. Sophie'd say, *You can't play their game. You never win by playing the cis game. You can win on so much, but you will never win that.* And Raina'd say, *I hate that they make me choose. I hate it like I hate almost nothing else.*

What more was there to it?

On this you will never win. There could be comfort giving in to that, in a certain light.

Five minutes later, she felt a tap on her shoulder. "*What*," she snarled.

"Whoa, turbo," her manager raised his hands. "It's just me."

"Oh. Hey," she said breathlessly. "Sorry, I—I thought you were someone else."

"Can I talk to you?" he said. He looked uncomfortable.

Her heart sank. It had been years, but ... she'd seen this look before. "What's going on," she said bluntly.

"I just need to talk to you," he said calmly.

Wendy followed him into his office, her fists balling and unballing. She closed the door. Sat down. Smoothed her skirt, then put her hands flat on the desk.

"I know," she leaned in pointedly. "You think I'm great. It's not you. Right?"

"Of course I think you're great," said the manager.

"Right." Her voice shuddered. She massaged her head. "Look, just fuckin' tell me."

"Hey, settle down. Just calm down, okay? Just calm down."

"*Don't tell me to settle down.*"

"Jesus!" he said. "Do you even know what you're on about? The store's closing."

Wendy lifted her head up. "Huh?"

"They sold it," he said. "To a company in Calgary."

"What!?"

"Yeah. Speculator. Something or other. Don't even know what they're doing yet," he said. "But they're going to rip it all out and—do something. They bought next door too. I had no choice in this. I think Tammy wanted to get out of the business anyway, to tell you the truth."

"Jesus." Wendy shook her head.

He gave her a moment. "We have to close right after Christmas."

"Right, of course. Jesus," said Wendy. "Well, shit. What are you going to do?"

He waved his hand. "I get a severance, I'll be fine."

"Sounds nice."

"Yeah, I know," he said darkly. "You kids are the ones getting the short end here."

Wendy's brain sank a little further. "I'll be fine."

"I'll write you any letter of reference, you know that, right?"

"Hey, I appreciate that."

"No problem." He spun ninety degrees and looked at the wall, then back at her. "So. I called you in here. Because if you're *interested*—I need you to help me liquidate. Would you be into that?"

"Probably. What would I do?"

"You help me close up the store and keep it running till the last day. You'll get forty hours up till just before New Year's. And I can raise your pay fifty cents. Not much, but it's something."

Wendy put her palms up in an *of-course* gesture. "Shit. Well, yeah, I'm not gonna turn that down, now am I?"

"Everyone else is getting hours cut right away," he said grimly. "Next schedule. We are not in what you'd call a position of strength. We've been overstaffed anyway."

"Don't they usually hire outside people to liquidate?"

"Like Tammy's gonna shell out for that! Anyway, that's big store stuff." He let out a pathetic blast of air. "What are we, we're—we're a middle-of-the-road gift store in a strip mall outside the real mall."

Wendy stared at the window. "I need to get another job soon then."

He coughed and nodded. For a second she felt a stabbing, unbridled hatred for him. Understanding the difference between them in how their days were about to go. And then, quick as it came, she was calm again.

"How long you known about this, Michael?" Wendy said.

"Since yesterday evening," he said solemnly.

"Damn."

"Yeah." He drummed his fingers on the desk. "You need a minute to think? You want to chill out in the office? Meditate? Go outside and smoke a fatty?"

She laughed. "You nerd. I'm fine."

"You got any questions for me? Anything I can clear up about the whole thing?"

"No."

"Well, if you're sure," he said. "I need to tell the others. This week you'll have your regular schedule, but starting next week you'll be at forty. You watch the register? I'm telling everybody here, then I'm making phone calls."

Wendy got up. Suddenly, on impulse, she shook his hand. "Appreciate you asking me to finish out with you," she said.

He shook back firmly. "It's always been a pleasure, Wendy. How long you been here, two years?"

"Two years."

"Always been a pleasure."

Wendy sat at the register while Michael guided the other three employees into his office. Kids, all younger than Wendy. *Getting to be a hell of a winter*, she thought.

Wendy barely slept that night. She watched TV with Raina and Genevieve, who were drinking wine (Wendy didn't tell them anything), then went to bed and stared into nothing. She did the same math equations over and over again in her head, cycling through employed friends who might hook her up, returning to a mental image of her thin, scattershot resumé blinking and loaded on her computer. Making copies of it the first week of January.

She was not filled with despair. She went through her whisky, arms on each side of the bedspread, spinning and thinking. She got up for the bathroom every half hour. Eventually, Wendy watched an old *Buffy* episode—the one where she gets telepathy. *It looks quiet down there.*

Wendy did drift off at five a.m. She dreamed that she woke up, and the sun was gone. It was noon but dark outside. She made coffee in her housecoat and bumped into furniture. Outside, everyone was driving and walking, but the sun never came up. And it wasn't the focus of the dream either—the pressing issue was being on time to work to get a tattoo; if she missed her appointment, she'd have to make too many espressos while she planned her next tattoo.

She only registered there'd been no sun in the dream when she woke up for real, and it was light out.

That evening, Wendy bought a pack of cigarettes, searched her e-mail, and found a phone number.

She cracked her desk window, took out her ponytail, and lit a smoke as it rang.

"Holly!" said a deep voice on the other line.

"Hey there!" said Wendy, inhaling, brushing her hair back from her face. "How you doing?"

"Good, very good to hear from you! Been a while!"

"Hasn't it," Wendy chuckled. "I know it's out of the blue. But I have a question for you."

"Shoot!"

"Well. You still doing photography?"

"Oh!" he laughed nervously. "Not as much these days. Not as much these days. Work's just been so crazy, it's hard to, it's hard to find the time. It's a shame. God, just hearing from you, I remember how good you looked in those shoots, but ... No time."

Shit. "Sorry to hear that," Wendy said, turning on her old phone voice, a precise edge of sultry and cockiness added to her usual rasp. "I was kinda hoping you might want to take some new photos of me."

"Oh, I would. Believe me, I always thought you were very beautiful, and

I liked our work we did together," he stammered, whispering, "it's just hard for—hold on a second, my wife just came home."

"Sure," she said. She sat on her chair, smoking deeply.

Could she still blow smoke rings?

She could.

"Okay, I'm back. I'm in my den now," he said. "So yes, anyway, I'm sorry to turn you down. It *is* nice to hear from you."

"It's nice to talk to you," Wendy said, exhaling smoke through her nose. "Sad we can't get together again."

"Yes, yes, if only there was ..." he said, sounding helpless.

"Tell me this. What if I waived my fee this time?"

"You'd do that?" he said, shocked.

"Yeah," she said, pretending to think about it. "Yeah. If you could get 'em done soon. I'd do that. And any time of day or night."

He tittered and spoke in a different tone. "You must need some photos bad then."

"Yeah," she said. "Yeah, I do."

"It's still a time thing, unfortunately," he said. "I *would* love to see you, and I can in a bit probably, it's just now ..."

"Would you," Wendy said. "I *am* in kind of a spot. I'm sorry, hon. I just thought you might be able to help me. You were always so nice to me."

She could've just taken iPhone photos. But she'd always thought that if she ever went back, there'd be no compromises. She would do it one-hundred percent right, as professional as she could, and work every day and take every client and make money. Real money. Lots of it. Like, lots of it. Maybe it was silly to start now, but January doldrums were around the corner, and who knew how the whole post-op thing would shake out with clients. And she'd rarely done outcalls before. Also, she was never good at waiting.

So.

"I've got a friend with a video studio in the Exchange," he'd said when he called her back the next day. "In the basement. Cool building. You around tonight?" Wendy arrived at eleven o'clock, every part of her body freshly shaved and her usual flyaways ironed into shiny black sheets, wearing new thigh-highs and an old merry widow under her coat, with a couple changes of new lingerie in her bag and an empty, empty bank account. They set up, shot, and tore down in two hours. Wendy wondered if he was expecting more—but no, he just shot the pictures, and true to his word, sent her a file two days later.

"It was so much fun seeing u again!" he emailed. "U got such nice hair and nice long legs. Hope we can see each other again soon. U are a blast to hang out with. Maybe we could have a drink when my work is less crazy ...?"

The pictures were good. Her hair shimmering down the side of a couch, her lingerie raised just enough to show a smidge of ass, her smile real and full and no circles under her eyes. She built profiles that night on Backpage and Shemale Canada and was done by one a.m. She pointed her mouse to the "Post Ad" button—

She saved everything and closed the browser.

Take a bit, she thought. *Who knows how long before you get to not be a ho again.*

She took the last cigarette out of her pack, changed into one of her new pieces of lingerie, and mixed an actual drink—an amaretto sour. She put on a Rainer Maria album and smoked and drank and looked out her barely cracked window.

Slivers of air blew in and over her bare shoulders, pure and cold. The kids across the lane on the second floor were silhouetted in yellow through a curtain. Above them, a sitting man washed in the blue light of a TV, the light filling the room.

Wendy remembered walking at night in the dark of winter as a kid, alone, seeing whole buildings lit up that way. Blue in almost every window down the street, whole blocks of black and white and blue.

Wendy'd never truly despised ho-ing—but she had hoped to never do it again. Oh well.

15

The next morning, Wendy's stomach was a wire ball—the sugar thing again. (She'd made a few more amaretto sours.)

She forced her body up and to the bathroom and peed with her head slumped between her legs. Cradled her torso. She shuffled back to her room with her hands touching the walls, drank down some T1s with water, and fell back into bed. She didn't have to work at the store today.

Later, she almost put her ad up, then Sophie texted: *Mom and I going to Stella's for breakfast. Love you to join.* She stared at the phone a good five minutes before texting back, *yes.*

Sophie and her mother looked exactly the same—six feet tall, neck-length hair, and long icy-pale faces, with flushed cheeks and diagonal sloping lines under their eyes and noses. They looked like cartoon versions of a Menno mother and daughter.

Well. Some cartoon.

They ordered coffees from a girl Wendy knew from high school, a brunette in a scoopneck with a flower in her hair who'd always referred to herself in the third person as *this lady*. She'd dated one of Wendy's guy friends once. She'd never gotten comfortable with the whole sex-change thing.

Sophie's mom folded her scarf and put it on the back of her chair, then unfolded it and put it back on. "I'm always cold," she explained to Wendy. "They never heat anywhere good enough for me."

"Ah," said Wendy.

"I'm Lenora."

"I'm Wendy."

"Yes, Sophie talks about you a lot."

"You do?"

"All the time," Sophie said quietly, taking off her gloves.

"Yes, well, just certainly glad this could work out," said Lenora. "We love Stella's Cafe. It's so nice they put one around here."

"I like it. I grew up in this neighbourhood. Partly, anyway."

"Oh my," said Lenora. Her eyes went wide. "Well, you've seen a lot of changes then."

"Have I?" said Wendy. On one hand, her life and her neighbours' lives were *mostly* the same as when she was a kid. On the other hand, she hated this conversation.

"I live on the other side of Portage now though," Wendy added. "Near Sherbrook."

"Ah," said Lenora. She looked at her food and cleared her throat. "So do you then ..." she trailed off. "Sophie tells me you work out by Polo Park."

"Yeah, at Tammy's Gifts and Books."

"I've shopped there! And how's that?"

"It's fine. It's great. And you, what do you—?"

"She's a nurse," said Sophie.

Their coffees came and they all emptied the cream bowl. "*So*," said Lenora, "Sophie told me you've discovered some interesting family history."

Wendy looked at Sophie, who was serene-faced and blank.

"Yeah," said Wendy slowly. "Yeah, that's true. What'd she tell you?"

"Well, that your family is from the Landmark area, for one," said Lenora. "I grew up in Kleefeld, but my uncle Jake married into Reimers from Landmark. You're a Reimer, yes?"

"Isn't everyone?"

Lenora laughed. "So you *are* a Mennonite. Yes, we can play that game later. But if I remember what Sophie said, it's that you think perhaps your grandfather"—her voice went exactly one shade quieter—"you think your grandfather may have been transgender. Transgender like you two. That's, that's correct, yes?"

"Yeah," said Wendy. She was still hungover and coffee wasn't helping. "Yeah, maybe." She realized Sophie still didn't know any of the new Anna stuff. "I'm not exactly sure," Wendy explained. "This woman called when my Oma died. She knew my grandparents. She said my Opa was like me—except she didn't know she was talking to me, she thought she was talking to someone else." Wendy dug into her bag for more T1s. "They don't like me being out. Out there."

"Sacrifices, yes!" Lenora said immediately. "I understand very much about that."

Sophie shook her head almost imperceptibly.

"She has letters from my Opa," Wendy said. "She wanted to tell my Oma, but, you know."

"She will have carried around your Opa's things for a long time, I imagine," said Lenora.

"He died twenty years ago, yes."

"Did she know about you? That you're—transformed?"

"No, she thinks I'm cis."

"Beg pardon?"

"She doesn't know I'm trans," said Wendy.

The flower-haired waitress came back. "You folks ready to order?"

"Oh, geez," said Lenora. "I haven't even looked at the menu. Though I think I know what I want."

"I'll have a two-eggs breakfast," said Sophie. "With hash browns. Are they shredded? I always forget."

"No, they're diced," said the waitress. "I guess they're like big pieces. More like slices."

"That's okay." Lenora ordered a grilled chicken burger.

Wendy scanned the menu. Her stomach was still churning; she didn't want to eat much in the first place, and she had only about seven bucks anyway. "Can I just have a plate of fries?"

"We actually don't have fries," the waitress said, looking embarrassed.

"No?"

"No," she said. Then, again, "No," the embarrassment gone. "We don't do fries. We just have the hash browns."

"Well, I'm going to the washroom," said Lenora.

"I hope it's okay I told my mom," said Sophie.

"It's fine," said Wendy. Her brow was furrowed. "I knew you lived with her, but I guess I never really realized it." Sophie and her mom lived out in Fort Richmond, where they grew up. Wendy and Lila had visited her there once, at night.

"Yeah," breathed Sophie. "Well ..." She took off her arm warmers, white with black criss-cross designs, and cupped her hands around her coffee. Wendy scratched her hands.

"How you doin' anyway?"

"Shitty," said Sophie. "I mean not cause of the—whatever," she muttered. "I wasn't doing great before that. That didn't help, though. I hadn't had a call for a while, you know. I wanna get my own place after Christmas. I just don't wanna ..." Her face was blank. "I'll get over it. Sorry I haven't called you. I wanted to see you. I just been like—"

"Yeah," Wendy nodded. She took Sophie's hand.

"You doing anything after this?"

"No, can I come over?" said Sophie.

"Yes."

"Thank you." Sophie slugged her coffee. She looked thoughtful now, more peaceful. "You know I'm twenty-nine years old? Did you know that?"

"I'm thirty," said Wendy. "What's on your mind?"

The waitress came back and refilled their coffees. Sophie gestured, trying to speak, but then her mom came back.

"So here's a question for you! Was your family EMC?" Lenora asked, sitting down.

"Yeah."

"Mine too. I think I *do* know your family. I think I've heard about you, in fact! You have a Timothy in there? Would be about my age."

"Yeah," Wendy said, surprised. "That's my dad's brother. How'd you know?"

"Well, *my* dad's friends with a Timothy Reimer from Landmark. He used to work for my dad." She smiled thinly. "And word travels fast in the Mennonite world about those who are—unique."

"Right." Sophie rolled her eyes, peeling the top off a creamer.

"Got it," Wendy mumbled.

"The EMC Church your grandfather would've grown up in was very restrictive," she said tonelessly. "They thought laughing was unbecoming of a Christian, for instance."

A memory floated into Wendy's head of Henry apologizing for a joke that was the epitome of harmless—the knock-knock joke you have to start.

Start the joke.

Okay ... knock knock.

Who's there?

... ...

He'd grinned like an imp then looked embarrassed once Wendy got it. He had asked Wendy to forgive him for being hurtful.

"And they believed in sacrifice," Lenora continued.

"I know that," said Wendy.

"Quite strongly," she said. "Well, great."

Sophie drummed her fingers on the table.

"Your grandfather would've had a long, quiet process to deal with his issue. And you realize, of course," she said stiffly, "he would not have had the options you two have today. That he could be so fortunate would not have been remotely on his radar."

"I know," said Wendy.

"Would've been quite different for him."

"I know."

"Sorry. Rude of me to presume you wouldn't know. I'm sure your parents have told you all sorts of things. Though," Lenora seemed to reconsider, "it wasn't as oppressive as some think. Or as some remember, for that matter."

"What do you mean?"

"Well, men would leave often—not before they had families, of course."

"They would?" said Wendy.

"Oh yes! There was an understanding that young people will be rowdy or wild. Drink, or ... Would've been extended only to boys, of course. But if a young person happened to do things the church wouldn't approve of, or if he happened to go to the city for some time and come back, it wouldn't have been unheard of, nor unforgivable. Some boys you probably expected it, honestly. Like, oh, that one, he needs to get something out of his system. It makes sense to me even now, really. No matter what you believe in life, why wouldn't you give young people some leeway before coming back to what's probably best for them?"

Sophie took a long drink of her coffee.

"How would I find out if my Opa ever did that?" said Wendy.

"Well," said Lenora, "you would ask this woman Anna, that would be my guess."

Wendy was silent. "I think I'm afraid of meeting her," she said, surprised at her own candour.

"Of course you are! This must be a big deal for you," she said.

Sophie snorted.

"Thank you," Wendy said to Lenora.

"What is her name?" asked Lenora.

"Anna Penner."

"And where does she live?"

"Morweena. It's very little, up in the Interlake."

"Oh, Anna Penner from Morweena!"

"*What?*"

"I've heard talk of her, yes! Very short woman. Bit of an odd bird, people said, her husband a little broody, I think. Very into her faith. Very religious. Likes animals, I think."

"Funny that."

It was storming and cold as they waited to cross at Broadway. Wendy glanced at a man standing beside them.

"Ernie?"

He was right beside them, all done up with a toque and face mask. Wendy had stood chatting for a minute or two without noticing him.

"Oh, hey!" Ernie said. "Hey, Wendy, how are ya? I didn't see you there. Oh, Sophie! Well, look at you two. Hey there!"

"Been wondering when I'd hear from you," said Wendy.

"Oh, for fuck's sake, I'm sorry," he said, embarrassed. "I've got, like, I didn't tell you this, but I have a kid ... it's hard to ... my free time. I'm sorry, I should've texted you. I still want to hang out with you again. I do. I understand if you don't. I'm sorry, I fucked up."

"That's okay," Wendy said genuinely. "Oh my God, I get it, it's okay, please don't worry about that. I—look, I have to go now." Sophie was silent. "We have to go. But text me anytime, please? Like, anytime. I want to see you again too." The light changed, and on the other side of the street they went separate ways. "Okay, 'bye."

He grinned. "It was nice to see you again. We'll hang out soon."

At the house, Sophie shrugged off her coat and looked up the narrow staircase leading to their part of the house, painted and carpeted several times over. There was an indent near the bottom of the staircase that was once a fireplace, now filled with boots.

"You know when I lived in Chrysalis, I lived in this big old country house," Sophie said. "Just on the edge of town."

"That sounds nice," Wendy said.

"It was," Sophie said, momentarily dreamy. "I had to share it with a bunch of idiots. But still. Hey, you've never lived anywhere else but here, have you?"

"Nope," Wendy said, bored. "I've always been here."

Wendy sat in her chair, and Sophie sat on the bed. "You wanna, like, watch some TV or something?" Wendy said.

"Okay."

"Can I get you anything to drink?"

Sophie laughed. "Would you judge me if I wanted a *drink* drink?"

"Girl!" Wendy hooted.

"Aw, you get me."

Wendy went into the kitchen and made whisky sours, even though she still felt a little sick.

The two girls walked up to the third floor and sat in front of the living room TV. It was chilly up there, and Wendy got blankets from the side closet. They watched some awful reality shows while the wind beat from outside and whistled through the house. They flipped through more channels and found a religious show, a preacher gesticulating as he spoke, wearing a big robe and big glasses, and with short grey hair.

"My grandparents used to watch him," said Sophie.

Wendy's head turned. "Yeah?"

"Still do maybe, I wouldn't know."

"Mmm."

The man on TV spoke grandly about the hidden nature of sin. Now and then the camera zoomed out to show that he was in a huge megachurch. It was sunny and there were palm trees outside.

Sophie lowered the volume. "Did you ever believe in God?" she asked.

"As a kid, yeah," said Wendy.

"No kiddin'. Wouldn't have thought, with your dad."

"My grandparents," Wendy said sleepily, snuggling into the armchair. "They knew I wouldn't get it at home, so they made sure I—" she let out a high-pitched yawn, "they made sure I knew about the Bible. All that."

"Got it." Sophie studied Wendy's face. "I didn't," she offered. "We went to church now and then, but my mom always made it clear she didn't believe in it. Kinda weird that way."

"It stays with you," said Wendy. "In ways you don't expect."

Sophie waited for her to go on. Finally she said, "I'd like to hear more about that."

Wendy redid her ponytail, her hair momentarily billowing around the chair. "I stopped believing in God in high school. My dad was doing well for the first time in my life—maybe I could take the loss, and it wasn't as bad. I don't know. I guess that sounds like horseshit, but it's linked in my head. Anyway. I stopped then, though I still like going to church."

"Me too. Though I never—yeah."

"I missed things about God you can figure—security, hope. And for years, I was angry about the bad things religion can do to you—this had nothing to do with gender—but there were things I didn't figure out for a while."

"What's one?"

Wendy let out a breath. Sophie tucked the blanket around her. "You know how, when you lose something that's been legit meaningful in your life, your brain kinda wants to swap something else in? Like, right away?"

"I do, yes."

"Like how addiction gets swapped with other things. Though addiction and religion are two completely different beasts. My dad likes to make that comparison, and he's wrong. Anyway," said Wendy, "when I was a kid, I thought of Him as someone always watching me and judging. When I was very little, I thought any bad thing would send me to hell where I would be tortured and burned for eternity, you know the whole thing ...

"But in my *last* few years as a Christian, like my early teens, I realized that's not true; the world is full of terrible people, and lots of them believe in Jesus, so for this to make any sense then God had to be forgiving. And, of course, people *say* God is forgiving, but it was only then I *believed* it. I think God really is kind. I got that then. But—I still had to impress Him. I thought, The Lord can see every bad thing I do. I began to think of Him as more unhappy with me than angry. And I really wanted God to be happy with me. I believed He loved me, and I had to just," Wendy jerked her head, "not screw it up."

Sophie nodded and sucked at her drink. "Yeah."

"But then, I stopped being a Christian. And that fear didn't go away, it transferred. Probably fuckin' pop psychology or whatever, but there was always someone I was trying to impress. Usually women. Even when I started dating guys—always women in my head." She sipped from her glass. "Whenever I did something bad, they were reacting in my head. Shaking their heads! Admonishing me that I had done something so wrong. I had these *detailed* apologies with so many different women that didn't exist! The conversations didn't exist. Obviously, I didn't literally believe they saw my actions like God could—but it didn't matter. I did something wrong, and I would imagine them hurt. Like I said, they were usually women, women a few years older than me. Never women I wanted to sleep with either." She emptied her glass. "Guess there was stuff about gender. Heh."

Sophie was silent for a moment then said, "I feel like everyone has a rotating list of people in their head they're trying to impress. It was specifically about God for you?"

"It was exactly like God," said Wendy. "Being forgiven more than you deserved. By someone good-hearted. Someone sad and exasperated you weren't doing better. Someone who was *right*. I was pissed off when I figured this out. You know how many years I wasted giving this power to other people?"

"Who is it for you now? Not that you have to tell me."

"Nobody," she said. "I was so pissed off at myself when I figured it out. I don't think there's anyone; not in that way." Wendy thought for a minute. "Hey, never thought about it that straight up."

"That's good."

"No one has ever understood my life," said Wendy. "I have given up on anyone understanding where I'm coming from. And it's fine. And I actually mean: It's fine."

Sophie curled herself further in the blanket and looked at the preacher. They changed the channel to a stupid sitcom and sat for a while, watching mindlessly. *This is nice*, Wendy thought.

"Is your dad different than when you were a kid?" asked Sophie.

"Lots," said Wendy. "In a good way. Why?"

Sophie was silent. "When I was younger my mom was—nicer."

"About trans stuff, you mean," Wendy said, bored.

"No. She's nicer about trans stuff now. Never mind."

"I'm listening," Wendy said, looking at her.

"Nah."

"Hey, Sophie?"

"Yeah."

"I'm fuckin' sorry to ask this, but are you suicidal?"

Sophie barked out a short laugh. "Yes. But that's not new."

"Oh, honey."

And then they were quiet for longer than before.

"It's not because of that ... bullshit—whatever," Sophie mumbled. "I've always dealt with ideation. It's been harder in the last few years. I guess I'll be fine. I don't feel like I need to check myself into the psych ward or anything." She shivered. "Though I hate that fuckin' place."

"I understand," said Wendy.

"Thought you might."

"Hey," said Wendy. "I had a friend who killed herself years ago. Her name was Clara. She was trans. I know I can't tell you to do anything. I can't tell you not to kill yourself because that doesn't matter because I can't stop you. No one can stop anyone." Wendy coolly stared at her friend. "But I miss my friend who's dead. And I want you around. I want to grow old with you. I want you to stay here with me."

Sophie cracked a smile. "You've known me eight months, bitch."

"Shut up!" said Wendy. "I fucking love you! You're fucking important to me, okay? You're one of the best friends I'm ever going to find in this shithole! I want you to stay alive! Sorry."

"Thank you," Sophie said softly.

Wendy shifted gears. "Would it be helpful if you had people around when you're feeling particularly suicidal?"

"I don't know ..."

"Sorry."

"Don't tell Raina, okay?" Sophie said suddenly.

"I won't. Hey, look, thanks for telling me. I want to be there for you how I can—you can leave that as open-ended, okay?" Wendy said. "You want to text or call me with a way I can be there for you, you can do it. I'll *want* you to do it. I know that sounds high school, but I'll never *not* want you to call me. Is that okay, can I say that to you?"

Sophie gave her a warm look. "Yes."

"And if I want to check in with you more than just every once in a while, can I do that?"

"Yes," Sophie said. "I would like that." Then Sophie laughed. "I just remembered something. You know Morgan Page, eh?"

"I read *At Land*."

"You know how she doesn't like the word transgender?"

"No," said Wendy, confused. "Why? I think it's fine."

"She said the other day: 'I refuse to call myself anything but a transsexual. I earned all those syllables.'"

"Ha!" said Wendy. "I'm going to use that."

16

Wendy finally posted her ad at four, after a nap. Almost right away, she got two calls, both about the size of her cock. Fifteen minutes later, a text asked if she'd take fifty bucks. Sigh.

At nine she got a real call.

"Hi, hi—what are your rates?"

"One fifty for a half hour, two hundred for an hour. Outcalls only."

"I'm sorry, I only have eighty dollars." She inhaled sharply but he continued, "Would you just come cuddle with me maybe?"

She clucked her tongue.

" ... sure," she heard herself say.

"How long?"

She considered. "Twenty minutes. Why don't I come over for twenty minutes." To her surprise, he said okay.

She bussed out to his place in East Kildonan—a little far for that much? Whatever, she definitely wasn't cabbing it, and she needed to re-break this damn cherry—and texted Lila where she was.

Wendy felt squirrelly walking up to his door. She'd rarely done outcalls before. This was a house. There were safety practices, but after that thing with Sophie ...

His place was a little bungalow, clean, with nice furniture. He was a short Indian guy in a black T-shirt.

"Hi."

"Hi." He stood nervously.

"Well, can we settle up business, then we can—" He hurriedly dug his hand into his pocket and handed her an envelope; she opened it and counted the cash.

"Would you like to show me to the bedroom?" She smiled warmly. She set a timer. They laid down together, clothed, and she cradled his head on her chest. He hugged her, vibrating at first, then unmoving. He smelled clean and scentless. They lay there for a few minutes. He nuzzled her neck, and she let him. He nuzzled her chin. He tried to kiss her on the lips, and she said, "No, no sorry ... that's more." He nodded and fell back onto her shoulder.

Minutes went past. The timer went off.

"Thank you, call me again anytime," she said. He shrugged nervously in the doorway. She left.

At the bus stop, she looked at the eighty dollars in her wallet.

The rest of the night was more wankers and timewasters, and at 1:40 a.m.:

Ernie: Hey fierce stuff

Ernie: Lol jk what u up to

Her heart sank at this. The sadness and weight of the last few days hit her hard. She took a huge slug from her mickey of whisky and felt tears in her eyes that she swallowed and pushed away. *Should text him my fuckin rates*, she thought moodily.

⁂

Around two a.m. she got a real call to an apartment in the Village, not even that far away. She texted Lila the address (*U got it ladypants*) and cabbed over, snow wild and blowing around the ankles of her boots as she walked through the courtyard. It was a young, drunk white guy with a soft beard who barely spoke, in an old building where Wendy knew you could hear anything between rooms.

She blew him in minutes then walked back with a brown and a pink bill, each zipped into her pocket, sipping from the last of her whisky. The storm was still going, but she'd dressed for it and the whisky warmed and radiated from the soft roll of her centre to her double-gloved fingers, and her hair whipped and flowed around her, dusted in snow. She laughed, drunk, beautifully tired and at ease with her whole aching body by the time she was home. A couple days like this a week, and this outcall stuff could actually be pretty alright.

The next morning, she was groggy and bumping around, almost late to go to the store. Her phone rang. At first she didn't look, but then—

"Anna!" she said.

"Hello. Um. This is Wendy?"

"Yes."

"Ah. Good. How are you?"

"I'm fine thank you," said Wendy, wriggling into her sweater tights. "I have to go to work soon, so I'm just getting ready, just—having my coffee." There was silence because—of course there was. "How are you, Anna?"

"I'm well, thank you. Yup. Have my grandchildren coming later today."

"Yes, that's good," said Wendy.

From the back lane came the sound of a car starting and fizzling out and a woman yelling, "*Get your fuckin' mom!*" A child said something back. Wendy put her arms through a tank top without disturbing the phone.

Anna took a breath. "I want to apologize. For last we spoke."

Wendy felt ice and iron inside of her. "Thank you," she said coldly. "And maybe you would like to tell me exactly what you are apologizing for? Why don't you say it to me very clearly. That seems like a good idea," she said.

There was a long, long silence. Then Anna said, "For being negative. Toward your. Idea of Henry's desires."

Wendy didn't respond at first, then thought *Good enough*. Her irritation evaporated. She put on a stretchy black-and-white-striped skirt and moved to the washroom. "Thank you for that, Anna. That is considerate of you." She put the phone down and waited for a response, put her hair up into a long, high ponytail, looking at nothing. If one of her roommates walked into the kitchen and looked her way through the open bathroom door, they would've seen a side view of her staring at a wall, phone balanced on the sink.

"I would like to continue talking. About Henry," said Anna faintly through the speaker. "Not many people interested in this part of him, I think."

"Yes," Wendy said. "Yes, I hope we can."

For all of Wendy's anger at Anna, which had built over the interim days, it was mixed with frustration and sadness. She had loved her grandpa. She had loved the shit out of him. And she was ready to believe he'd been like her, that Raina was right, and Anna just didn't realize that Henry was trans, and maybe Henry hadn't understood it himself. Wendy wanted to love this old woman. She was so, so tired of loving her people and them not loving her back. Sometimes this made her angry. And sometimes, like now, she found it spookily easy to put her hurt and baggage on ice. She was aware how strange this was. On some level.

"Anna, may I ask you a question about Henry?"

"Oh, go ahead."

"Was he ever angry? About his—situation?"

"Never," Anna said immediately. "Henry was not an angry man. Of course, no matter how Christian a person may or may not be. Anger is still very much there."

"Yes," said Wendy. "I understand that."

"Not him," Anna responded definitively. "Never saw a hint of it. You'd think he had. A thing or two to be angry about. However you want to look at it, now. I have no doubt he is in Heaven. Had his soul straight with God when he died. Forgiven. But no Christian gets there easily."

Wendy had to go to work soon.

"But Henry," Anna continued, "didn't bear grudges. He was never harsh. For whatever else he might have done—" she trailed off.

"He told me a joke once," blurted Wendy. "It was silly and harmless, but he apologized afterwards," she said. "Because I was confused and didn't get the punch line."

"Oh, mm-hmm," said Anna blankly.

More silence. "I think I get what you mean," offered Wendy.

"Oh!" Anna said suddenly. "And how is your family keeping? With Aganetha's passing."

(*Jesus*, Wendy thought to herself. *You do remember your grandmother died this month.*) "They're doing just fine," she said. "All things considered. We knew she was near the end. Ben seems to be doing okay, and I believe his brothers are coping as well."

"Oh, good. Death is never. *Not* painful but. I'm thankful she is with Jesus. I take great comfort in that. That a loved one's suffering is over."

"Nettie wasn't suffering when she died," Wendy said.

"Well," said Anna.

"Hey," Wendy said. "Another question. I was looking over some family photo albums. And there's some periods where Henry's not in them."

"Oh, yes. Would be in the eighties, I think."

"You know this!" Wendy said. "Why?"

She was silent for some time. Then said, "One should not take delight in one's self."

"I beg your pardon?"

"The church didn't like cameras. Back when we were children. Idolatry too of course. Graven images. Looked down upon, in general, as vain, selfish. I think that was the old saying. 'One should not take delight in one's self.' I think the elders changed it in the fifties or sixties. Goodness, can't remember. But there was a period where Henry. Went back to this. I think it was the eighties."

"But Nettie had a camera."

"Oh, yes," said Anna. "Aganetha loved her camera. Quite the shutterbug. You perhaps remember."

Wendy sighed. *That's not why he avoided cameras, Anna,* she thought nastily, *it was never about fucking religion.* For fuck's sake, Occam's Goddamn Fucking Trans Lady Razor.

"Henry," Anna said, "had no interest in judgment. He didn't judge anyone for using a camera, no, my goodness. He loved Aganetha deeply. *Very* deeply," she said sharply, as if correcting herself. "He said he thought the elders were right, years ago, and that was his decision. For himself. He would leave the room when Aganetha got a new roll of film back, if I recall." Anna's voice dropped off. "Did irk her somewhat."

"Anna, can I come visit you, still? I have to go to work, but I want to talk with you more," Wendy said rapidly. "I would like to do that, and I'd love to do it soon. Can I come up and see some of those letters you're talking about maybe?"

"Oh, uh. Sure! Yup, that could certainly happen. I could make some coffee and some sandwiches."

"How about next Friday," said Wendy. "One week from now. I could come up for lunch."

"Absolutely! I'm right on Highway 329. You have the number?"

Wendy stared at the ripped-out page of the phone book that had lived on her desk for a couple weeks now. "Not in reach. What is it, just to be sure?"

"The house number is 36492. On Highway 329. Brown house, it's on the north side of the road."

"Sure."

"I'll write it on the calendar." Anna gave a short laugh, a fuller sound than Wendy had heard from the woman so far. "Looking forward to this, Wendy!"

That night she got a one a.m. call-out to the motor inn on Henderson—a trucker who wanted to fuck her in his cab. He was short and clean-shaven in a polo shirt—looked more like a pampered hockey player than a trucker. Barely older than Wendy. He had a 519 area code and Ontario plates.

He was drunk and couldn't come. He throat-fucked her, standing as she lay on his bed for a long while, and she vomited in her mouth a few times but swallowed it down fine. She hated doing this. But they liked that. Wendy always marvelled, in a grim sort of way, how so many boys liked this. The velvety sliding feeling of her puking and swallowing with her mouth closed around their dicks.

Then he wanted to fuck her ass. He wriggled a hand into her pussy at the same time. "You feel that?" he said breathlessly.

He never managed to cum. She left after half an hour, and he didn't make a fuss. Her hands and face were a mess from his dick. She walked over to the Sev across from the motel and bought a thing of Wet Ones and wiped herself off right out front, in the cold, still air, where the stars for once were out.

She put on her headphones and listened to Hole as she waited for her cab.

She listened to the song "Violet." She listened to it over and over on repeat. She had an early shift at the store tomorrow.

As she fell asleep, she thought about the moment when he'd had his hand in her pussy and his dick in her ass. He didn't even look like he was having fun. His body in hers felt as sensual as foam peanuts.

The next morning, Wendy heard hymns. Beautiful, haunting hymns. It was a Sunday. She heard them for a few minutes, then they would go away and come back a few minutes later. They sounded recorded, like maybe a loudspeaker van was driving around. They were beautiful. Wendy had no words for how light, sad, and peaceful this made her feel. She lay in bed listening until the last second before she had to get up.

It wasn't a recording. It was people standing in their coats near the church down the street, listening to an outdoor service. Wendy hadn't known that was a thing—in any season.

The minister led the gathering again in a hymn as she walked to the bus. She kept stopping to stare over her shoulder at them as she walked, until they were out of sight.

17

The next morning, the phone rang as Wendy was rubbing her eyes and shuffling back from the bathroom, getting ready for a noon shift. She ignored it, then saw it was Lila.

"Hey—"

"*Dsomebatjouyet?*" Lila's voice was frantic and garbled.

"What?"

"*Did someone tell you yet?*" she repeated, obviously crying.

"No, oh no, no, what—"

"*Sophie killed herself.*"

"NO!" said Wendy.

"*I know I can't fucking believe her!*" screamed Lila.

"NO! No! No!" Wendy screamed. "No. No. No. No."

There was a moment when neither spoke; both were crying.

"Who found her?" said Wendy.

"Her mom."

"*Fuck!* Sophie!"

"She didn't tell me how she did it," Lila said manically and breathlessly. "She found her this morning. She did it last night. She thinks late. Her mom thinks late. I hung out with her yesterday evening. She seemed fine. We were out at Cousin's. We didn't get drunk. We made plans to hang out again today. I—"

"FUCK God fucking damn it!"

"I haven't told anybody else," said Lila. "I was the first one her mom called. She wanted me to tell her friends. Her new friends, she said. She was going to call everybody else."

"I ca—I ca—I ca—" Wendy was hyperventilating. She was staring at the wall unable to think, or speak. "Lila—she was—oneofmyonlyfriends. She was one of my only friends."

"I'm fucking pissed off at her!" sobbed Lila. "What the fuck was she thinking! What the fuck! What the fucking fuck! What the fuck is wrong with her!"

Wendy didn't say anything. Her mouth wouldn't open. She stopped hyperventilating. She listened to Lila cry while tears silently dripped down her cheeks. One of the quiet cis roommates came out of her room and Wendy waved her away like a vampire in sunlight.

The two of them cried together on the phone for about a minute.

Then Lila said, "I need to call other people."

"I can't," said Wendy. "No. I can call Raina."

"I'll do it," Lila said shakily. "I don't know what to do," said Lila. "I'll call you later today," she said. "No, I'll call you in just a bit. Please. Okay?"

When Lila hung up, Wendy sat on a stool in the kitchen, crying. She didn't move. She sat there with the phone in her hand.

Sophie's face and laugh and body ran through her vision.

She just sat. The fridge turned on. There was quiet. Nothing happened.

She sat and cried loudly and horribly.

She sat there for almost an hour.

Wendy'd known many people who died suddenly. And more than a few who'd killed themselves. Only Clara, the girl from Charleswood, had she been close to. She'd had reactions before. Strong, screaming, raw reactions. They weren't there now.

She called Raina at work. "Hey ..." she said. "Can I tell you something where you're alone?"

"Sure," Raina said cautiously. Wendy heard scuffles and then Raina going outside. "Okay. What is it?"

"I don't know how to say this," Wendy said (though she did). "Sophie killed herself."

"No she didn't!" said Raina.

"She did."

"I ... I ..." Raina said nothing for a long time, and Wendy heard yelling in the background. "I don't know what to say," Raina said in a voice half-crushed and half a sob.

"I know," Wendy said in a dead voice.

"Why?!" said Raina.

"Yeah."

Raina was crying. "I'm leaving work," said Raina. "I can get out of here."

"Lila's coming over." (She'd texted.) "I have to go to work soon," Wendy said.

"Are you ... Wendy, no ..."

"I have to," Wendy said. She sounded dead. "I have to go. I need the money." She had to go to work.

Lila and Raina came to the house, and the three of them held each other and cried and sometimes yelled. Raina said, "This is such a waste." And they called more people when they thought of them. Soon Wendy really did have to go.

Wendy walked to the bus stop. She didn't hide her crying. A man's voice beside her asked if she had some change. Wendy'd gone to the bank on Sunday and literally had no cash in her wallet, and in a dead voice, she said sorry.

He put his hand on her shoulder and said, "You have a good day."

Wendy slapped his hand away. "Don't touch me."

A guy in a pickup with a John Deere cap was stopped at a light. "He bothering you?"

"I'm fine," Wendy said.

"You sure?" the guy said, eyes wide and smiling big.

"I'm okay!"

"Want some hand sanitizer?"

"Go AWAY!" she screamed. "Get. The Fuck. Away. From Me."

She worked her shift like she was in a dream. She cried in the back room more than a few times. No one thought it was weird; everyone had sort of been fired.

For the rest of the week, Lila came to the house most nights, and she and Raina and Wendy spent a lot of time crying. The first night they all drank, and a few others came over. Only a few. Sophie'd only been back in town for eight months. She hadn't made many new friends.

Every morning, Wendy woke and felt normal for five, fifteen, thirty seconds, then remembered, *Sophie is dead.*

On the fourth night, the three of them sat around the kitchen table. Lila put her head down, lifted it up, and said, "After we left Cousin's that night, she called me."

They were all silent. Then Wendy said, "Oh yeah?"

Lila sniffled. "She said she was in a bad place. I said, do you want to be with someone, and she said no. I said, do you want to hurt yourself, and she said yes and I said I love you, I want you to stay around, and she said thanks. And then," said Lila, "she said, 'I'm not going to kill myself. I'm not. I'm just in a bad spot. Will you stay on the phone with me?'"

"Sophie liked the phone," Wendy said suddenly.

"Oh my God! And she would call you up for no fucking reason," said Lila, laugh-sobbing, like she was clearing her nose. "Like it was 1985! We talked for, God, like, two, three hours, just going on and on. She sounded better at the end. Like two a.m., she said, 'I'm probably gonna sleep.' I asked if she still wanted to hurt herself. And she said not as much. And that she was going to be okay.

And that was it. I thought everything was fine."

"Did we ever find out when ..." said Raina.

"The morning, it turns out," Lila said.

"When she got up maybe," Wendy said gently. "If she slept, I guess."

Lila looked desperate. Finally she said, "Lenora told me how—"

"I don't want to know," said Wendy. She was cold about it.

18

"I'm not angry she killed herself," said Wendy.

"I am," said Lila.

"I'll want her back," Wendy said clearly. "I will want her back the rest of my life. Someone will have a stupid argument on Facebook between people I love who are starting to hate each other, and I'll wish she had been there to de-escalate it or say something smart. I'll see some horrible fucking thing on the news, and I'll wonder what Sophie would have to say. I'll be at a bar and wish I could harass her, wish I could see her sitting alone and surprise her. I did that once, a few months back, and I will never get over the fact that I will never get to do that again. I thought we would be in it together. I'll miss her in a way that will never stop and will never heal." She drained her beer and looked away from the other women as she spoke. "She should have been here. We should have grown old together. I've had a lot of people die. She understood me. She knew where I came from. I'm alone in a way I'm never going to not be alone again. I'm not angry. I'm just alone. There's nothing else to say."

Wendy's memories of the immediate days after Sophie's death quickly grew patchy. She went to the store like usual. She took her number off the Backpage ads and deactivated her SMC. She cried. She went to work and came home and watched TV with the other two, and at night drank whisky and took melatonins and slept. She slept easily and long and sometimes had good dreams. Sometimes Sophie was in these dreams. The seconds after

Wendy woke that week were the last moments when Sophie existed as alive to her, before Wendy remembered: *Sophie is dead.*

When Clara had died, she had been numb like this too but with flaring screams of anger. Wendy'd needed to talk about it, and she'd talked about it a lot. It had reordered how Wendy looked at things.

Not now. There had been a woman she loved, and now there was nothing. She and Sophie had only known each other for eight months but had quickly become familiar with each other's roughnesses and edges, like siblings. And she knew—could feel growing—a dark spot in her brain that was blank and empty in a way she couldn't fathom; keeping herself alive would be harder, at least for the next little while.

Wendy was intimately aware of how she mourned a death that had no warning. Even without rage or anger, these were processes beginning in her that she felt and understood and submitted to.

Well, except she'd had a very clear warning here, hadn't she—they all did. *Fuck fuck fuck fuck, Sophie! God damn it.*

Of all the dead people in Wendy's life, only her grandfather had been closer to her. (But he'd been old and sick. Old people were supposed to get sick and die.) She didn't even have memories of her mom. She thought of her Oma, who had kept a picture of her Opa on her dresser until she'd died.

Right. Which had only been a month ago. Ben was probably still intimately mourning her.

And now there was Sophie.

⁂

She hadn't even been thirty.

⁂

The next day, Ernie texted her at work: *You still want to hang out sometime?*

Wendy snorted and put the phone back in her pocket.

An hour later: *Wendy?*

You there?

Are you ignoring me?

19

When Wendy woke up on the fifth day after Sophie died, for a morning shift, it was early and she couldn't get back to sleep. She made coffee, added a stream of Feeney's, took a shower, washed her hair. Running conditioner through the split ends that were down to her ass, she remembered she was supposed to see Anna the next day. She had to call her. Tell her she wasn't coming.

Then she thought of talking to her dad. But he'd never met Sophie, except for once. (She'd always thought she and Ben would see more of each other.) Well. He'd find out about all this later, eventually.

If Wendy missed anything about her boy life, she missed what she had had with her dad. He'd always known how to cheer her up. She thought randomly of that time he'd persuaded her to drop out of university after one terrible year—"Look, you don't need to piss yourself into debt to be miserable," he'd said. "You can do that for free."

She didn't make much of the fact that her transition eight years ago had coincided with his last meltdown. Ben *had* begged her to stay a boy and taken a while to call Wendy anything but a son—but he always knew he couldn't actually stop her, and he knew (and had explicitly said at the time) that having run his own life through a blender, he wasn't exactly Mr Role Model for telling her what to do, was he?

So she silently thanked God for such minimal troubles among the larger ones that were brewing for the both of them.

And, she reasoned, soon enough Ben would call her his daughter. With time. And after a couple years, she was right.

But Ben had never been able to protect her as a girl, and Wendy had wanted that, always.

What could he even relate to about my life now, anyway.

Dressed but still early for work, she curled in an armchair upstairs by the window in her black pencil skirt and blue tank top, covered by a blanket.

As a kid, she'd lived with her dad in rooms exactly like this. They usually shared a bed. He'd been adept at raising a little boy. Full of magic and games and distraction from the grimness lapping at their lives. He was like a kind man from a Heather O'Neill book.

She should call her father. *Call your dad. Call your dad and tell him one of your best friends is dead. Call him. It's not like you have a mom. It's not like Raina or Lila or Sophie had dads! You have a dad! Call your fucking dad!* Ben had good intentions; he loved her. He would want to hear from her. He would want her to reach out. Wendy could at least—*No. No. No. Stop. Go to work.*

She got Anna's voicemail. Thank God. Wendy couldn't bear the thought of talking to her right now.

One thing Wendy wasn't prepared for was the flood of others from Sophie's past. Her feed and inbox filled up with Sophie day after day, with messages from people she didn't know. Inadvertently, Wendy began to piece together Sophie's life.

She had lived in New York a couple years. And spent some time in Minneapolis.

She had gone to the U of M and got a degree in *chemistry*—she would have started right after Wendy's shit year.

She had a dad! Technically, anyway. Split his time between the oil patch and some hideout in the bush. They spoke like once every two years. Someone was trying to get in touch with him.

Wendy knew one of Sophie's old grade-school friends, a guy legit-birth-named Winston who bartended at the Toad. (He'd eighty-sixed Wendy one night when she was beyond shit-housed; he'd been nice about it.) Winston'd gone to kindergarten with Sophie down in Fort Richmond. Apparently, Sophie would purposely get in trouble with the teacher because she liked time-outs. "We were mean to her," he told Wendy.

"I will always remember when Sophie came back from visiting home for the first time since she transitioned," said one girl out in Oregon, a former roommate, a cis girl who, to all appearances online, seemed like a Very Together Punk-Queer. "She didn't want to talk much, but she wanted to hang out with me more. She stopped being that girl who only hung out in her bedroom. She became obsessed with hearing about my life in high school, for some reason. I never understood why. She always made herself be in a good mood for you, that was always a trait of Sophie's, but there was something desperate about her that winter, where I could feel she needed me to like her. It made me mad sometimes, though I don't think (or rather, I hope) I never got mad at her. I don't know why we hadn't spoken in years. I'm heartbroken and angry and I don't know what to say. Please please please please don't kill yourself."

Wendy started to hear a lot of stories like this. They jumbled and turned and bled into one another, and they soon became too overwhelming to process:

We had to do a presentation one day in Queens you were dating Raina if you had asked me about her last week I would have told you I'd vowed never to speak to Sophie again she was the first trans woman I ever met I would've told you about the time she ghosted me not the first or the second that she taught me chess I don't think it's unfair to say or at least that many wouldn't disagree Sophie was fascinated by people jump to them like a grasshopper had the stupidest things to say and would never let you go of them she could be so quiet and god that girl loved to drink she was so fun I always had fun with her she could get her fucking paws into collected people in that sense in uni she drove me in the middle of the night to Grand Forks to get my mom never let me pay for her hormones not a year ago I just started hormones yesterday surprise everyone btw and I wanted her to be the first one to know I don't know what else to say I just met her two weeks ago fuck her I'm done with her we never stood in line waiting at the door in rain for hours joke of hers was she did this for me she did this to me

Lila and Raina and Wendy were showered with condolences and queries and, strangely, friend requests. Them being physically closest to this woman who had made friends everywhere, it seemed, between the fortieth and fiftieth parallels in the six years she had been away from Manitoba. Or at least people who claimed to have been her friends, or at least people who were desperate to share the stories and feelings they had. Their Facebook feeds became newspapers of mourning. It overwhelmed them all in different ways. For Wendy, when she was alone and picked up her phone or computer, her brain would just fuse. Sludge in her neurons backed up and shut everything down. She would pour a huge glass and slug it and lay down. She wanted to sleep. She wanted nothing.

She would sleep for hours and wake up with her brain softly thudding and, for seconds, peacefully study the wall. *Sophie is dead.*

Lenora somehow got Sophie's funeral held at the First Mennonite Church on Notre Dame, a week after she died. Some of the Internet folks wanted to come from out of town, but only some were able to in the end.

Wendy didn't know any of Sophie's old-old friends. Like, her pre-transition friends. Besides Winston.

Half the people in attendance were from Sophie's extended family. More than twenty of them. They looked like carbon copies of Wendy's family—Southern Manitoba Mennos. She didn't speak to them. She did say hello to Lenora, and the two women hugged with tears running into the shoulders of their dresses for a very long time.

The first person to speak was a composed middle-aged blonde woman with square glasses and a black smock dress.

"Sophie's mother contacted me a year ago to tell me her daughter was coming home. Some of you will know that at the time my own personal life situation was not the best. So the week I was settling into my new house, Sophie herself knocked on my front door. Now, I had no idea she was even coming or even that she was in Steinbach at all! And I opened the door and she just stood out there in front in the sunshine all tall and majestic with that big grin of hers. And I tell you I almost cried. The first thing I said to her was, you look just like your mother. You look exactly like her ..."

"When Sophie was a little ... girl," she said.

This was the point in the funeral where Wendy began to cry.

"When Sophie was a little girl, we looked after her often. She was such a bouncy thing. One particular trait I will always remember. She would tell me she wanted to be a cartoon. She would watch Saturday morning cartoons and say—she would whisper—'Oh look, that's me, Aunt Jeni, that's me, I'm going to be like that when I grow up!' Well. Whoever heard of a small child saying a thing like that? She was always a strange child. I don't think I ever imagined I would overestimate Sophie, even when she was that young. You just knew she would end up somewhere, her name might be in lights or in the paper, whether through her writing or music or ... or just anything! And she grew into such a strong, mature, responsible young woman. Even during the time she was out of touch with our family, I always knew, I always just knew in my heart the Lord was looking after her, that she was making something fantastic happen. She had such a pure soul, a soul that was too pure to stay with us. I never realized how much pain she was in—I prayed for her every day, and I will continue to pray that she is with God."

The woman sat down and put her head in her hands.

Wendy and the others were sitting in the front. None of them spoke. Some people got up and told stories like the aunt had—light, beautiful, melancholy stories, stories both adjacent to and a thousand miles away from tragedy.

Wendy had a flask for the washroom at the reception in the fellowship hall. She stayed in there for a while. She silently prayed, *Lord, please keep this woman with you, and may she rest in peace.* She said out loud, "Fuck you, I'm not joining you for a long time." She laughed. She poured a splash in the toilet. She said, "You better be getting drunk now, you cunt." She leaned against the wall and sobbed. Wailed, really. Ghoulishly wailed. Snorted and heaved, with gobs of makeup-ruining snot running down her face.

She sucked on her flask. She looked at her trimmed pussy, one hand on her vulva, the other on the wall, her flask on the floor. She said, "Man, you stayed alive, you coulda had one of these!" She hiccupped. "You stupid dumb fucking *bitch!*" The door opened and someone walked in. Wendy flushed and stumbled to the sink. An old woman a full foot shorter than her with neat short crystalline hair looked at her politely. The woman could have been Wendy's aunt. The woman could've acted in a movie version of the latest Miriam Toews novel.

Back in the fellowship hall, everybody was friendly. Everybody chatted and everybody talked to everybody else, the family included. It was different than it'd been at Wendy's Oma's funeral. "*Faspa* time," said an old man to Wendy, waiting in line for another helping at the food table.

Sophie's family went back to her mom's place. Her friends went to Cousin's. At the bar, Wendy and Lila and Raina sat at one table, with a few younger girls with short hair and black dresses and two women from the States who'd come up. Sophie's old straight friends sat at another.

One of the women from the States sat down next to Wendy, a white lady with rat's-nest hair, wearing a cardigan and jeans under a huge fucking coat. Carrying a pint glass filled with ice-black liquid.

"Hey," said Wendy. "Your name's Carla, isn't it."

"Yep."

"I'm Wendy."

"I know who you are."

Wendy smiled.

"What are you drinking?" she asked Carla.

"Whisky and Diet Coke."

"We call it *rye* up here, Yankee."

"Oh, whatever! You speak the same language we all do. I haven't been to Canada in years, though—it always been this expensive?"

Wendy rubbed her eyes. "They raised the fuckin' ... liquor taxes again. Last year I think. It was in the paper. The PST went up too."

"Socialism ain't all it's cracked up to be, huh."

Wendy shook the ice in her drink. "You lived with Sophie, didn't you?"

"No. She lived in my town for a bit."

"Chrysalis?"

"Yup," Carla breathed. "That's the place."

"Were you close?"

"Kinda?" Carla coughed. She hacked. "Sorry. Hey, you don't got any weed, do you?"

"No. I could hook you up, though ..."

"Don't worry about it. I'm going home tomorrow. Anyway, like I said. Sophie lived across town from me. Big old house full of assholes. For a while, she was the only other trans girl running around. I'm from a small town, you know. We saw each other around but we never got close. Except this one time, right?"

Carla raised her voice over a sudden change in music.

"So, you know—well, you know Sophie was ... I don't know if you know—fuck it, she's gone, you're a sister, I can probably trust you, huh? She was—like, well, she was a sex worker."

"Yes," Wendy said, her voice sterile. "I did know that. I am one too. I am a sex worker."

Carla's face went blank as a potato. "Okay, great," she said. "That's cool. I mean, I don't know if it's cool, maybe it isn't. You tell me. Or not. I mean I'm just trying—"

Wendy blinked a few times.

"Right, I'll just go fuck myself right now," said Carla. "Sorry. Starting over. So Sophie. She would borrow a car and drive to other towns for work, right? Where I'm from, there just ain't a lot of people; she couldn't make much money, I guess. So one time we ran into each other at the bar. And Sophie's bitching how she doesn't want to go, she's always lonely and wigged out on these trips of hers. I thought hell, I get weekends off now. So I said to her, 'You want me to come with you? It could be fun. I have a real job now, it could be like a vacation! You know, you and I never legit hang out. I dunno—that a good idea?' I thought, *Damn, maybe I'm fucked up, is this a jerk thing to even suggest?* But the look on her face—did it just light up. This was a couple summers ago."

Carla'd already finished her drink.

"I got a room beside hers, we watched TV, had some drinks in my room. She saw two or three guys every night, said she made a decent amount of money. Fuck me, I never realized, you know—I never realized how much sitting around you girls do! Heh. She'd be, like, waiting for the phone to ring. Sussing out all the guys just wasting her time or who wouldn't show up. All for not getting paid. I was, like, Christ, that'd drive me up the wall. I didn't realize."

"Yeah, that ain't fun," Wendy said. "Kinda no end if you tried to talk about it. It's boring and crappy. So I don't. Go on. Tell me more."

"Sorry, sorry, you know," Carla said abruptly. "So over, like, four days we went up to Grand Forks then down to Fargo, and it was just great. The last night, we said to hell with it and slept in the same bed. We watched that one movie—*Heavenly Creatures*, I think it's called? Garbage movie."

"Oh yeah! That movie's boring as hell!"

"Piece of shit," Carla agreed. "What's next, *The Well of fucking Loneliness*? Fuck me. Anyway. So afterward we're talking. And you know," she hiccupped again, "the thing about Sophie. You probably know. She was one of those girls who didn't grow up with it that hard. I mean, she grew up being loved and she grew up with security and believing the world would protect her. I guess what I'm saying is—"

"Why don't I get your next drink?" Wendy cut her off, looking around. No one was listening.

"I didn't grow up with it easy," Carla said again right away when Wendy brought her drink back. "My mom loved me. My dad didn't. We didn't have money, but my dad always had a job; we weren't trashy." Wendy's eyes flickered at this. "But my mom loved me. Now she doesn't love me. That was hard. That was one of the hardest things. I don't know what it's been like for you. I'm guessing you've lost some things. Maybe you've lost more than other girls. Maybe you've lost less. But Sophie grew up loved and she grew up with security and dreams. Do you get what I'm saying? Am I pissin' you off? I know this is dicey."

"I do know what you mean," said Wendy. "And I didn't grow up with security. Mostly. I had it for a few years as a teenager. I don't fuckin' know. Look, go on."

"What I'm saying," said Carla. "Sophie was a girl who lost a lot. For me, I didn't grow up thinking my dreams would ever be real. Like, sure, I used to say I wanted to go to the city and be a fabulous writer or whatever, but in all honesty I knew I wasn't going to be famous and I wasn't going to be rich and I wasn't ever going to move to New York City or anything like that. I'm the GM at my store, you know; I make more money now than I ever thought I would. I'm not saying everyone who grows up like I did feels that way. But that's my read on myself. And Sophie had a different experience. She had such dreams. She believed in *good,* and she wanted there to be *good.*"

"Hey," said Wendy. "Hey, Carla!" Wendy glared at her, suddenly and instantly flaring. "Why don't I buy you another drink, and you maybe think about what you're saying?"

"Sure," said Carla. She swivelled her head around. It fell forward for a second then she caught it. She pulled on her cardigan. "Yeah. Whisky-Diet in a tall glass." The drink Wendy'd just got her was half gone. Wendy took her time with this one.

"Carla," she said, sitting down, politely and icily. "You were telling me a story about a motel."

"Yeah, yeah. It's a sensitive time. Sorry." Carla cast around like she was looking for something. "She told me that when she was little, she wanted to be prime minister. Isn't that a thing?"

"Ha!" said Wendy.

Carla shook her head and burped. "I'll finish my story and get—" she burped again, "get the hell out of your hair. I know, I'm a goof. So like I said, we were lying in bed. And she was dealing with some asshole. Insisted he only had forty bucks. Said she was a bitch. A bit later, he re-appears, says he has more money, sorry, he'll pay full price, please forgive him and see him. She gets all ready and he keeps saying he's just about there. And then he ghosts, he just doesn't show up. Well. Again. You're probably used to that stuff."

"It's daily," said Wendy. "More of an incall thing. Outcalls still flake plenty though."

"Huh?"

"Never mind. Go on."

"I mean, Christ. I don't know what it was like to be her." Carla hack-coughed again. "She'd made money already like I said, so she wasn't really bummed. After that guy, she said, 'I'm calling it a night. I'm taking my ad down. I'm turning off my phone.'"

"Yeah, sure."

"And then we just got *hammered*," said Carla. "Watching stupid TV and telling stories, we talked *shit* about people in town. That was fun, heh. Y'know, people who hate gossip aren't any better than anyone else. They just try to put political justifications behind their shit-talking. They're just as bad as everybody else *plus* they're boring. I trust people who gossip. Anyway, it was fucking fun. And then I went out for more beer, and I came back in. And Sophie." Carla paused, set her drink down and made a hand motion. "She's sitting straight up on the bed. I'll never forget it. She's sitting straight up in this huge T-shirt. And pyjama pants. And Sophie kisses me. I don't usually ..."

Carla faltered and her eyes grew vacant. Wendy wondered if she'd just crossed over to blackout.

"Anyway we had, um. We had sex. She fucked me. I didn't think. From just stuff she'd hinted at. She even ... liked doing that. But she fucked me. It was *rough*. Good, just rough. I don't know. I don't have a lot of sex. I mean. People usually don't want to have sex with me. Nobody likes having sex with me. Anyway. She fucked me through my panties. She had this big, manic grin on her face. We'd never even flirted before! I don't think we had that—energy. Or whatever. And we were SO drunk. It was sloppy. You know? You know. It was that kind of thing." A glimmer of a smirk flashed on Carla's face. "It was fun. And we fell asleep at the same time."

"Sure."

"Hours later," she continued, "I woke up in the middle of the night. Sophie was bucking on the bed, facing away from me. Still naked. That red bob of hers going up and down. And this creepy sound, like a *skriitch skriitch*. And I lay there—I was still pretty drunk—just looking at her back, dumbfounded. Didn't say anything."

"Okay ..." said Wendy.

"Eventually, I realized she was shaving. She was dry-shaving her legs. At least I assume it was her legs. I don't know what else that sound could have been or what else she could've been doing with how she was moving. I watched for a long time before I fell asleep again. I didn't want to move. It felt like I'd done something bad by waking up and learning this. I didn't want her to know I could see her. I had to pee bad too. I fell back asleep. Next day, she was totally normal and we're driving back home and she says, 'I'm sorry, you know I love you, but I don't think we should be sexual again.' I said, yeah, yeah, that's fine." Carla swallowed. "That's all," she said hollowly. "I guess that's the end. Nothing happened after that. I dunno. Never mind."

Wendy's mouth was dry. She wanted to change the subject. She wanted to talk about anything else right now.

Lila was across from both of them, silent, not speaking to anyone. "Hey!" Wendy said to her and Carla. "Okay, random question: What was it with the aunt? How she thought Sophie would be famous for writing or music? Like, I didn't know she wrote or played music."

"I don't think she did," Lila said.

"Never heard shit about that." Carla shook her head.

"Me neither," said Wendy.

"People like to exaggerate," said Carla, sucking on her straw at the dregs of ice, "a person's accomplishments after they died. I get it. But the girl doesn't need exaggerating."

Wendy clinked her glass against Carla's. "I get you on that."

"Her family was all Mennonite, huh?" said Carla.

"Yup," said Wendy. "Just like mine."

"No shit."

"All shit." Everyone laughed at that.

"There's nothing else to it," Wendy said, later in the night, when it was near closing time and they'd steered Carla into a cab with Lila's roommate. Wendy was drunk and in a bad, ugly mood.

"We'll slowly forget, and then this will happen again, and it probably won't be someone I loved as much as I loved her, and Sophie will still be gone, and another person will be gone, and I will think about all we should have done together till the day I die. And I won't miss them like I miss her. That is all there is. That's what suicide means! It's death! She's just fucking gone, and she should fucking be here! And it's her fault. She did this."

There was a lot of silence. Everyone looked the other way. "Thought you said you weren't mad at her," said Lila.

"I'm not," said Wendy. She didn't feel angry. She felt hopeless.

"Oh, okay."

Raina coughed and got up from the table.

Wendy put her head in her hands, pressing her cheeks out, almost off her face. When she looked up, an Amazonian girl from the straight-friends table was making her way over. Wendy readied herself to tell her to fuck off.

"Hi," said the girl, pulling out the chair beside Wendy.

She realized the girl was trans.

How the fuck had Wendy not noticed her earlier? And how did she not know who she was?

Wendy was speechless for only a second. "Hello," she said, visibly confused. The girl looked at her drink and sipped.

"I don't know you, do I?" said Wendy.

The girl arched an eyebrow and said, "I don't think so."

Wendy latently registered through her fogged brain the details of how the other woman looked.

The girl was tall, taller than Wendy, with short, shaggy jet-black hair, thick black eyeliner. She wore a studded belt and a loose, huge threadbare white T-shirt under a maroon hoodie under a dark-blue jean jacket. Tattoos creeping around her neckline that Wendy couldn't decipher. And freckles all over her body.

"No, you don't know me," the girl said. And then Wendy registered: She had an English accent. It wasn't an upper-crusty accent, like the ex-pat Brits who came into her work, but it wasn't, like, Cockney either. Wendy felt embarrassed she couldn't place it. "My name is Aileen," said the girl.

Wendy laughed.

"What?"

"My name used to be Tulip."

Aileen laughed. "Well, I like my name better'n your old one."

"Yeah, me too. Where are you from, Aileen?"

"Me? *I* am from the Internet."

"You look like a trans girl from the Internet." *Oh, you suck, Wendy*, she immediately thought to herself, but Aileen snorted.

"Right," she replied. "Girls in my city think I'm a weirdo too."

"What city's that?"

"I live in Dublin. But I'm from the north of England, outside of Sheffield," said Aileen. "I came to visit a friend. Aside from—you know."

"You chose a hell of a time."

Aileen didn't break her gaze. She sipped from her drink, put it down. "Cheap to fly here this time of year."

"Oh, right. Well, so, how'd you meet Sophie?" said Wendy.

"I didn't," Aileen said. "We talked online for years. We'd made plans to meet in person for the first time. I been here five days."

There was something confident and frightened in the girl's eyes.

"And instead you're here, in this bar," Wendy finished.

"Yes."

"Will you buy me a drink?" said Wendy.

"Yes," Aileen replied instantly.

"But first, do you want to talk about Sophie?" Wendy said rapidly. "Then you should talk to someone else. Because I can't do that. I can't do that anymore for a while. I know you knew her online, but if you want to talk about her, you need to do that with someone else."

"Maybe," said Aileen—she had wide, deep-brown eyes—"maybe I came over to talk to you."

Wendy's head fell forward. She was drunk. She was so, so, so drunk. "You've got pretty eyes," she heard herself say.

"You've got a pretty face, love. Now, let me get your drink."

When they kissed, it was magic. The others were gone and they'd done shots at last call and now were alone outside Cousin's, wind blowing and snow melting on their faces, their lips. *Well. Thank goodness that's mutual,* Wendy said, a finger on Aileen's lips, her swirling breath a cloud moving up and over the taller girl's face. *You tit,* said Aileen. *Like you don't have pretty girls all over you all the time.* In her head Wendy's first thought was *Well no, I'm kind of straight,* but she caught herself midway and just said *No*. Aileen said *Oh no?* and kissed Wendy deeply, her shaggy frizzy hair gradually speckling with white. Wendy said *I don't mean to be bold and I don't know if you like walking but I don't live too far away*, whispering though they were truly alone on Sherbrook in the hushing icy swirl of dark. *You think you're bold,* said Aileen, *I was going to say I've got a room around the corner I'm betting you look good naked in.* Wendy hooted. She laughed her guttural heard-down-the-block laugh with a pickled brain hundreds of feet above herself, spiralling off to the moon. *Why don't you show me yer fuckin room then, I guess* Wendy said, grinning, suddenly and dumbly aware of her own drizzly McKenzie Brothers-like accent. They walked around Wolseley and up Furby—Wendy briefly flashed to the guy on the stoop. *Three weeks ago that happened, Jesus, only three weeks ago? Stop, STOP, you're with this girl not him*—mulched grey and black snow everywhere, the air now still, their boots squeaking and crunching. Wendy pinned Aileen against the side of a corner store, grinning and fondling her face and rubbing hard on her tits through her layers. Aileen gasped. *You are a treat Miss Aileen*, Wendy said. *I can already tell you're a treat.* They made out in front of the stucco wall. There was nothing around them. It was all quiet. The girl's flesh felt soft and safe and beautiful in this way Wendy had forgotten was possible. An old feeling. Aileen led Wendy onward and up Spence and when she turned into a gate Wendy said, *No fucking way. Action House? You're staying at Action House?* Aileen said, *Yeah I'm friends with Randi. She came through Ireland last year.* Wendy nearly fell over in the snow *You know Randi? We got on like mad, she kept begging me to come visit,* Wendy snorted. *Fucking punks. Action House? I've been going to parties here since I was ... well, anyway.* Aileen led her through the front door, hung their coats on the overflowing rack, through the kitchen with the two fridges and impossibly tall black cabinets, through the back the decaying stairs, down into the basement past the laundry into what Wendy recognized as some boy's bedroom who'd lived here forever, who Aileen explained in patches was away ... somewhere ... doing ... something. A slippery memory rose and fell of hanging out in this room with people at a party—years ago. And now this girl Aileen was here. There were posters. Wendy couldn't focus on them. She was so, so drunk. There was a tiny bottle of Jameson on the bedside table. Aileen kissed Wendy on her breasts, the breasts that were both fuller and rounder from the new medroxy and also getting baggy from the years—wait, when did Wendy's top come off? Aileen had the smaller, perky fresh-on-HRT tits she remembered both on her own past self and others (when did both their tops come off?). Wendy pressed the other girl down onto the bed, straddled her and held her firm. It didn't take long for Wendy to figure out what she liked; drunk as she was, she intuitively made sense of Aileen's shuddering skin and a light hiss of air when Wendy touched certain things. She pressed on Aileen's nipple and whispered, *You like that kind of thing.* (*Yes!*) A courtesy, building trust as opposed to gathering information. Wendy's ponytail was coming loose, her huge black mane draping and expanding down her back. Wendy smiled inside herself. It really had been years. Sex with another girl. Wendy screwed her hands into Aileen's chest, and she bucked like fire and screamed, *Fucking shit yes yes! Shit!* Wendy ground against her crotch and Aileen said, *Hurt me. Come on. Be rough with me.* Wendy's pussy was wet and stinking, soaking her panties, God, that fucking smell—she pulled Aileen's hair back. Her hands were on her throat—how did her hands get to Aileen's throat? Aileen was wriggling and vibrating and her clit was hard against Wendy's through their underwear. She released. *Am I,* Wendy said dumbly. *Is that too—? No, fucking choke me! Oh, okay.* Her hands slippery and sweating on her neck. The picture of Aileen below her snapping patchy in and out of focus. Suddenly she is here. Suddenly she is here.

The next morning, Wendy woke up aching in every hungover and sexed sense with all of her body. Aileen was fast asleep beside her. It was noon. *Sophie is dead.*

Her phone had a *babe u free today?* inquiry from a repeat client and a text from Raina: *Wendy-burger. Are you okay?*

I'm fine. I'm at Action House.

Oh my. Scrub yourself before you come home please.

You're hilarious.

Wendy grabbed clothes that weren't hers off the floor and wobbled to the bathroom that had three different colours of gunk between the walls and toilet and sink. When she came out, she saw a cheerful boy doing laundry.

"Wendy!?" he said.

“Yeah. What’s your name?”

“Travis. We’ve met before.”

“Oh. Sorry. Well, nice meeting you again.”

“You stayed over last night! You with, ah, what’s her name—Aileen?”

“Yeah, Aileen. We met last night.”

“Hey,” he said solemnly. “I heard about Sophie. I’m so fucking sorry, lady. That’s just. I don’t know what to say. She was amazing. She was so amazing. I’m going to miss her.”

“You knew her? Did you know her well?”

“We weren’t close exactly. But I saw her around at a couple things, and she always seemed so cool, I always wanted to, like, get to know her better but—”

“I’m going in here before I throw up on you.”

“You know there’s a washroom right behind you! Please don’t throw up in our—”

click

Wendy spent the first hour awake in bed. Aileen’s lips were open and wheezing onto the pillow. Wendy sat with her knees to her chest, her long soft fatty arms tucked around her legs. Brilliant light came through the window above them. The *shkkkt shkkkt* of windshield scrapers and muffled creaks of boots on snow. There was a space heater in the room, and they weren’t cold. Wendy tilted her head and looked at Aileen’s body moving and up down with her breath.

Around one, Aileen was still sleeping. Wendy threw her clothes together and scrubbed off her crusty makeup. She went upstairs and asked Travis if he'd be around while she got coffee.

By three, Aileen was still sleeping. Wendy sat dressed on the floor with an empty coffee cup, feeling stupid. The repeat client really wanted to see her. It'd been over a week since she'd seen a client—well, since Sophie died.

She checked herself out in the mirror. She looked okay. She even had condoms and lube in her bag. She put her hands on Aileen's side and rubbed. "Hey, I'm getting out of here."

Aileen made a deep-sleep snorting sound and smacked her lips and rolled over.

"Come on," Wendy said louder, "I want to say goodbye to you, what the hell." Aileen bodily pushed Wendy back from the bed. Wendy stared at her, then went out the door and called a cab. On the way, she put her ads back up, then found Aileen on Facebook and sent a hope-I-see-you-again message. *Okay, there. Jesus.* The sunlight was starting to fade.

Right after her call, waiting for a cab in the dusk, her phone buzzed. "Bring back the dick parade, boys," Wendy said, reaching into her bag. But it was her dad. *Busy tonight? I wanna celebrate! I worked all my shit out with my brothers! Lemme take you to dinner.*

"So you got it worked out, huh?" Wendy said, pulling out her chair at the Toad.

"Yeah! They all figured it out. I drove out to the old country last night, and we all shook on it and made up."

"That's great!"

"Fuckin' A it is!" Ben said. "So I got back into town today, and I thought, hey, haven't seen you in a while, what kind of father am I? Hey, I got ya a beer."

The waitress came over with Kokanees. Wendy knew her from the music store on Portage. They said pleasant hellos.

"So what's been going on, huh?" Ben said. "You good with your work and everything, you got Christmas season coming up."

"Yeah, it's all fine," she waved a hand. "Everything's great. So your rickshaw thing's rolling along then, eh?"

"Oh, naw, forget about me! What's up with your life, kid? I've always got my own shit. You're always like, 'Oh, everything's fine, it's all fine!' *Talk* to me. You can't be all be rose-coloured piss."

My best friend is dead. My best friend killed herself. I'm getting laid off and I'm doing tricks again and I'm scared a thing that happened to my friend is going to happen to me. But I'm making money. I'm almost certainly making more money than you. A man did something to me in an alley weeks ago, and I'm burying it because too much else has happened. Your father might've been a woman, but I can never tell you that, ever, ever. I don't want to kill myself, but I don't know if I want to live either. I'm taking new hormones and I like my boobs better and it's made me calmer and less angry, and they might also kill me faster. Maybe. No one really knows. My best friend is dead. Every man I like and am attracted to would never love me, ever. Every man who thinks they like me is either an awful creep or is paying for the privilege and sometimes both. More and more, I feel like life is something that's just happening to me. My choices don't feel like choices at all. It's like they're things that have been decided and I just react to them the way anybody would. The older I get, the more life feels like a blank, gauzy haze where every direction is just the same thing. It seems like other people have this way of pushing back against things in their life they don't like, and I just don't have that. Doing tricks the second time is harder. I think sex work is work like anything else, but there isn't agency the way the smiley ones say there is. I feel like it was all predetermined and inevitable and it was silly to think I could ever stop. I feel that way like I feel about the fact your grandpa had to be a farmer and your dad had to be a man. I could never tell you this, nor could I tell you that I'm safer than you think, being white and working indoors. I don't mind I could never tell you any of this. Could I get a different job? I don't know. Jobs never worked out for me, except for the one I'm about to get laid off from. I'm always either too much of a goon or they don't like that I'm trans. What would my life be like if only one of those things were true? I can't tell you any of this. I know I can't. But I don't think my life is bad. It's funny—does all this stuff seem dark to you? Even though you're no stranger to hardship. I don't feel like my life is bad. I have friends I can trust; I have a good house; if I feel weird about a trick, I don't have to take it. Yet. I feel hopeless and powerless, but I'm genuinely grateful. That's a true thing. I don't know if you'd understand that. Maybe you would. What can I tell you about my life? Last night at my friend's funeral, I hooked up with a girl for the first time in years. It was hot and sweet, it was so nice. But you know what, Dad, I barely remember it. I only remember patches, bits and pieces, I got so fucking dru—

"Sometimes I think I'm an alcoholic," she blurted.

"Fuck off, don't talk like that."

She was silent. "Sorry."

"Your uncle," Ben said instantly, "when he was in rehab, he met a guy who every morning would get up, go out, and bring back to bed a sixty-ounce of vodka and a bucket to throw up in. That's being an alcoholic."

His eyes softened. "You don't drink *that* much, I don't think."

"I don't know," said Wendy, but her first thought'd been *I have the money to drink that much now. I could if I wanted, and it wouldn't matter.* She lifted her glass and tried to look at her father, but her eyes wouldn't focus on him.

"*Are* you drinking like how my brother used to?"

"No." *But I can't remember the last night I wasn't drunk.*

"Even close to that?"

"I don't think so ..." She drank about a mickey a day. Sometimes more. Usually a mickey a day or equivalent thereof. She knew this.

"Kid," said her dad, folding his hands in front of himself. "If you're worried about it, count your drinks. If you count your drinks, you'll know a number for when you're in trouble. And if it turns out you can't count your drinks? Then yeah, maybe you want to take it easy for a bit. Look: I don't think you got much to worry about. If you do? Count your drinks. Try it. It's a thing you can do."

"That's good advice, Father." Wendy was genuinely surprised. She lifted her beer bottle and set it back down. "Number one. Geez, that was easy."

"See?"

Ben reached over with a kindly look and squeezed his daughter's shoulder, and the warmth of it almost made Wendy cry.

"See? There you go."

"I fuckin' love you, Father," Wendy choked.

"I love you too, kid!"

December

20

In Wendy's dreams some nights later, a man had gotten into her. She was clothed, wearing jeans and a plain shirt, but a man was in her. She pulled him out, and he was like a long string of beans coming out through her fly. She shrieked and pulled and pulled, but he was laughing. A woman tonelessly told her that certain things happened with celebrities. She was screaming—

Wendy shocked awake, sweating under the blankets with her bladder pulsing. *Sophie is dead.*

Later, getting ready for work, her phone rang. She ran to it with adrenaline and dread—

Anna.

Wendy watched the phone ring in her hand until it went silent. She took a nip of rye before moving back to the washroom where she heard the ding of a voicemail.

She went to work, putting up displays and doing markdowns. Business was steady with the holidays, and she had mindless work eight hours a day, five days a week. Between this and boys in the night time, her distractions were many. She was grateful for this. Wasn't sleeping much but building a pretty decent nest egg for when January rolled around.

An hour before her break, she went in the back to box up damage claims.

"Wendy, how you hanging," said a voice behind her.

"Shit!" She threw her hands up.

"Hey!" Michael started. "I didn't mean—" He put a hand on her shoulder and Wendy hit it away like a bug.

"Sorry, sorry."

"It's okay," Wendy said, already recovered. "I'm sorry. Shit. I—I was startled."

"Nice reflexes," Michael said, massaging his hand. "So, how *are* you holding up? Are you okay?"

Wendy glared at him. She turned back to her box.

Michael chuckled. "Yeah, I know, Captain Asshole over here. Sorry. Look, here's a real question: You wanna get drunk before we head out of this place?"

Her manager's face was hopeful. " I can pick you up," he added.

She didn't want to fuck him. But that was the face she made. "Yeah," she nodded slyly. She had put on her phone voice too, without intention. "Yeah, let's do that."

"Cool. You give me a day."

She smirked. "Give *me* a day, bossman."

"*Bossman.*" He put the back of his hand to his forehead. "Who are you? Let's go next Friday. You have a closing shift Saturday, and I have it off."

"Done."

He walked off. She ignored the sinking feeling in her chest. *Whatever! Do you have to fuck him? Just milk him for some fucking free booze and leave!*

"Hello! Yes. Message for Wendy. This is Anna Penner. Wanted to. Offer condolences again. I am very sorry. For the loss of your friend. That pain. Never eases. You can only be thankful they are with the Lord. If you. Believe they are of course but well. Don't mean to. Bless me. Well."

Anna coughed a few times. "*Pardon* me!" she said. Wendy grimaced, smoking her cigarette, and went to delete the message but accidentally dropped her phone on the sidewalk with a quiet clattering on the ice.

She bent down and heard: " ... my prayers every night since you informed me on my answering machine, dearest Wendy. I have been thinking about you. And wishing God's angels may surround you and bless you. I know you are loved, Wendy. You are welcome in my home at any time ..."

Wendy stayed kneeling on the sidewalk, staring at her phone, wind blowing her scarf around, the horizontal sun lighting her against the snow bank by the parking lot.

"You have yourself a good day. 'Bye now." There was a long, scuffling click.

She got home and listened to Anna's message again.

Then she got a call from a guy she'd never seen before. He sounded real.

Out by St. Mary's Road, a short bald white man with tattoos and dense muscle was waiting for her outside a garage, wearing a blue T-shirt and khaki shorts. He showed her into the garage. "It's kinda messy."

There were tools and a couch piled with crap on one side and lawn chairs and an armchair around a table on another. There were beer cans all over the floor, a fridge at one end, and a big stereo behind the table with the radio on.

"You okay with drugs?" he said.

"I'm fine with drugs."

He flicked a baggie of powder. "Want any?"

"No thanks."

"Mind if I do some?"

"I don't mind at all."

He fucked her as she sat in a lawn chair. It was more comfortable than she thought it'd be.

"You want a beer?" he said after he came.

"I would love a beer." She put her feet on the table.

"You don't have to sit naked," he said by the fridge. "I'm not going to." He put his shorts back on and wordlessly she put on her lingerie.

"That was fun," he said. "Your pussy's good. It's good. Shit, can it ever get wet on its own? It's just amazing what they can do, like—take something out, put something else in. I see girls all the time. You're one of the good ones, I can tell. I work up in White River, Ontario. Putting in a hydro dam. It's brutal. I work twenty-one days on, ten off. I'm a carpenter. I used to be married. I didn't have a good marriage. One of the girls I saw fell in love with me, eh? It was trouble, she really liked me. My wife found out, started calling her—it wasn't good. See these tattoos on my arm here? Those are my girlfriends. Just kidding, they're my kids. They're good kids. Two of 'em—Ashley and Robert—they're out in Vancouver right now. I don't see 'em often. Whatever, I'm not gonna fight. They'll come find me when they wanna find me. I don't worry about it. I like to go to bars. I like dancing. I like to go to the Lincoln, go to the Sherbrook. My friends don't like to go there, eh? Guys I work with too, big guys. I grew up in Norwood. When it was bad. You'd be walking around at night, all the gangs would be out, these guys would be like tryin' to steal my hat and coat, and I'd be like, 'We go to school together! Fuck!' One of them ended up my friend. I work with him now. Guy gets into fights all the fuckin' time. He's on the run from the cops now, actually. I went out last night, picked him up out of a ditch in Assiniboia Downs. A fuckin' ditch. Not fuckin' days ago, we're on our way back from White River and we go to a strip club in Thunder Bay and the guy gets into a fight before I even get to see a stripper. And he's a huge guy, like, arms twenty-eight-inches-around big, like the bouncer doesn't want to mess with him. And, you know I'm not a big guy, but I go put an arm around him like this and the other around him like this, and I'm like, 'Hey, let's get the fuck out of here.' The bouncer's looking at me like, 'You gonna be okay?' I said, 'Hey. He ain't gonna hit me, and if he does, it won't be that bad.' I've been hit hard. You don't wanna do it again for free do you? No? Even though I'm a nice guy? Okay. Okay. Want me to walk you out?"

"Hello, Anna?"

"Yes. Oh, is this Wendy?"

"I got your message. Thank you. Can I come up to visit this Thursday?"

"Well! Can't see. Why not. Yes, why don't you come up for lunch?"

"That sounds lovely. Noon then?"

"I'll make sandwiches. Do you like ham and cheese? I can also—"

Wendy felt herself about to cry. "Love it. Thank you, Anna, I'm sorry to cut and run, but I have to go. I'll see you in three days. I'm looking forward to it," she choked. "See you then."

She put a hand on her heart, made coffee, and called Lila.

"Hey, can I borrow your car?"

"Oh, cool lady, it's nice to talk to you too."

"Sorry. Look. Tell you a quick story?"

Wendy filled her in on the whole thing with Henry and Anna.

"Damn, girl."

"Yeah."

"How long has this been going on?"

"I found out, like, a month ago, I think? A month."

"You didn't tell me."

"Sorry."

"What day you going? I'll need a ride to work."

Wendy was emotional and exhausted and still a little drunk. So she only noticed by touching her first mug of coffee that her wrist was hurting.

Like, hurting a lot.

She set the mug down and turned her hand. There was a bubble on her wrist, like an amniotic sac. The skin on her wrist had opened up around it, and there was a clear, grey film with fluid inside. Away from the heat of the mug, it didn't hurt anymore, but it ached.

"What the fuck," she said numbly to no one.

She looked at the rest of her hands. Two parts of her palm had cracked and there were flat round red sores on some of her fingers and dead skin. Her joints had been hurting—for a few days, now that she thought about it. With everything happening, she'd kind of subconsciously written off the pain.

The medroxy, she thought with a chill.

How long had it been? She pounced on her phone and found her text history with the dealer. Three weeks. *(Jesus, only three weeks.)* Still in a window where the drugs could be making new and fast changes to her body.

She frantically Googled everything she could about the synthetic hormone. She'd done it before, but she did it again. She found a warning about the possibility of cracking skin. That was all. She'd go to urgent care after work.

Hours into her shift, the red sores on her fingers had also turned into bubbles, smaller ones. They also hurt to touch. It hurt to do things with her hands. The big bubble on her wrist was growing too, the skin splitting further to make room for it.

Wendy worked uncomplaining through the pain, and mid-shift ran over to the LC. It was so big and calm when she walked in, mid-afternoon on a weekday; usually she came in after work, and it was packed. But now it was quiet. Bottles for miles. She walked past the sale rack—the province's idea of discounts made her depressed—and past the half bottles and into the main part of the floor.

Usually she headed for her vodka or her whisky and maybe a chilled king can of something. But today, when it was so quiet, she really noticed how big the store was.

It could be strange to disturb a routine in a store where you have consistent habits. Regular customers in her own store could have no idea where certain things were. Wendy moved down the rows. There was cheap Russian vodka beside Alberta Ice. Expensive ryes a foot above her usual shelf that she had not known existed.

The Manitoba Liquor Control Commission's *raison d'être* was to make money off booze and curb its consumption at the same time. They trumpeted eleven-percent ABV craft beers and ran Be Undrunk ads under the same roof. They had a Twitter account. There was this one TV ad with these soused seniors bopping around at a party—old guys without shirts, an old lady with a lampshade on her head. The idea was to shame them with the final message, Act Your Age, but Wendy and her friends all took it the other way: *Those old people rule! That ad's not working at all!*

Her dad once said this province had one of the higher rates of alcoholism in the country—which, considering all the abstaining Mennos, was impressive. Or extra bleak, depending on your point of view. Was that true? It was the kind of stuff her dad would look up. But her dad said a lot of things. She did remember reading in the paper that the MLCC pulled in a profit of close to $276 million for the province last year. Only 1.2 million people lived here. And $276 mil was the profit. The profit.

Wendy knew it was childish to be bothered by any of this—she was an adult, she knew what she was doing to her body—but it was something she remembered.

Right, I'm supposed to be counting my drinks. In the bathroom at work, slugging long from a mickey of Forty Creek, she felt the pain in her hands ebb and a fuzzy glow warm her brain. *One.*

As Wendy bussed home, she wanted to collapse—from the lack of sleep, from being on her feet for eight hours, which was getting harder day by day—but her hands, her freakish bubbled hands. She had to go to urgent care. The hospital was a reasonable walk away. Wendy got off the bus and thought *Just go.* But she was so, so, so tired.

She'd nap! *Duh.* She climbed up the stairs, set the alarm for half an hour later, and fell into bed.

When she woke up, it was two in the morning. *God damn it.*

She had slept in her clothes with no blankets. She was cold, and by now her hands were in incredible pain. An EMS vehicle went down the back lane, strobing red and white around her room then vanishing and leaving the room dark and soundless but for the dripping of a tap.

She turned on the lamp and put her feet on the floor with a creak of wood.

The bubble on her wrist was huge now, a golf ball cut in half. There were bright air bubbles in the lake of fluid sloshing around inside. And there were more bubbles on both her hands. She counted. Six on her left, eight on her right, one more coming up slow and visible on each of her thumbs. And another on the heel of her right palm. And they hurt.

They really, really hurt.

She felt tears. "Stop it," she whispered. It looked like a horror-movie virus. "Stop it," she whispered again. A big hulking cracked monster who would only grow like this more and more, and it would spread to her arms and the rest of her body. She would infect her friends, her loved ones—

Wait. Could she?

She wanted to wake up Raina. She wanted to say, *Raina, I don't know what's happening to me, I'm so scared, these illegal hormones made this happen to my body, I feel like I'm dying, I'm so tired and I can barely walk, please, please, please help me ...*

The hospital wasn't far. She could go to urgent care. She wished she had something more to drink. She'd finished her mickey by the end of her shift. But the vendor closed at two-thirty, if she hurried ... *What the fuck, Wendy, just walk to the fucking hospital!*

The wind was brutal and loud, like a shrieking person she had to push through. Her headphones flew out of her ears. She put them back in, and they flew out again right away. It was so loud. It had hurt to pull on gloves, and now they were rubbing on the bubbles. Her mind simplified and descended like it did in these temperatures: *I am in pain, and soon I won't be. I am in pain, and soon I won't be. I am in pain, and soon I won't be.* She thought about literally nothing else until she walked through the door.

Everything in the hospital was orange and brown. The triaging nurse was nice. "Yup, that's strange. You'll probably need a dermatologist, but I'll get you in with the doctor anyway."

An hour clicked by. Eventually Wendy asked for the washroom and was directed around the corner, near the patient rooms. She passed by a room with the door half-open. A tall Black doctor with his back to the door moved his hands over a person she couldn't see.

"And how did this happen again?" said the doctor.

"I smashed a plate in someone's face."

The doctor must have sensed Wendy as he then turned around. They stared at each other for a few seconds before Wendy said, "I'm just going to the washroom."

Then he saw her hands, and his face relaxed. "You're the girl with the skin issue."

"Probably?"

"Forgive me one second," he said to the other patient.

"No problem."

The doctor took his gloves off and sat down at his desk. "I can tell you right now no one here will know what's wrong with you. You'll see a dermatologist. Call this number tomorrow morning. I'll leave a referral message for them in the next hour so they'll know to get you in right away. And I am sorry about the wait." He handed Wendy a slip. He seemed only a few years older than Wendy and had specks of a tattoo sleeve poking out from the arms of his lab coat.

"Thank you, doctor."

"You're welcome. Have a good night." He turned around to the patient Wendy couldn't see. "I apologize."

"Hey, that's okay."

She went back home. It was almost five in the morning when she got there. She was sober now and wide awake. She sat in a chair, read a little, played with her phone.

Maybe this was it. Maybe she wanted too much.

It wasn't enough to transition, to get bottom surgery; she had to have this too. And now look at her. There were two more bubbles growing on her hand since she'd woken up! It wasn't stopping! She hadn't taken her medroxy that day, of course, but the bubbles were still growing ...

She'd been ignoring her phone too—she couldn't do calls like this.

Wendy sat in the dark, in the cold, staring at her knobby, bubbled hands. The only sounds were a tap dripping and a car every few minutes in the back lane. Someone screamed in laughter, maybe a block away, then a primal "Whooooo!" then quiet.

The ache was getting worse. If it kept going like this, she couldn't even work at the store. She already had a small stockpile of savings from these past couple weeks of ho-ing, but ...

What's going to happen to me?

She sat there for hours until nine o'clock, the sun peeking and shining through the upstairs window.

She had sat there not thinking and letting her brain go beyond overdrive.

Then the door flew open and Raina yawned and stretched in her pyjamas. "Wendy! Are you alright?"

Wendy numbly held up her hands. "No."

"Shit!" Raina said uncharacteristically. "What is ..."

"I don't know," said Wendy. "It's time for me to call someone. I'll tell you in a minute."

Raina padded downstairs, and Wendy dialled the dermatologist. Raina's girlfriend poked her head into the room and waved. Wendy nodded.

"Hi, my name is Wendy Reimer. I have a referral to come see you urgently. Oh, excellent. This afternoon? I have to work. I could come right now. Can I come right now? Oh. Tomorrow morning? Okay, ten-thirty, you got it."

Raina came back upstairs with coffee and Wendy gingerly accepted a cup, leaning over the table to sip it. "Have you ever heard of anything like this happening before? With any kind of hormones?"

Raina shook her head. "Never."

"You don't know anyone who's taken medroxyprogesterone, do you?" Wendy said desperately. "Anything?"

"I read something on a message board," Raina said slowly. "Years ago. I doubt I could find it now."

Raina's girlfriend emerged with a frown, and Raina looked pained. "Could you give us a second, love." The girlfriend's face turned to ice. She retreated and loudly closed the bedroom door.

"Look at me," whispered Wendy. She had her hands flat on her knees like a punished child. She felt like a monster.

"You have your appointment soon?" said Raina, still looking uncomfortable.

"Tomorrow morning. How the fuck are they supposed to fix me—how will they know what to do?"

Raina stood up, bent over, and kissed Wendy on the head. She put her arm around Wendy and hugged her fiercely with her lips near her ear. "You are beautiful, and I have every faith you will press on and remain."

Wendy couldn't move her hands.

Raina stood up. "Whatever happens after tomorrow, my dear, I'll be here."

Their eyes locked and Wendy whispered, "Thank you. I love you."

Raina looked away bashfully and went back into her room.

Wendy worked another shift. She tried it sober, gulping T1s like Pringles. Michael wasn't around, so she fobbed off most of her work, but still barely made it through. Got off shift at eight. She didn't want to be around anybody, didn't want to try to work. She bought a two-six and bussed home staring out the window. *You had to have it all, didn't you?* The bubble on her wrist was truly huge and couldn't be covered with a glove without extreme pain. The temperature had fallen off a cliff in the afternoon. Minus-forty wind-chills on her walk back to the bus.

At home—sweating, freezing, swearing—she drank down two, three, four booze-and-water bombs, followed those with melatonin, and slept for twelve hours without dreaming.

Raina was knocking at her door before her alarm went off. "Wendy?"

"Hafsdhf. Huh? Hi."

"My dear, I'm afraid I have to tell you something."

"NONONO who is what is it—"

"Nobody is dead," Raina said gently. "Nobody is hurt. Come upstairs in a minute if you would. I just need to talk to you before I go to work."

Wendy got up and made a coffee, tied her hair back, spent a solid sixty seconds emptying her bladder, then put on her slippers and housecoat and trundled upstairs.

"What's happening?" Wendy said, using pot holders to carry her coffee. "I have my appointment in an hour. It's still fucking freezing as balls out, isn't it?"

"They're not renewing our lease. We have to leave this house soon."

"*Are you fucking kidding me!?*"

"I'm not, I'm afraid."

"*I don't—what the—*I'm sorry, I'm yelling."

"Yes. I imagined you would."

"You did? Why is this happening?"

"Our super is getting fired, and apparently we're fired along with him."

"That doesn't make any sense."

"It doesn't, does it? You know how our lease expired a few months ago, and he kept saying he was going to get a proper new one?"

"But we've been paying rent to that fucker!"

"Yes, and for reasons mysterious to a law-hating social-service worker like me, apparently that doesn't matter and we have no valid claim to living here and we can be evicted basically any time with thirty days notice. That would be January fourth, of course, but they're offering us half a month's rent plus deposits right away if we can be out before month's end." She handed Wendy the letter. "They delivered it about half an hour ago and explained the whole thing."

"Oh my God. Oh my God, those goddamn motherfucking sons of fucking bitches."

"Yes."

"What do we do?" Wendy said, sitting down on the floor with a creak. "Can't we ... can't we ... aren't there tenant's rights organizations? There have to be. There's, like, a million of those, aren't there? You know this shit, right? I can't ... isn't there some kind of organization that helps us? Isn't that why we pay taxes?! Do you know someone?"

"Indeed, there are many. But you need to at least currently be on a lease. And legally we are not." Raina was sitting on her bed with her head cupped in her tiny hands. "We could try to fight it, I suppose. We would have some standing. But I wouldn't be confident about it. Or, we can each take our precious four hundred dollars and find a new place. If we sign this other thing they gave me, we get our cheques immediately."

"Shit." Wendy breathed out deeply. She took a sip of coffee and rubbed her forehead with her clear thumb. "Well, hey, lady, you got surgery coming up. You can probably get off this rock after that, hey?"

"I'm sorry?"

" ... Leave," said Wendy after a beat. "I always thought once you got surgery you'd leave."

Raina looked out the window and made a quizzical sound with her lips that was halfway between a buzz and a horse snorting. "Yes. Me too. That was the original plan."

"So?"

"Well, there's Genevieve to consider, obviously. If she were to leave, it wouldn't be for some years, not until she's finished her master's."

"Right, of course."

There was an awkward silence until Raina said, "I think I may have also moved around enough. In my life."

"Sure, that makes sense," said Wendy.

Raina clapped her hands. "Anyway! I would still like to live with you. Do you want to still live with me?"

"Of course."

"Then I'll start looking on Kijiji tonight. I don't know about the other girls. I haven't spoken with them yet."

"Barely ever notice those two," Wendy said abstractly.

Raina raised her eyebrows. "Who can figure out cis people, no?"

"Ha!"

Then Wendy looked at her globuled hands. A wall of anger appeared in her. She wanted to hurl her coffee mug at the wall. *What the fuck is next, huh?*

21

"Ms Reimer? Geez, you're tall."

"That's me."

"Ms Reimer, I'm Dr Freedman. How are you?"

"Awful. Look at my hands."

"Yeah, that's some stuff you got there. Do you have them anywhere else on your body? Your armpits?"

"No."

"You're sure? Absolutely none on your armpits."

"I'm sure."

"Weird. Any changes to your health recently? Or new medications."

"No and no."

"Okay, let's take more of a look here. I'm not gonna hurt you." The doctor strapped on gloves. "Tell me more about yourself—what do you do?"

"I work at Tammy's Gifts and Books."

"Tammy's! My mother loves your store. You probably know her."

"Yeah, probably."

"I get my son Moe to take her there. You ever see a young Jewish guy in there looking miserable with an old lady, that's my family."

"Oh, I know them! They come in all the time."

"My apologies," said the doctor dryly. "You can't pick your family, you know? I'm just kidding, I love 'em, 'course I do."

"They're nice. I like when they come in."

"You're a sweet liar, Ms Reimer."

"Ha! I like you, doctor."

"Don't get too hasty."

"You're funny—*ouch*!"

"Told you." She drew fluid from the burst bubble on Wendy's pinkie into a syringe and popped it into a vial. "Pretty sure I know what you have. Goes away with antibiotics. It's weird you don't have it on your armpits." She printed out a prescription slip and signed it. "Anyway, I'll have this fluid tested on the off-chance those antibiotics don't work. Call my office if your hands aren't clear in a week. They will be, though."

"You're sure?"

"Ninety-nine percent. Nice meeting you."

She watched the doctor's back as she started down the hall.

"Wait!" Wendy said. "Do you know what caused this?"

"It's random. You get this, it's just random."

A thought occurred to Wendy as the doctor was about to enter another door.

"Wait."

Dr Freedman turned around.

"Moe. His last name isn't Hirsch, is it?"

Her brow furrowed. "It is. That's his dad's last name."

"We were in daycare together. I just realized. I remember that name. That's your son."

"No kiddin'!" she said. "You remember little Moe. The daycare on Grant Avenue. John Dafoe."

"Yeah," said Wendy. "My mom got me in to that place just before she died. Not that I remember that. Parting gift, I guess."

The doctor's smile flickered. "Funny, I don't remember a Wendy. Thought

I remembered everyone Moe went to class with, even back then, but I don't remember a Wendy."

"Well, it was a while ago. And after daycare, I went to school in my own neighbourhood. I mean—I didn't even recognize him at the store. Guess he wouldn't recognize me either."

Wendy looked down at her hands. Her long ponytail fell in a sweep of black across her shoulder.

"What's Moe doing now?"

"He's a contractor. Plumber, I guess you'd call it. He likes it. Engaged to a real sweet lady."

"Good for him. I always remember he was nice to me." He had been. One of Wendy's few friends. Maybe her only. They were so little—four, five years old. But she did remember.

"Thanks again for your help, doctor."

"'Bye now."

Wendy went across the street to a Shoppers and filled her scrip, popped her first two pills, and went back out to the bus stop. Okay, so she wasn't dying. *Thank you, God*, she felt herself thinking. She took out her phone and texted Raina: *I'm not dying. They knew what it was. I got some drugs. Love you.* Then she remembered they'd been evicted. She wanted to punch something. She yelled "Arrrrhghhh!" to no one. A couple shrank away from her and hurried inside. She saw them pointing her out to a clerk. She hated them. *Hated them.* It was those kinds of people who kicked her out of her fucking house! It was those kinds of people who killed her friend! *Sophie— goddamn it!* She kicked the side of the bus stop, and flakes of ice showered to the ground. Then the bus came, and she went off to work.

Dr Freedman was right. The pain stopped in hours. By the end of her shift, the tinier bubbles had withered and faded. The bigger ones stopped growing and began deflating slightly.

She took more antibiotics at home, then looked at her little half-used foil sheet of blue pills, the medroxy.

Should she keep taking this stuff?

They did make her feel better.

Dr Freedman had said it was random, but Wendy also hadn't told her she was on these things.

Did anyone really fucking know what hormones did?

She wished she could trust doctors.

Wendy took the sheet and shoved it in a drawer with the vitamin bottles. *Not yet. Maybe again, later, but not yet.*

Then she remembered: Anna. She was seeing her tomorrow. Holy shit.

Her phone was pinging with timewasters and wankers. *Hey,* she thought to herself. *Tonight, just get a good night's sleep. You have a long day tomorrow.*

She poured her fourth big vodka-and-Fresca of the night and settled into her bed, sipping and smoking cigarettes and dreamily scrolling through Facebook, starting and stopping episodes on Netflix, listening to the soft hum of Raina's and Genevieve's voices talking above her. She settled on a movie called *Comet* and watched the whole thing without paying attention, poured another drink, and let herself float under her layers of blankets, feeling and thinking about nothing, her barely cracked window sucking out the wisps of her smoke and the returning tendrils of pure, clean cold filling the air above her.

Then, turning off her light, she got one last text: *U still awake*

Maybe, she texted back reflexively.

Up for an outcall by the perimeter to see a respectful gentleman?

Lol respectful gentleman huh

Pip pip cheerio

She tittered. Tricks were so rarely funny.

Maybe i'm downtown so thats far

Ill pay cab plus etransfer half the money upfront so you know it is worth your time. Whats your rate for two hours?

She told him, and he said yes. Shit. Couldn't turn that down.

Alright sweetie cakes. ;) I'll come once the money clears. Send to ...

She tossed her phone down. She was tired. She was so, so tired. It was so cold out, and she felt so nice and warm and the best kind of fuzzy-drunk-sleepy. Part of her didn't want the money to come. But she couldn't turn it down if it came. (This was ingrained into her skin, and it always would be. She could never turn the money down.) And it came, twenty minutes later. With extra for the cab.

"Alright, alright." She pressed her healing hands on her face. "Come on, champ, let's do this."

After long expanses of nothing past Kenaston, there were dots of luxury homes in undeveloped fields near the Perimeter. It was barely even suburban out here; it was like they expected the city would fill in to the space. Eventually.

The cabbie stopped at a row of thin, new, cheap-looking townhouses, the kind that technically had their own street numbers but were still basically just apartments with their own front doors. So he didn't live in a luxury home, then. Geez, if you weren't getting a nice place anyway, why the fuck would you move all the way out here?

The guy opened the door in a shirt and jeans. He was young and pale and muscled and he looked happy in a manic way, and Wendy immediately thought *Cocaine*.

"Fuck, it's cold! Come in!" he said.

She took her coat off, and he said, "Want a line? I just got this and thought, *fuck*, I should call you!"

"I'm alright, thank you."

"Fuuuuuck, I can't wait, thank you so much for coming over! Can I e-transfer you the rest of the money? I don't have any cash. Do you want some wine? I got wine. Got us a big bottle of wine!" A cold magnum of white. Wendy poured a glass.

Weights and video games were scattered in the living room. He sat down on the couch and intensely tapped on his phone to send the money. Midway through his head jerked up. "Sorry, I'm watching porn. I'm a pervert. "

Wendy hadn't even noticed. She swivelled her head at the big cocks on the screen. "That's okay. I like watching porn too," she said.

The guy's eyes were moving a million miles a second. "I like watching shemale porn. Does that make me a faggot?"

He didn't seem dangerous—but there was a possible *yet* that Wendy tagged onto that assessment.

"I'm sorry if I can't take it good," he said. "I never been fucked before, will it hurt?"

Shit. She played dumb. "Will what hurt?"

"When you ... when you—when you fuck me in the ass."

"Oh. Honey, I have a vagina. I'm a trans girl with a surgical vagina."

The guy gaped at her silently with his jaw open and moving. "You don't have a dick?"

"No."

"You chopped it off!"

"That's not—yeah, I did."

"Fuck! Oh, son of a *bitch*, I was hoping you'd fuck me with your cock!"

"I'm sorry," she said, "it says in my ad, I have a vagina."

"I didn't read your ad."

"Ah, well then."

"You don't got a friend you can call?"

Instantly Wendy thought of Sophie. What a laugh this would've been, doing duos together, trading off driving this loser wild, shit-talking him in the car ride home, and she went to the kitchen and said, "Maybe let me just get my phone, and I'm gonna have some more wine!" and she sucked at the magnum like it was a water tap and turned the faucet on full blast and opened the fridge door to let it run and left it all like that for a few minutes so he couldn't hear that she was crying.

"Man, I hope you got a friend or two," he said when she came back.

She didn't really know other hos these days.

Come on, Wendy. Save this. She didn't want to give back this much money, and no way she was running out on him here in butt-fuck nowhere.

"I'll text some people," she said, and then a lazy smirk crept onto her face. "It's a shame you didn't see me before, I had a huge dick."

The guy's eyes turned on like lamps.

"Why'd you have to cut that shit off," he said. "I bet your dick was fucking beautiful."

"It was," said Wendy. "You wanna see?"

Years ago, Shemale Yum had come through looking for girls. It was mostly a bust. But Dexedrina—a mother-hen ho and back then the only trans girl Wendy truly called a friend—phoned the bitches she liked when she heard about it. It was a decent gig. Three hours posing and touching herself and moaning. Paid her six hundred American bucks. The cameraman was a jolly ex-Navy guy in his forties with a beard.

Wendy missed Dexedrina. She'd moved to Toronto years ago. Dex's old joke: "Trans women in this city either leave or die. I know which one I'm doing." Trans women like *us,* Dex had clarified after. It'd been ambiguous whether Wendy was included in that us. Dex was from an older crowd. Well, maybe only five or seven years older but that was a lot in trans years. Wendy was no stranger to hardship, but she knew that being poor and trans in this city used to be much, much, much harder.

She'd no idea what Dex was doing these days, a thought that flashed to Wendy as she cooed to this guy about her old huge cock, clumsily typing a name into Google with his PlayStation controller. Dex had fallen off Facebook, but Wendy's Yum shoot was still online.

"Whoa," he said. "Your cock is beautiful! Why'd you cut off a beautiful huge thing like that?"

"I know," Wendy giggled, massaging his coke-soft dick through his pants.

"You text your friends?" he said.

"Oh right, thank you for reminding me!" She took out her phone. *Already been here 20 minutes. Good.* She texted Lila to check in at four if she saw this—she hadn't been responding, was probably asleep—and then (what the hell) texted Aileen the address with the same request. *I'll explain later*, she added.

"In the meantime," she grinned, "check this out." She thumbed at the controller with her bra hanging off her.

On the screen, Wendy-from-five-years-ago wanked and moaned. The camera focused on her gaping perfect O of a mouth.

Her balls were so big. She'd forgotten about that.

"Fuuuuck, that's hot," the guy said. "Am I a faggot for loving this? I'm a faggot. I just *like* this—it's *hot*. Will you call me a faggot while I'm getting fucked? I just, I don't know. I like girl's clothes too."

New sissy. "It's very common," she reassured him, stroking his flagging dick, kissing his neck. "You want to get dressed up, be a little bitch?"

"I'm a little faggot," he said. "I don't know. I'm ex-military, eh? I just got discharged a few months ago. And all I've been doing is this." He leaned over and did another line. "Fuck. This is hot—that dick of yours— damn it, I wish you could fuck me with it."

"Ssshh, look, I'm about to come," she whispered. They watched as twenty-five-year-old Wendy worked up to jizzing in her own mouth.

I looked good in this, she thought. Her hair and nails never looked that good anymore. Wendy'd primped for this shoot more than for nearly any other occasion in her life. Seeing clients included. She always thought that was funny. Drunk boys in the dark won't notice armpit stubble, but a camera damn well will.

She tried to blow him afterward, but he just leaned over and did another line. He was getting more nervous and worked up. A kettle about to sing. "Do you have clothes you can put me in?" he said.

"I didn't bring any, sor—"

"I have heels—you wanna see me wear 'em? Me, the little faggot?"

"You little faggot sissy," Wendy laughed. "You're new to this, aren't you? You little faggy shit. You ever been put in girl's clothes before? You like being dressed up and taking orders?"

"Oh shit." Those darting coke-head eyes.

Alright, we can do this. "Show me your heels, faggot!"

He led her down the hall to his room. Back in the living room, the video of Wendy jerking off re-started on the screen.

The bedroom was barren but for delivery boxes and random papers littered across the room. Nothing on the walls. A king-sized mattress and box spring in the corner, and on the bed, up against the corner, a human-sized stuffed koala.

Wendy's heart dropped into her knees.

Sweetie.

The guy turned back from his closet wearing clear, six-inch heels never meant to be worn outside. His face was moving like there were bugs on it. "See these? That's some faggy shit, huh?" he said excitedly.

She nodded. "Take off your shirt."

He obeyed.

"And your underwear," she said calmly. "Over your heels.

"To the kitchen. Move faggot." He did as he was told.

"Face the counter," she said. "Bend over." He did. "Don't you dare fuckin' even look or turn around."

"I wo—"

"Shut up, faggot."

She turned around and took her bag from the table. Took out a large condom, lube. Grabbed the magnum of wine and sucked, sucked, sucked, sucked, until she'd killed it to almost a third of the bottle left.

"Ah," she whispered.

He stayed bent over, quivering, waiting for her. Quivering boy. She wanted to cry again. She felt the wine rushing through her system, converting in her blood. *You're clear from here. You're fine. Do your job and go home.*

Behind him, so he could hear everything, she rolled the condom over her bunched fingers and lubed up her fingers and the outside of his hole. "You want to be fucked like a little slut?" she whispered.

She couldn't conceal the choke in her voice.

He didn't notice. "Yeah!"

Some guys were coy about their butt experience, pretending they were new, their asses then swallowing appendages like gumdrops. Not him. He breathed and shook at the first fingertip. "Ssssh, you little faggot," she said. "I've got you."

The monster slugs of wine were really hitting. Her naked body was tingling and warm and she felt a second-wind night-power of adrenaline charge through her, down to her bare feet on the linoleum.

"You want to get fucked, don't you girlie," she said.

"Yes," he said. "Fuck me."

A little deeper. "That feel good, you little shit?"

"It hurts but I love it. Holy *fuck* what the *fuck*."

Wendy massaged, slowly probing and opening him up. "You got a name for yourself, you little fuckin' girl."

"Kaitlyn," he said immediately. "Kaitlyn. With a K."

Wendy shut her eyes and breathed deep to open her body to her exploding brain.

"That's a ... lovely name. That's a lovely name, Kaitlyn." She reached into his ass deeper and he bucked again. She pressed up against his back, his soft, hairless muscly flesh, rubbed her clit with the heel of her hand, and fucked him slow and intense till her own eyes rolled into the back of her head.

"Could you, like, tell me, maybe?" he said, sitting on the couch quietly now, though his teeth were still grinding after his ass had taken her hand to the wrist. "What it was like. How you knew."

Wendy finished off the wine, drops spilling onto her lips and face.

"You're asking," she said, "because you want to do it too, don't you?"

"I don't know. Probably not—I don't know."

"Everyone starts somewhere," she said blankly.

"Do I want to cut my dick off? Like you? Fuuuuuuck, I don't think so! But your body's so fuckin' sexy, if I had a body like yours ..."

"Thank you."

"Can you tell me?" he said. "What it was like cutting your dick off."

"That's not how it works," she heard herself say.

"No? Damn, that's crazy! Do we still have some time? Before you have to go, right? I just. Maybe it would help me. I'm a mess. This is what I've done ever since I got discharged."

"We have a few minutes left, yeah."

"Tell me."

"Surgery isn't—look, sweetie, hormones are a much bigger deal. You transition and take estrogen and you look more like a girl and you feel so much better. You're probably a girl, and that's probably what you need to do."

He looked down, then up. His teeth still grinding away. His eyes weren't there.

"Tell me about the surgery," he said. "Tell me about chopping off your dick."

It was nearly three years ago that Wendy'd gone to Montreal.

Her dad tried to talk her out of it initially. *Are you sure? I mean are you sure-sure? It's so permanent. I know. You're sure you're gonna be like this forever. Look, I had my stuff I was pretty sure of in my twenties too. You know? Just think about that! You don't want to lose something good you can't get back is all.*

Besides, what if something goes wrong?

Wendy'd nodded, said *Yes Dad, I know, I'll think about it.* He was just trying to be a good dad. It did mess with her! Not that she wanted to detransition. But surgery in general squicked her out and she hated hospitals and the whole *procedure* of it made her—goosebumpy. The pain alone (*which was stupid right why would you let pain stop you from something so important*) but also while yes she hated her dick she'd sorta learned to work with it? She didn't know—you were supposed to know this in and out but she couldn't untangle everything in her brain. She would try to re-set her thinking about it and build her reasoning step-by-step like it was a regular mundane choice—do I want to get to Point

B, and if I do, is it worth the line from Point A? But everything folded in and out and back on itself. And her dad wouldn't give it up, he was so weird about it (*It's not that I don't want you to be a girl!* he said. *I know you're a girl. I know. It's just—*) but at the end of the day she trusted the jump in her stomach that had come with the announcement that the province had listed vaginoplasty for funding. She marched right up to Klinic's front doors the next morning and got there before they opened. She went to every appointment and filled out every form. Doubt and worry ate at her as it got closer, but every time she felt it was too hard, something mechanical in her just made herself do it. Right up until she left. It was like the only way to get it done was to not understand what was actually happening. To not think but just do.

When she left, Wendy barely told anyone she was going. She told herself the secrecy was rational: If cis people knew they'd be stupid about it, if trans people knew they'd be jealous about it—she didn't even know *anybody* with a vagina installed at the time, besides the rich old lady who ran the support group at Rainbow. But honestly, deep down: She didn't want a soul to know. She wanted to swap her junk out alone, in the dark, as if it was something not part of the world.

When Wendy first transitioned, there was someone to notice and comment every step of the way. Every physical twitch and surge and loss earned opinions from the mouths of strangers and lovers alike. She had no language for it at the time. And she didn't think any of it out of place. Barring the more harass-y things, the commentary seemed natural: Like, duh, if you grew tits, your friends were gonna talk to you about your tits. If the fat flew out of your stomach and into your thighs, your girlfriend would say something about that. Wendy's hair, Wendy's freckles, Wendy's jeans, Wendy's jewellery, Wendy's ass, it was all eligible for public remark. And some of it was benevolent and some of it was condescending and some of it was sweet and some of it was gross, but what it all seemed was inevitable. Of course people would talk. And then she started hooking up with dudes and they said a lot more things—it only occurred to her, years later, that no physical part of her womanhood had been allowed to be solely her own.

So by the time she was waiting out front at Klinic that morning, she grew attached to an idea, an idea that started off idle and grew into something large and unalterable, of her vagina as something that could be pure, new and untouched, something she could nurture, take care of, give only to those who would be good to it. Wendy knew it sounded silly, silly as the idea of virginity itself, and that was another reason she didn't want to talk about it. In the sense that regardless of what she wanted, people still talked about her body, gossiped about her body, men on the street still shouted and groped at her body, old women at work touched her body like they would a doll or a coat. She felt this way far before she ever became a prostitute. (And then *that* had happened—.) In every section of the city it seemed Wendy had a memory of someone who had treated her body with the casualness they would only treat their own.

And so Wendy wanted her vagina to herself. She wanted to fly away to a land where she'd never been, and come back with a part of herself she would shelter and grow from the bottom up. She was always bitterly, bitterly jealous of people who'd transitioned away from home. That seemed legitimately magical—scary, but magical. So here was this thing for her body she could do and it would be hers. She only told a couple friends. She claimed at her day job that the four weeks she'd booked off in advance was to help a sister due with a new baby, far away. The boss believed her, didn't know anything about her family, didn't like giving her hours anyway (didn't give her any more after she came back either).

She'd never been east of Minneapolis before going. And instead of flying both ways, she ended up going there on the train—she turned her phone off once she got on, most of the trip was forest, thirty hours, it was the middle of summer and lush and gorgeous—it was late getting into Toronto to connect and she had to run through the station—it was so busy, there were so many people—that train was delayed too—and when she got to Montreal it was night, and raining, and far to the hostel she'd booked, and it didn't occur to her a cab wouldn't really be that expensive. She was so tired when she schlepped in, wet and exhausted, squishing up with her wallet to a young, young Québécois boy at the front desk with sunken yellow in his eyes.

In the two days before surgery, she walked around the city, and she didn't turn her phone back on. She walked around the city and for the first time in a long time she discovered new things that were old to everybody but her. She loved this. She went into strip joints, cafeterias, museums, office buildings, dusty bookstores, surrounded by language she didn't comprehend (like most Anglophone Canadians, she'd taken seven years of French and remembered exactly twenty words). She spent five hours in a T-girl joint called Citibar, a place Dex had mentioned only once in passing and now by complete chance, she walked by as she was wandering, and she got blind drunk spending a fortune watching these beautiful tall strong girls and sweetly declining the trickle of men propositioning her. She wore a white T-shirt with the neck cut out and short black shorts and moved seamlessly through the rush of people, without a car, without a phone, didn't talk to anyone, meet anyone, run into anyone, or understand anyone. It was beautiful. Beautiful. If there had been a way for her to make peace, clear her brain of the weight and loaded-ness and false grandiosity of what she was there for, and leave in its place only the simple purity of her body exiting one state and entering another, that was it.

Two days later she woke up drugged and bleeding with the weight of a toddler pressing on the vagina that until she died would always remind her of a mush of uncooked dough. She didn't talk about her trip back home to anyone, any part of it, and she never would, with one exception. If other girls asked (as more and more would when more girls came out and the Klinic pipeline got long) she would say the one true thing she could: No she wasn't any happier, no she didn't feel any more like a real girl. But she was calmer now, like a small buzzing part of her brain had been turned off, and was now forever at rest.

That thought came to her gradually as she lay stoned and in pain back home at her dad's, who by the time she'd left actually ended up graciously cute about the whole thing. He'd demanded to put her up: *I'm still your father! You're gonna let me take care of you!* As if she would scream resistance—*Okay, no argument Dad.* (There were, perhaps, things he could do to help her as a girl.) The heat was awful and she lay on the couch in a haze in front of the TV and a box fan, under the window that opened to the back lane, the soft volume of voices mixing with the sounds of bikes and teenagers and dogs. Her dad made her cold soups (a different kind every few days, from scratch, Ben had always loved to cook), he made her coffee in the morning, made up her bed on the couch when she was in one of her mandated baths. He had, in defiance of all sanity and reason, watched a YouTube video of the actual procedure while she was away. *Jesus CHRIST!* he'd said on the drive back from the airport. *That was like, just, Je-sus, like, ahhhhh! AHHHHHH!* he said with his thighs squirming. *Dad,* she'd said, fuzzed-out with her head on the window. *Why. Would you. Watch something like that.* And he said, *I don't fuckin' know, I wanted to know what was happening to you.* There was a peace and gratitude from those combined weeks that she managed to wrap and carry with her far after she recovered, that would power her for many years in a way that was so much precious more than just her pussy. Like: Enough. Some things were enough.

Not even a month post-op, she was at a party at Lila's place. Wendy'd been sitting on a couch chatting with an older guy who already knew Lila was trans. He asked if Wendy was trans. He'd seemed like one of those dudes who was dumb and a drunk but fun in low doses. It was her first good night getting hammered since she'd went under, and Wendy was feeling pleasant and giggly in a weak, low-energy kind of way. She mentioned she'd just had surgery—that pulled the guy in for a lark.

"You're kidding me!" And then he tugged the front of her skirt out and stuck his hand in with a twinkle-eyed cry, like someone doing magic for his grandkids, and his fingers momentarily felt like insects on her poor, healing cunt.

"Eek! Not shaved! You don't shave like a girl yet, huh?" he said. And then patted it. Patted it like a teacher giving a friendly D; better luck next time. All these people around them. No one noticed.

Wendy couldn't characterize this as sexual assault, even though it was sexual assault. *He was just some dumb fucking guy!* He was just some fucking guy. And then she realized how dumb, pointless, childish, and princess-like it'd been to think any part of her body could be kept sheltered and untouched and loved. The thought went up in ashes without remorse or sadness. But she did feel calmer now, and she had ever since. She was calmer now, she was calmer.

"It was easy," said Wendy, snapping back to Kaitlyn's couch. "I just went to Montreal, and they turned my dick inside out."

Kaitlyn stared at Wendy glassy-eyed.

Then she said, "No shit."

"Girl, I think you're a lady," said Wendy. "And I'm afraid I have to be going. But you know Klinic with a K? On Portage?"

"No."

"Call them. Write it down right now. Ask for an appointment. At the trans health clinic. Klinic with a K. Look them up. You don't have to do it tomorrow, just remember. Klinic with a K."

"God, thank you," said Kaitlyn. She sniffed.

"And I'm afraid I must be going." She was already clumsily shoving herself into her boots and jacket and scarf. She turned around to grab her bag, then hurried into the wall. "I had a lovely time, thank you for hosting me."

"Do you need a cab? I can call you one, you can wait here."

"Nonono," she said, words toppling over themselves, that magnum sloshing around in her fucking pisstank of a body. "I'll get it!" She couldn't stay another fucking minute in this apartment.

"This has really helped me," Kaitlyn said at the door. "How can I thank you?"

Wendy walked out into the frozen air and crunched down the lane. She was *drunk*. And fucked up. Like, she'd seen plenty of pre-transition girls who talked like that. Like dudes. But ...

She came to Wilkes Avenue and gazed into the ink of air and dots of faraway houses.

When had she begun to feel this kind of despair?

Years ago, a rich and supple-toned trick with a yin-yang back tattoo had come over and said, "I dream about my wife divorcing me so I can have a sex change. Yeah, yeah, wash me, that's good," as Wendy licked his ass in her shower. He'd worn a pair of Wendy's heels.

Besides the yin-yang back tattoo, Wendy couldn't remember what that man looked like except that he was in shape and white. And already she could feel that forgetting with Kaitlyn; her face, her voice, disintegrating and blending and layering in with all the rest, like every boy did with Wendy, tricks or no. Soon all she would remember about that place was the layout of the counter and the way Kaitlyn's ass felt around her hand. And the stuffed koala. And all else about this night would dissolve in her memory.

She was so drunk and so fucked up, like every part of her body was going to come apart like it was going to spark on fire and burn up into frozen steam. She got out her phone to call Raina and silently pleaded for her to be up before calling a cab. *Please don't be at your girlfriend's tonight,* she desperately thought, *and please still be awake. Please*. But she took out her phone, and it was dead.

She'd known her battery was low too.

Okay. Okay. "Okay," she said unsteadily in the middle of the road. She could go back to Kaitlyn's house. Politely ask to use his phone. That would be fine. She turned around. What was the number? What did his house look like? His street was in the distance. She honestly couldn't remember how to get back there. His address was—in her phone.

Now. What. How? Wendy swayed and nearly fell over in the ditch. She'd been drunk before she even got there. It was brutal out. She didn't feel that cold, but that didn't mean she wasn't in trouble, even that fact filtered down to her fogged, slushing brain. It was minus-forty-five or something ... *fuck. Fuck, focus!*

Knock on doors? It was three-thirty a.m.

She put a boot forward onto the road. Kenaston couldn't be that far. Even if a gas station wasn't open, there'd be pay phones. *Okay.* "Come on, champ," she said, noiselessly slapping her sides with gloved hands. "Let's go."

It was really, really fucking cold. But she had walked for miles in this kind of cold before. That had happened. She'd lived.

Except—tonight, for some fucking reason, she was wearing sweater tights instead of pants, and her legs were numbing and her body was jerking and lurching around, she was so fucking drunk *damn it*—she concentrated on her breath and her feet, the muffled crunch her boots made in the snow, actively pressing her brain into pause. She walked. She walked. She walked and walked. For a long while.

Eventually, a street sign caught her eye.

Fairmont Road. Wendy stopped and did a 360 turn. She was nowhere close to Kenaston. Or anything. *Where was Fairmont Road ...?* Were those lights down there Kaitlyn's street? Was it somewhere else? *Where? Who ...* Maybe she was farther out than she thought.

Her long-numbed toes were now feeling tiny electric shocks with each step. She kept walking.

Then a car came up from behind her, going east.

She turned around to wave it down. The car sped past.

That's okay, she thought. *The next one. Someone will think they see a helpless girl and want to stop for her.*

The next car zoomed by her too. *That's okay*, she thought. *You'll be fine.* The next car slowed. A middle-aged woman, looking kind. Wendy gasped in relief and ran over. "Hi!" she said. She forgot how drunk she was, how she must have seemed. Had her makeup been smeared when she was in there—? She had no idea how she looked.

"Hi," she said again. "My phone's dead! Fuck, I'm so glad. I'm just trying to get to Kenaston. I don't know where I am. I have cash. I. Help me." The woman's face went white and she sped away. "Hey!" she chased after her. "*Hey!*"

She kept walking. She was so, so, so cold. Another car coming east. She ran right out into the road this time. Waving her arms. "Help me! Helpmeplease I just needa get—"

The car honked and swerved around her and sped away. "Oh, fuck you! Please! No!" she screamed. The red brake lights disappeared into the immediate dark, and farther on, the faint bright of the city lighting up the prairie sky in an ocean of peaceful, starry black. Wendy felt herself crying, horking up snot, ugly glistening gobs that froze as they dripped down her face.

She made noises that didn't sound like words.

She kept walking. She walked for a long time. Her legs felt like sticks.

A long time.

Then behind her coming east, a cab. With its light on.

Wendy stood on the road and waved desperately. The cab slowed.

Inside, before she could even thank him, there were also police lights.

A door opened and slammed. The cop came to the cab. He looked in, then looked back at Wendy. He was angry. He spoke to the cabbie. "You just pick her up?"

"Yes."

"Miss," he craned toward her, "we've gotten two calls now that a tall woman in a black coat has been freaking people out around here. Scaring the bejeezus out of them. Now, that was you, wasn't it?"

"No one stopped for me." Her voice came out heavy, as if behind static.

"Calm down! You run out all over the road! You scare people! So you just calm down. Where you going?"

"I'm going home, sir," said Wendy. Desperately she reached into the depths of her body for stillness. "I'm going home. I have money, and I'm just going to ask this gentleman to take me straight home."

The cop looked at her furiously. "I need your ID."

She was too frazzled to lie. She handed over her driver's license and the cop went away and she and the cabbie sat in silence for five minutes. Her head was slouched against the side window with the cop car lights strobing outside while her frenzied brain suspended itself, holding its breath.

The cop returned and gave the licence back. "Hey, *Wendy.*"

"Yes."

The cop started to speak, then cut himself off. He laughed like he'd just seen the most amusing thing and had to keep it in. "What you doing so far away from home?"

"I was at a party." The first thing that came to her head.

"Yeah? Where."

"Fairmont Road."

"What house?"

Wendy's head drooped forward, and she let out an "Uhhh ..."

The cop laughed again. "Don't ever let me catch you out here again, *Wendy*."

He drove off, and the cabbie moved east. The meter was already over ten dollars.

"Nobody *stopped* for me," Wendy said. "Nobody *cared*."

"Miss! You going crazy, that's why people don't stop for you."

"People should stop! They didn't stop!"

"Miss, *please!* Calm down."

"*Stop telling me to calm down!*"

"Miss. I need you to relax. No one can do anything for you if you don't relax!"

"*Augggh*!" Wendy howled. "*Theydidn'tnobodycaresnobod—*"

The cabbie stopped the car right there on Wilkes, his hazards flashing. "You want me to keep going?"

Wendy imagined her arms reaching in front of her and crushing the cabbie's neck.

"Yes," the word forced its way out of her mouth.

"Then you be quiet. You want to get home?"

"Yes."

"Good. You understand then?"

"Yes."

"Good. Now pay me up front. One hundred dollars."

"What?"

"One hundred dollars, I need the money upfront."

"No one ever needs ... It doesn't take a hundred dollars to get downtown. You fucking know that! Do you think I'm stupid?"

"You need to pay me. Pay me or I don't go. Cash or card, I don't care."

The cabbie got out, breath spiralling from his body in clouds. He opened the side door and a *dingdingdingdingdingding* echoed out into the dark and the flashing lights. "You feel that? It's fucking cold out," he snapped.

He looked like every endlessly angry adult who had dealt with her as a surly child. "You gonna be smart?"

Wendy wanted to fucking knock out his teeth. She wanted to fucking kill him. The rage demanding she hurt him enveloped her like a mass of fucking insects.

Wendy gave him the hundred. The exact amount of cash she had on her. Then she calmly engaged him in conversation on the way back until he was chatting with her like a normal guy. Passing Grant on Kenaston, she asked if she could charge her phone with his cable. He let her. She had always been smart.

The little apple flicked on at five percent as the cab turned off Route 90.

Aileen: 4:16 a.m.

Jesus goddammit tell me your okay I'm

getting cab in 20 if I don't hear from ...

(204) 612-1989 4:01 a.m.

can I fuck ur ass still

(204) 822-9532 2:36 a.m.

wd u do an outcall to morden! I got

100 plus party treats for u babe n im ...

It was 4:19 exactly. Cop car lights flashed again, stopping her heart then washing her in red and blue as they went past. She looked out at the silent, frozen grounds of Polo. They were right by the store. Like them, the cop car was heading east.

"Hello," Aileen answered cautiously.

"Hi!" Wendy organized her thoughts. "My phone died. I'm in a cab."

"Oh, thank fucking God son of a cunt, I was about to run over there with a bat, I swear to fuck like I just put my coat on—"

"It was fine. Actually it's not. Nothing is fine. I mean," Wendy's voice cracked. "I'm not in danger. Um, are you like, busy?"

"I have my fucking coat on, love. Tell me what you need from me."

Wendy swallowed. "Can I come over?"

"Of course," Aileen's voice soothed. "I'll have a beer ready. Get over here."

"Sir, I'm sorry," Wendy said after hanging up. "I need you to take me somewhere else. It's not much farther. I'm very sorry about this."

In front of Action House, she asked for her change. The meter was at sixty dollars. He gave her exactly forty back. *Decent of him*, she thought.

"Sir?" she said outside in the freezer-burn cold, reaching a gloved hand back through the door, holding out a tip.

He turned around. She snatched it away. "*Rot in hell!*" she shrieked and slammed the door in a whirl of snow.

22

Aileen was in a housecoat and holding a bottle. She kissed Wendy on the lips in the doorway and pinpricks of snow from Wendy's coat melted into the girl's robe.

You are so beautiful. Wendy shucked off her boots and lipped her coat over the others on the rack. *You are so goddamn unfairly fucking beautiful.*

"You don't have to talk," Aileen said. "But if you want to talk, I'm listening."

"It's cold out there," Wendy said dumbly.

The two women sat on opposite ends of the living room couch with their legs stretched and touching under the same blanket.

"I saw this boy," said Wendy, fighting her way through the fog in her head. "But he wasn't. A boy. He was one of us."

"Damn. Right."

"I just ... He was this ex-soldier or something. Doing a bunch of coke. I *hate* coke," she shivered. "And he, he just ..."

Aileen waited attentively. Wendy could almost focus her eyes on her. She felt something rise and clear in her chest.

"When I transitioned," she said, "I didn't think things would get better for trans people. I thought it'd be the way it was forever. And now. So much has happened that's *good.* In the last few years. I—I have a pussy. I'm out at my job. I know. But there's still. Girls like her. Are still ... I don't. Why can't ..." She moved her arms. "She has so much, but she still. Like I don't ... I'm saying, like, my heart breaks for this girl, you know ..."

Sophie said her brain and she pressed hands to her makeup-smeared face and started to cry. Aileen scooched over, put her arms around Wendy's huge, heaving body, and said, "I know. I know, love."

Wendy cried into Aileen's chest for a good minute.

Then slowly, mush-brained, she gathered herself and took a long open-throated drink from Aileen's bottle. "Do you get what I'm saying?" sniffed Wendy.

Aileen looked grim. She appeared to think, then said, "I met a girl a few months ago. She'd just come out. Seemed like she had friends, had her hormones, no big disruptions. Quiet girl, been in the hardcore scene most her life. Forty years old. I liked her heaps. And I sort of had it in my head that things were right for her. Fuckin' stupid, right. Next time we're out, I ask her more about her past, said she had a thing for hurting herself at shows, that she kept doing stupid fucked-up shit hoping she'd die because she hated her body so much. Said she'd eat glass on stage." Aileen swigged from the bottle.

They shared a long silence after that, then Wendy said, "Did you have any girls around? When you were coming out."

"Of course not." said Aileen. "Not where I'm from. When I moved to Dublin, I first met gay people period. Then I was a gay boy for a while. Had some *fucked* boyfriends. There's more trans girls now in town, though. Deffo more weirdo lezzas like me than I ever expected, and Christ, I only crossed over four years ago. Why, what about you?"

"No. God, no, no. There was a support group." There was a beat, then Wendy laughed. "Support groups—like they're not people," she laughed again. "There was this woman named Dex," she added. "I miss her. I met Lila through her, actually."

"Yeah?"

"This was about five years ago ..."

She got up for another beer but her legs buckled and she crashed to the floor.

"Fuckin' hell, you alright?"

"I trip—" but Wendy felt her brain commencing shutdown just from lying on the wood for a few seconds.

"Shit, I'm *tired*, Aileen." She'd been exhausted and drunk even before the call. Then three hours and a magnum later, out in the cold, her melting brain had animalistically forced her to stay conscious so she wouldn't fall over and die in the snow. And now.

The remaining deflated bubbles on her hands throbbed very lightly as she pulled herself up. "I've. Had. A very. Long. Day." Wendy crawled back up on the couch then softly kissed Aileen, stroked her freckled face. "Can I stay here tonight," she whispered. "Would that be okay?"

Aileen's eyes were amused glee. "Yes love, you may."

They kissed more, in an instantly familiar way, familiar and old even though they'd only fucked once, and even that just patches in Wendy's memory. That'd only been a few days ago—but already it seemed so far in the past! And their bodies easily clicked into place, turning the same pages in an old book, following a progression both already knew, one both women had known the first time they touched each other: *Here, here is my skin that feels like your skin, my muscles and frailties that feel like yours, the lift of your flesh something I intuitively know from my own body, inner maps that, for most of my life, I thought were purely shameful and mine alone. And here, with you, with me, for minutes, for hours, if nothing else*—a line from a book Wendy couldn't remember appeared to her in a slippery ripple of memory—*If I loved you, this is how I would love you.*

"Okay, then," Wendy said, guiding her hand up. "Let's go to bed."

"You'd rather not sleep up here?" Aileen said.

"No. No I would not. I would like to sleep on your bed. What, did you lose your bed?"

"Raina's sleeping there."

"*Raina*?"

"Ah. Bugger. She didn't tell you, then."

Wendy dropped back on the couch. *Jesus, this day.* "You fucked Raina?"

"I thought she told you."

"Figured she was at her girlfriend's."

"Not unless she meant me. And I hope she didn't. I'm leaving town soon. Though I heard you're getting the boot from your house, eh? That's shit."

For fuck's *sake. That too.* "I didn't even know she was poly ..." Wendy whimpered. "Wait. Of course she's poly. Of fucking course she's poly, how would I ever imagine that Raina would not be poly."

"Said she's got two sweeties at the moment."

"Who—oh my *God*, trans dykes."

"Yes?"

Wendy laughed her long, deep-throated guttural laugh. She kissed Aileen suddenly and ferociously. "How good. Goodnight!" she said. "Go downstairs and fuck my roommate."

"I'm not going to do that, Wendy."

"That was a joke." Wendy threaded out of her bra.

"Right." Silently, Aileen got up and retrieved pillows from a closet.

"Raina and I slept together too, you know," Wendy blurted. "Years ago. When she first moved here."

She didn't know why she said things like this.

"Was she the last girl you had sex with?" said Aileen.

"I—yes. Years ago. Now that you mention it, yes."

"She said you two used to be intimate—but you generally went for the men now."

"Did she."

"Funny world."

Wendy's exhausted brain was overpowering her again. "Thanks, lady. I'll be out of here in just a few hours.

"You don't have to be ..."

"You're sweet," Wendy balled up under the blankets. "I'm sorry I'm a mess. Have a good morning."

Aileen didn't leave the room. She stayed by the couch with her hand on Wendy's hair until she went to sleep. Sang something low and melodic that Wendy couldn't understand. In the dark. She had a beautiful voice.

In her dream that night, she was in a room playing in a band with guy friends from junior high. They were all laughing while the old, bearded man John grumbled that Wendy wasn't being quiet. She'd get it from him eventually, but the guy friends and Wendy were having a good time. They sat on couches in a long room. The old man John exploded and followed Wendy to the other rooms, and Wendy knew she'd get punished and there was nothing she could do to stop it.

The house ended and the rooms stopped. She turned around, and old man John stood fully clothed in a button-down and khakis, looking furious, with his long penis out. Wendy woke up flailing on the couch sweating and jumpy in the crisp-cool house air. It was almost eight o'clock. That idiot Travis was puttering around the kitchen. Her clothes and bag were in a pile beside the couch. She had her underwear on.

She hated waking up alone like this. With these dreams. She was still kind of drunk. *Sophie is dead.*

"Hello?" Wendy knocked on Aileen's door in the basement.

"Hey," she knocked again. "It's Wendy. I have to go."

Silence.

Quietly, she turned the knob and peeked inside. Raina was alone and motionless.

Raina's raven-coloured hair rose up and down with her breathing. Most of what Wendy could see of Raina was hair, her small body covered in blankets.

She leaned over and kissed the sleeping girl on the head.

"Muhhh."

"Aw, shit. I didn't mean to wake you up."

Raina's eyes flew open, but she didn't move. "Wendy?!"

"Good morning, roomie."

"You must truly miss it when I'm not home."

"Heh," Wendy said. "I do, but that's not—well. Long story."

"Are you alright?

"I'm going to see Anna today."

"Anna?"

"The woman who has the letters about my grandpa being trans. Or gay. Or whatever the fuck. I don't know. I don't even want to fucking go anymore. I guess I can't stand up an old lady, though."

"Goodness." Raina closed her eyes. "I hope the best for you. And her. Are you home tonight?"

"Yeah, it's my weekend."

"Aileen and I thought all of us should go to Cousin's. She leaves Sunday. We could bring Lila."

"Let's do that."

"Excellent. Wendy, I'm afraid I'm going back to sleep."

Wendy leaned over and kissed her forehead. Raina blushed.

"Goodnight, lady," Wendy said. "I'll see you in the evening, then."

Aileen was in the kitchen with a grocery bag as Wendy walked up the stairs. "Sunshine!" she said.

"Beg pardon?"

"Aren't you a ray of sunshine!"

"I—have you slept?"

"Nope!"

Wendy's phone rang. It was Lila. "*Hey!*" she said frantically. "Are you okay? Where are you?"

Aw, shit. She'd never checked in. "Yeah, all's good," said Wendy. "I'm sorry I didn't call. I just had a weird night."

"*God damn it,* you fucking scared me!" said Lila. "I just woke up to your texts! Like right now! I thought maybe you were—"

"Sorry. I'm sorry."

"It's okay," Lila said rapidly. "I'm fucking glad you're alright, just please remember to check in! Please! I thought you were maybe—I don't fucking know, you know?!"

"I promise, okay!"

Lila sniffled. There was the light sound of a Kleenex pulled from a box.

Wendy kept forgetting how close Lila'd been to Sophie too.

"I should know better," Wendy said. "I'm sorry."

"Are you still using my car today?"

"Yes. Please."

It was true. Wendy didn't want to see Anna anymore; it was an obligation now. Go keep an old woman company. She *was* curious to read the letters, kind of. But the sporadic mental energy it took her to care just didn't currently exist. *Oh, well. In six hours it'll be over.*

"I'm off. I'm getting Lila's car. Have to drive her to work."

"You like company on the way?" said Aileen. "I ain't sleeping."

"I'd have to come back here to drop you off."

"If you'd like the company!" said Aileen rapidly.

"I—no, girl, it's really not on the way." *Jesus, what was her deal?*

"We're going out tonight, yeah? All of us?"

"You bet," Wendy said, doing up her coat.

As Wendy opened the door, Aileen came up and kissed her and said, "See you tonight." Like a wife seeing her off to work.

She walked to Lila's house. They got into Lila's car and stopped at the McDonald's on Pembina where Wendy got them both breakfast. Lila had some new office job out by U of M that she hated, but it paid a few bucks above minimum. "I shoulda done the social work thing like my mom," she said.

"Sophie told me this funny theory she saw online once," said Wendy. "That there's, like, a square of trans-girl careers, and it's anchored by four corners, and everyone fits somewhere on the square."

"Oh yeah?" Lila said, her voice tight.

"It was like, one corner is social work, another corner is sex work, another corner is, like, arts and academia, and the other corner is tech."

Lila lit a cigarette and cracked open the window. "I don't do any of that." She exhaled. "I do hang around a lot of hookers."

"What exactly is your new job again?"

"Driver coordinator for Skip the Dishes. They just moved out of downtown."

"I woulda thought the Internet did all that," said Wendy. "Coordinate drivers."

Lila sipped her coffee. "Someone's gotta yell at those fuckers."

Wendy snorted. "So last night," she said, lighting a smoke and juggling her food. "I did this call, hey? And there was this guy. Coked out of his mind. Nothing bad happened. But, like ..."

Wendy told Lila the whole thing, down to the Yum video and the koala bear and Kaitlyn's open, eager ass. She left out the part about getting lost and the cab.

"Damn," said Lila.

"I'm feeling kinda messed up about it," muttered Wendy.

Lila was silent for a moment. "Why's it so fucking hard for us to stay alive, man?"

"Oh, I don't think this girl's gonna kill herself."

Lila flicked her butt and rolled up her window.

They got to the building, a bland grey block right on Pembina. Wendy invited her out for the evening with the rest.

"Hell yes, girl," Lila said. "You can buy me a drink for using my car."

"Sure."

"Alright, fine, two drinks."

" ... sure."

"Look," said Lila. "Four drinks is an okay thanks. I'll take four drinks."

"Get to work, you bitch!" Wendy laughed. Lila got out and flipped her off walking backwards toward the building. Then she tripped and fell over into a snowbank.

Wendy hooted and honked the horn and drove away. She got a text: *Six drinks. And I hate you.*

Wendy trundled down to the Perimeter and turned west, swinging around past Oak Bluff and the Number 3 highway, up past Wilkes and over the Trans-Canada, through spurts of houses and acres of blank fields. At the exit for the Number 7, she turned north, with only traces of city behind her. The day was perfectly clear and still, flecks of sunrise visible in violet streaks on the snow.

It'd been a while since Wendy'd driven a car. She stuck the cruise control at eighty and found the CBC station that played classical music. She drove in peace past the occasional farmhouse or traffic signal, light veils of white blowing over the lines of the road.

⁂

For a while, the only sounds were the hum of the engine and cellos and the quick roars of passing cars.

This was the first time she'd left the city since her grandma died. Which was over a month now. It felt like a fucking year. Christ. *Sophie is dead.*

⁂

Then she noticed the gas tank was almost empty. *Shit.* Lila'd even told her, too.

She slowed to seventy. There was still nothing around. More specks of farm buildings, the dustings of snow blowing over the highway like shreds of fabric softener.

Wouldn't someone pull over for her if she ran out of gas, if she were stranded out here? They would.

Despite the previous night, not eight hours old, Wendy assumed this unquestionably, for no reason, none at all.

⁂

Fifteen minutes later, a speck of green rectangle in the ocean of white. Wendy parked at the Co-op, put her hands together in prayer, and thanked the Lord before getting out of the car.

"Co-op number?" said the young guy inside.

"No."

"Forty-two seventy-five. Debit or credit?"

"Cash," Wendy shivered. "Where's your coffee?"

"Next to the Slushies. Gee, that's a nice coat you got, eh?" the guy continued. "You made a—how can I say this? You were filling up out there with the sun and the highway behind you, that belt ya got on yer coat flyin' around—I. Ah. You just looked cool."

"Cool, eh?" Wendy grinned. "You're sweet."

The guy seemed embarrassed. They might've been the same age, yet he looked so, so young. "You need anything else, give me a shout."

"What don't I need," said Wendy. He laughed.

Once she had her coffee, Wendy grabbed a pen and scribbled her number on the receipt. "Pardon me," she said. "I know I'm being bold, but if you ain't cute! If you ever drop by the city, give me a ring. My name's Wendy."

The guy looked shocked. "Wow." He held the paper and gazed at it like a first-grader. "Wow. Okay. Okay. I'm Troy."

Wendy touched her forehead. "See you around, Troy." She stuck her hands in her coat pockets and left, and for two seconds the wind blew violently inside the store before the door slammed behind her.

She drove on, through glazed fields of waist-high snow, a four-way stop here, a grain facility there. A farmer in a padded spaceman suit plodding around a long livestock barn.

When Wendy was a kid, she imagined the prairie land outside the city stretched forever in every direction. Now she knew that barely minutes from where Anna lived, this all turned into bush, bush for a thousand miles, up into Nunavut where the land broke into tundra.

She stopped in Arborg to touch up her makeup (*You need to be cis for, like, a couple hours, don't forget*) and a final coffee for her sleepy nerves. She drove around the town looking for a Tim's but they didn't have one here, just a community centre and a hockey arena and churches and a school and a Chicken Chef and a bakery and a huge machine shop and another little Co-op gas station. She stopped on Main Street, and her phone confirmed that the closest Tim's was half an hour south, in Gimli.

The whole place reminded her of the little towns around her grandparents' place when she visited when was small. Wendy'd liked those towns. It disquieted her as she grew up, as those isolated Southern Manitoba burgs turned into Canuck versions of American Bible Belt mini-suburbs. With the fireplace stores and the megachurches and the sterile late-night coffee shops and the liquor stores open till ten. Not that the burgs of old were better—any less xenophobic, homophobic, racist. She was drawn to the isolation of those humble desperate towns of old, but their isolation, too, was a myth—Mennonites had been some of the first settlers in Western Canada to colonize the countryside.

Outside, the weather was now quiet and calm. Wendy got out of the car and went into the bakery between the Chicken Chef and an empty lot where she bought a huge weak coffee and a roll with icing for her blood sugar and sat in a little booth with a *Coffee News*. Most everyone ignored her except a Hutterite man in suspenders buying donuts who glared at Wendy as his wife looked forward, immovable as a train. Wendy wordlessly met his gaze, staring blankly into his angry eyes as she sipped her coffee and ate her roll. She flipped over the *Coffee News*. Among jokes about women and Liberals was a box that read: "The commandment God gives most frequently in the Bible is *Do not be afraid*."

"Ya want another coffee there?"

"Huh?"

The guy behind the counter lifted a fresh pot in Wendy's direction. A big ticking clock behind him. "Oh, crap," said Wendy. "Thank you, but I'm late, I gotta go!"

23

Anna had a bungalow surrounded by poplar trees and a trampoline out front. She was waving from inside a big picture window. Short and wearing a long skirt and a head covering.

They stood in the doorway facing each other.

"Nice to finally meet you!" said Wendy.

"You as well," said Anna. She was stooped and walking like she might've needed a cane, but she didn't have one. She was so short. Wendy was so huge. "No troubles on your drive. I hope."

"No, none at all," Wendy said awkwardly, nodding. "Nice and easy."

"Good weather?"

Wendy gestured to outside. "Like this the whole way up."

"Very cold out this week," said Anna. She spoke with an absence of body language. "But the wind. Wasn't too bad."

"Yes, absolutely," said Wendy. "Could've been worse. Very pretty drive on the way up here," she said. "I haven't been out of the city in a while."

"Oh. Haven't yuh," said Anna.

The entranceway had dark blue linoleum flooring and a big grey rubber mat for boots and a stairway to the basement. Wendy took off her layers, and memories of sandy-faced Mennonite kids running into houses for family visits went through her like wind.

She wondered if Sophie would've felt as much like a boy as she did just then.

"Oh. Are you. Having trouble," asked Anna.

"I'm fine, thank you," Wendy blinked back tears. And then rapidly, "I like your trampoline! Is it for your grandkids?"

And Anna said, "Oh, yeah! Even in winter time. Have to be. Ready for the grandchildren."

"Well, I bet they love that."

Wendy towered over the tiny lady. Anna nearly disappeared under her coat when she took it to the closet. Wendy wore a sleeveless bottle-green dress over blue jeans and under a zippered wool sweater. When Anna hung up her coat, she turned around and looked Wendy up and down.

A deep smile formed on Anna's face. "Very nice to have you here," she said. A grin flashed. "Get a look at you!" She slowly made her way to the kitchen. "Made some coffee." Off in the corner was a plate of *päpanät* on a little table next to an old wooden box. The cabinets were beige-yellow with silver handles, and on the other side of the sink was a mirror. The top of the mirror had a short wide bell curve with a small design in the centre.

Anna invited her to sit down. She had a lined face and large glasses.

Wendy crunched down on the tiny biscuits at the table, and they filled her mouth like sand.

"So," said Anna, in words that alternated between drawn-out and clipped. "Tell me about. Yourself, Wendy. So you live in Winnipeg."

"My whole life," said Wendy. "And you? Have you been in Morweena your whole life too?"

"Oh. No." Anna momentarily looked taken aback. "Morweena was only. Built in the fifties. I was born in Kansas."

"*Kansas*?"

"Yes." Anna looked unsure whether to go on, then proceeded. "My parents, they were from Steinbach area. And then they and other Kleine Gemeinde Mennonites went down to West Kansas. Satanta area. They stayed there for about twenty-five years."

"I had no idea," said Wendy. "I knew there were some Mennonites in Kansas, but I didn't realize they were related to our Mennonites."

"The American Mennonites were more central. Around Wichita. The school is somewhere around there, I know. A small number of our Manitoba families went to the western part. For the better climate. Most of them came back in the Dirty Thirties. That would've been my childhood. My parents stuck it out. Until the end. We moved back, 1940. And I was born. In Satanta, Kansas. In 1930."

"Oh, yikes," Wendy said. "What was that like?" *Oh, what the fuck, Wendy!* "Sorry," she immediately said.

"Difficult," said Anna. "Very difficult. For my mother especially. But tell me about yourself, Wendy."

Wendy crunched down on more *päpanät* and sipped more coffee. "I work close to Polo Park." Wendy said. "In a gift store."

"Oh, yes."

"I'm a supervisor," she said. "I work directly under the head manager."

"Oh! Very good."

Anna was quiet, smiling, waiting for her to go on. She had the open, grandmotherly look of someone who genuinely wanted to listen to this stuff. Like she would listen to Wendy talk about her life for the next hour. She was just waiting.

"I have a boyfriend," Wendy said. "His name is Ryan. He lives with his parents in North Kildonan. They attend the North Kildonan Mennonite Brethren Church." Anna nodded in approval. "I know, those MBs," she added, and Anna made a short cackle.

Wendy propped up her head with her hand.

"I do well at work," she continued. "I'd like to go back to school at some point. I'd like to be a bookkeeper. I've always been good with numbers, and I keep track of my money. That's part of why I do so well at work. I hope Ryan's going to propose to me sometime in the next year. I really want him to. He needs to finish school, though. He goes to the U of M. He teaches music. He's a wonderful guitar player and singer. He helps the choir church a lot. I think he'll be a high school music teacher. It seems like that's what he wants to do. I want to get my bookkeeping certificate before we have children."

"You want children!" Anna said. "Very good. Some young people today ..." she trailed off. "Well."

"Yes," enthused Wendy. "And goodness, Anna, can I tell you, Ryan's going to be such a good father. He's such a sweet man. He drives to my house just so he can drive me to work so I don't have to take the bus in winter. He'll sleep over on the couch and wake up early, and he goes out to pick up breakfast just so it's there when I wake up. I'm no cook myself, I—well. It's awkward to say this, but I ... I didn't have a lot of female figures looking after me in my younger years. There are some normal girl things I missed."

Anna nodded impenetrably. "We are not all. Blessed the same."

Wendy tucked a long strand of hair behind her ear. "He puts up with dinners I make him," she said. "I'm so lucky, Anna. I'm sorry, I don't mean to be so emotional. You asked me about me, and I'm just talking about him. He sings for me when he plays guitar. He's good to me when I'm upset. I get frustrated ... kinda easily. He's so much better to me than I deserve. He loves me. He loves me. I'm so very lucky."

"The Lord is. Looking after you well," Anna said.

"What else?" Wendy said, wiping off a stray tear. "I've lived in the city all my life. I went to high school in River Heights. I've lived in Crescentwood most of my life. You remember Ben, I know. I live with him now. You could say he's taken me in. I had—" she paused "*troubles* with my own parents. My mother is still alive, but where she is I don't know. My father I never knew. But Ben has taken very good care of me."

"How's Ben? And. Uh ..." Anna stumbled over her words for a brief second. "His family."

"There was tension for quite some time," Wendy said. "I think that's more in the past. I wish he went to church more, I will admit. A few times a year he comes with Ryan and me. I attend Ryan's church," she clarified. "That's where I met him."

"Well, praise the Lord. I'm sure you'll. Be a good mother."

Anna's face glowed. Wendy felt held, as Anna listened to every word; here she was. Here she was.

Safe.

Understood.

"You'll be a good mother," repeated Anna. Her tone was the same, sitting there, unmoving. "I can already see this about you."

⁂

"Well," added Anna. "Ryan sounds nice. What about. His family."

"Ah, they're great," Wendy said. "His grandmother and I are very close. I often go with her earlier on Sundays for the German services."

"Oh, *jo!*" Anna said, immediately giddy. "*Kjenn jie noch Plautdietsch?*"

Wendy smiled with what she hoped this woman would take for sadness.

"Sorry. I never learned Low German. Or High German. I just go because she needs someone to take her."

A mischievous look crossed Anna's face. "*Scheissarei.*"

⁂

They were silent for a few moments, then Wendy politely asked about Anna's grandchildren and heard all about how some lived here in Morweena and some lived in Winkler and how one of her children was now out west in BC. Anna showed her photos in the living room in front of the picture window. Tiny Menno kids, cheery and bright.

When they returned to the kitchen table and Anna had poured more coffee Wendy said, "So. I suppose I did come up to hear more about Henry."

Anna nodded. "What would you like to know?"

"Would you say he was happy?" Wendy said without thinking. "That's a stupid question, sorry. I'm sure he wasn't happy."

Anna did not respond right away. Then she said, "He was not a man in pain."

"No?"

"That's what you're asking," she said.

"Well. Um," Wendy said. *She's lying*, she thought. "I'm glad to hear that."

"His faith was strong. I would never call him anything but a committed Christian. I hope everyone knows that."

Wendy was taken aback. "I don't think anybody would say otherwise." She tried a different tack. "Could you tell maybe a bit more about his early life? Where he came from? I don't know these things. Ben doesn't like to talk about Henry much." She tried a joke. "Don't tell me he was born in Kansas too?"

"No," Anna replied, unmoved. "Think he was born in Grunthal. Or Steinbach? Can't remember. I think it was Grunthal. He moved to Landmark when he met Aganetha."

"Wait a minute," Wendy interrupted. "I thought you went to school with Nettie."

"We lived in Landmark a short time before I married my husband," replied Anna. "I went to Prairie Bible Institute. With Aganetha."

"You were a teacher?"

"I never got to," said Anna, flat-lipped.

"I—okay." Wendy was getting disoriented. "Okay, so Henry. What was he like when he was younger? Like my age? Maybe that's something I'd like to know."

"Henry," said the older woman. "When I met him—we became friends fast. Though it was. Unusual at the time. Men and women having that kind of. Friendship. But Aganetha never minded. Anyway. Henry judged himself greatly on what he viewed as. Personal inadequacies in his faith. He said he often felt stupid he didn't understand more of the Bible. That he did not grasp what his elders were able to grasp. He was always a strong believer. As I said.

It never wavered. But he thought he was stupid."

"He said that?" said Wendy.

"Yes. I told him often. Whatever you understand, well. If your faith is strong. Then that must be part of God's plan. No one can understand all of Holy Scripture. Not ministers. Doesn't matter. How much you read," Anna was no longer looking at Wendy, as if she'd said these words many times. "If you are physically opening the book and sitting down and asking to be guided, the Lord will draw you to what you need to hear. That won't be every word, every book! No life is long enough for that. And which part of the Word of God you need to see will not always be the same as everyone else's. Isn't that faith? That is part of faith, I think."

When she was younger, Wendy had tried to read the Bible, especially the parts with Jesus. She had trouble focusing. "Then two *men* will be in the field: one will be taken and the other left. Two *women will* be grinding at the mill: one will be taken and the other left." What? This was the Word of God; it meant literally more than anything else in the world! What was stuff like that supposed to mean? She'd felt so stupid. She'd wanted to get it.

"Like to think. That gave him some solace," continued Anna, looking pained at what she took as Wendy's bored expression.

"Oh, yes," Wendy snapped back. "I'm sure it did." She paused. "Might I ask when Henry told you about—the way he was?"

"The seventies," Anna said after staring off into space for a minute. "We had been good friends for decades. By that point. Our families knew each other well. He swore at the time he was not. Doing. Acts. Found out later that wasn't completely true," she said, then shivered. "Can't think about that. He smartened up. I do believe at least the last ten years of his life, he was right with God and living. Christian. He righted himself. It was always a burden. I'm sure but. He carried out his final years in peace and asking God for forgiveness. I believe he is in heaven. I do."

"I do too," said Wendy. "I wouldn't think for a minute otherwise."

"I'm glad you think so," said Anna. "Don't want anyone. To get the wrong idea. He struggled. And he fought."

"I'm sure he did."

Anna didn't say anything more. The two women sat there with their coffee at the table in the noon light.

"Well," Wendy eventually said, breathing out. "I don't suppose you might let me take a look at a letter or two he wrote you? I don't want to pry, but I seem to remember you mentioning that."

Wordlessly Anna reached over to the old wooden box on the table and opened it. She withdrew an envelope from a small stack and pushed it over to Wendy. "This one. I thought you might want to see. Talks about his thoughts. About cameras. You mentioned."

Dear Conrad and Olivia,

Given that it has been some time that last we seen each other at my Fathers funeral, it seemed prudent to write.

We have been blessed with good weather season here. The snow has melted and we are readying ourselves for a busy year. Neighbour Peter Ungers are aging and we are assisting their sons some what around the farm. May the Lord bless the whole effort.

My poor Mother has not coped well with death. She cries often and other times will say "Wheres Dad?" The rest of the family has stayed in good spirits. God has helped us well.

Loren has gone on to attend Mennonite Brethren Bible College in Winnipeg. Agnetha and I discussed this at

"I can't read this," said Wendy.

"No? It's in English."

"Look."

"Didn't know you couldn't read cursive."

"I can read cursive, but this doesn't make any sense to me."

"Oh, for heaven's sake. Of course. Gothic script. Was a certain way of writing. Mostly used for German of course, but. Many wrote English as well." She thought. "I suppose it wouldn't take too long to transcribe this one. You came all this way. I could just read it to you. But this one in particular, I thought you might want to look at and see for yourself. In 'black and white,' as they say."

"That's extremely kind of you."

"Let me make some more coffee. I'll just type it up on the computer here." She smiled shyly. "I spend enough time on there for. Useless things."

"Don't we all," said Wendy reflexively. *Lord help me, don't tell me she's going to friend me on Facebook.*

Wendy sat in her chair as more coffee burbled, looking out the window to the poplars and behind them empty fields under a bright sun. She didn't take out her phone. She got up and refilled her mug then sat there with her hands on the gingham tablecloth, looking out at the land, with the clacking of a keyboard and ticking of a clock coming from deeper in the house.

Twenty minutes later, Anna returned with a fresh sheet of paper.

Dear Conrad and Anna,

Wendy looked up. "Conrad?"

"My husband."

"He also knew about Henry?"

Anna grinned in a way Wendy couldn't interpret. "My husband didn't read English."

Given that it has been some time since we last saw each other at my father's funeral, it seemed prudent to write.

We have been blessed with good weather down here. The snow has mostly melted and we are readying ourselves for a busy year. Neighbours Peter Ungers are aging, and we are assisting their sons somewhat around their farm. May the Lord bless the whole effort.

My poor mother has not coped well with death. She cries often and other times will say, "Where's Dad?" The rest of our family has stayed in good spirits. God has served us well.

Ben has gone on to attend Mennonite Brethren Bible College in Winnipeg. Aganetha and I discussed this at length but we considered it appropriate in the end. We have our hopes with him. The rest of the children continue to live at home, though Peter has been spending a great amount of time with George and Helena Barkman's daughter.

I have experienced renewed faith in our Lord and Saviour Jesus as of late. For this I have the Holy Spirit to thank but also yourself, Anna. I am and will always be grateful for your patience and compassion, for your words and your listening. Your invocation of Romans 12 has been of great solace as of late, in matters of my own personal grief.

On a lighter topic, but not unrelatedly, I have reconsidered the matter of cameras. I have not told Aganetha of your influence, but should at some point you find yourself in need of her good graces ...

Through Christ all things are possible. May that the sins and misjudgements and many errors of my past be forgiven. May the Lord bless and keep your household, and please send news and announcements, etc.

With love,

Henry Reimer

Wendy looked up.

"That's it?" she said.

Anna stared back at her.

"You have a question," she finally said.

Wendy chose her words carefully. "I feel like I may be missing something."

"I wanted to share the point," Anna said, "where he overcame."

"Did you," said Wendy.

They stared at each other for some time until Anna said, "You perhaps would not have heard. About his friend who died around this time."

"No. His friend?"

"Yes. In the city."

When Ben saw Henry in the bar, Wendy thought. *He'd been looking for someone.* She was starting to lose patience. "When you say friend, do you mean lover?"

"I wouldn't. Know anything about that," Anna said.

"How'd the friend die?" said Wendy.

Anna said nothing.

"Was it AIDS? Oh, holy shit, did Henry die of AIDS too?"

"No!" Anna said. "Henry never got it." Then she realized what she said. "I mean ..."

"But his lover did," Wendy countered in sudden vindication. "Didn't he? And he couldn't share this. You know it, and he couldn't even name it in a letter he wrote to you."

Anna was quiet again.

"He must have been in such pain," Wendy said softly. "There are no words for this."

"Do not underestimate," Anna replied, looking at Wendy anew, with a strange, haunted look in her eyes. "The strength he had in the Lord."

"No," said Wendy. "I guess I can't do that, can I."

In the sunlight the two women sat at the table across from each other with the letter and their cups of cold coffee between them. At one point, Wendy folded the letter in half and then half again and put it into her bag.

Finally Wendy said, "I'm sorry. I did not mean to pry or get emotional."

"Oh," said Anna, the mischievous look returning. "That's alright. All old people. I suppose I. Myself. Decided some secrets had to come to an end." She got up. "I'll make those sandwiches I promised you."

As they were eating, Anna said, "Wendy, you seem like a young woman whose faith is particularly strong."

"I do?"

"You do," said Anna. "Many young people are all full of excitements and gadgets. I don't hear much of that from you. Tell me, what are you excited about? What's that new nifty gadget completely missing from your life?"

"Huh?" said Wendy. "Anna, I don't know what you're talking about. I have everything I want. I told you about my life. Does it sound bad? Why would I want anything else?"

"No," she said. "That's because you have your head on straight." Anna smiled warmly. "I get the impression you don't know Scripture too well. There is no shame in that."

"No ...?" Wendy said. Her voice cracked.

"As long as you open the Word of the Lord," said Anna. "You only need to open the book and let it guide you. God will have no anger if you cannot recite every book of the Word in order. You only need to open the book and let Jesus guide you. You told me you have what you want, didn't you? Your life has been blessed by God."

"Yes, it has," Wendy whispered. "Thank you. Thank Jesus you are here to say these things to me."

"There are hard things God asks of us," said Anna. "I'm sure Henry went through. Difficult times. But I don't know. It's just. My grandchildren, even my children. They always talk about happiness. My word, they spend so much time and energy chasing this—*idea* of happiness! But you're gone of this Earth before you know it."

"Sure," said Wendy genuinely. "That makes sense. Go on."

Suddenly Anna looked shy. "Oh—I'm eighty-four, you know. And it still feels like yesterday I was a little girl. I don't think unhappiness matters much in the end. My parents never said much about it. They had many difficult times, but they were also very blessed. I don't think they got cheated."

She looked heavy for a moment, staring at Wendy, then said, "I know you had this idea that Henry. Wanted to be a woman. Do you still think that?"

"I don't know," Wendy said, surprised. "Maybe. I wonder if there is a possibility if he had that desire, and he wasn't aware ..."

"There is much he didn't tell me," Anna said. "Won't presume to tell you that you are wrong."

Wendy finished her sandwich and looked at Anna with gratitude.

"Henry might even be a woman in heaven for all eternity," said Anna. "Perhaps that's his Godly reward for enduring on Earth. I don't think it's inappropriate to say that's a possibility. I don't think it's sinful or wrong to consider. If you feel sad for him, maybe you can think on that."

"Do you think that?"

"I think," she said eager and grey, "that it would be as presumptuous to assume that he is not, as it would be presumptuous to assume that he is."

It dawned on Wendy like a bird settling into a tree.

"You're gay."

"I've never touched a woman!" Anna said immediately.

They were both silent for a long time.

Then Anna talked again and her face was curled. "There's so much that is hard in this life that God asks us to weather, for reasons we cannot understand.

That's faith. Not judgment. I am very grateful for what I have been allowed in this life. I don't feel cheated for what I have let go for God. There are so many delights that I would like from the world. I can acknowledge that, but I don't have to feel cheated. Now, you must think I'm rather stupid," she continued flatly. "But you don't know what you're capable of. Maybe you haven't had to be strong yet. You don't have any more or less strength in your marrow than I do. You don't know you have so much strength. God has *so much* strength to give! And He will replenish you! And replenish you for every day you can wake up and lift your hands! You will think you can't possibly take another day, but God's power will flow through your bones for an ocean of time. He already does. I can tell that. I can see it in you. And I am perhaps presumptuous enough to guess that Jesus isn't as much your Saviour as you say, but if that's true, that doesn't matter here. Most people think you don't get things if you don't pray for them. But it is un-Christian to believe God must be asked in order to give. He makes His sun rise on the evil and on the good, sends rain on the righteous and the unrighteous!"

She looked at Wendy furiously. "You obviously think I am stupid. That I don't see anything. About you. Who you are. How you have lied to me. Though I have certainly been nothing but gracious!"

"I—"

"You have no excuse," Anna cut her off. "The choices you have made in life. All of you people. None of you are lazy. None of you are stupid. There is much you could have weathered. But you don't believe in yourself. And you're not sorry. I can tell right now: You are not sorry. You *learn* faith. Tulip. Marvin. Whatever you want to call it. God's fire is pure. You may have thought you needed to be a woman or die. Have you any idea what you can manage? You think you're weak. And because you think you're weak, you can't actually do anything. So you choose the easy, selfish path. Now, I'm telling you that."

—

"You'll want to take along the last of these sandwiches," Anna added as Wendy put on her coat and thanked her for her time. They were already wrapped tightly in Saran wrap and neatly placed in Tupperware. "Thank you for dropping by. Very nice to meet you."

24

There aren't any freeways in the city of Winnipeg. The few highways—what are called highways—are six-lane roads on the major streets with dozens of crossed-time stop lights. A light turns green and a block down, a light turns red. None of the streets have directionals, and nothing is numbered, but a dozen major roads assigned out of sequence, which have no meaning to a stranger, have markers like ROUTE 70 TURN HERE. The map is a collection of stitched, makeshift grids, dozens of blocks that follow an order, then hit a main road and scatter in all directions. In winter, the main roads are ice-capped with trails of snow streaming across faint, barely visible lines. Every minor street is covered in bumpy intractable white-grey ice. But there aren't any freeways. There is no fast way in or out. The closest thing is the Perimeter. The circle that barely touches the city. Ben would say, "You know, in most places they built highways to get you *into* town faster. Here we built one so everyone else could go *around* it."

25

When Wendy got home, she crawled into bed and napped for three hours. When she woke up, it was dark.

She got dressed after Raina knocked on her door. They went to Cousin's where she opened a tab, ordered shots, then a double, and shuttled the thought of money into a blank spot in her mind.

"How was your trip?" said Lila, who'd met them there.

Wendy stared straight ahead. "Um."

"Did that woman turn out to suck?" said Aileen.

"I—"

"We're here for you if you want to talk, Wendy-burger," said Raina.

"Well—so—"

They waited.

"I don't think I can talk about this," Wendy eventually said to her friends. "I'm still processing it. It was terrible. I think I'm really sad. I can't talk about her right now. I don't know what I think."

There was silence. The others murmured. Somebody coughed.

"How's your father's rickshaw service, Wendy?" said Raina.

"Oh, that fuckin' guy!" Wendy hollered, grateful to boomerang the conversation. "Motherfucker thinks he's gonna be a millionaire pulling his goddamn bicycles around."

"He sounds like quite an adventurer," said Aileen.

Wendy put her hand on Aileen's face, the lovely freckled girl's face. "He's a fuckin' psychopath," she said.

"Your dad rules ..." Lila hiccupped like a mouse.

"He's a good guy, he's a good guy," Wendy said. "He's a good dude, he did his best."

Aileen kissed Wendy on the top of her head.

"Oh my God. Surrounded by lesbians, man."

Raina smirked. "I logged my time on such matters yesterday, Lila."

"Jesus *CHRIST!*"

"I'm not a lesbian," Wendy slurred.

"You are!" said Lila. "I've known you longer than anyone. The only reason you fuck dudes is that you finished going through every carpet-muncher in this city five years ago!"

Wendy turned her head to look at Lila.

Lila was grinning like a chipmunk. "I'm not wrong."

"Fug off," said Wendy. The shots were hitting.

"This polite Canada I kept hearing about," said Aileen.

"My dear," said Raina, "you will likely find that I, the American, am by far the most polite of this bunch."

"Right."

"Yeah, you haven't even seen a fuckin' cabin or, like, a bear," Wendy said, slouched over in her chair.

"I have seen concrete and dirt and ice."

"*Canada*," spat Lila.

Wendy soon finished her drink and came back with another and also bought everyone shots. They cheered, and Wendy announced, "I feel better."

"Woooo!" said Raina, lifting her hands up.

"You're cute," said Wendy. Raina blushed.

"You know what I saw today for the first time?" Lila said. "The COGIATI."

Wendy and Raina exploded in separate pitches of "*Nooo!*"

"What's the COGIATI?" said Aileen.

"It is—" said Wendy.

"The worst ..." Raina trailed off.

"The worst what?" said Aileen.

"Maybe just 'the worst,'" said Wendy.

"Very possibly," said Raina.

"Seriously, what's this fucking thing?" said Aileen.

"It's like an online test some trans woman made in the nineties," said Lila, "where you answer all these multiple-choice questions about yourself and then it tells you whether you're a transsexual or not."

"And the questions are so ..." Wendy said.

"Fucking ridiculous!" said Lila. "It like, asks if you're good at math and how you would feel if you were in a meeting with all men and the boss says everyone has to hug."

"You're kidding me," said Aileen.

"That's literally a question."

"I can't believe it's still up there," said Wendy.

"I remember it looking like a GeoCities site," said Raina.

"It's still up there, and it ain't on GeoCities, man," said Lila. "Also the backgrounds are all, like, pink clouds." She shivered. "It was fucking creepy, like, it reminded me of all that shit from when I first came out, you know? You know what I kept thinking of? It kept reminding me how they dressed up the woman in *Transamerica*."

"I remember that," said Wendy.

"Like a bunch of frilly pink nonsense, that kind of thing?" said Aileen.

"Nice neat middle-aged white ladies who fretted about their fuckin' handbags, and if you weren't dead thirsty for a vag then you weren't a real woman," said Lila. "I dunno if that's Miss COGIATI's experience or whatever, but, like, you know. When I was a teenager, that's what I thought being trans was. That's why I was a gay boy until my mid-twenties."

Everyone nodded, murmured understanding. "I wonder," said Wendy, "how much that shit has hurt us in ways we don't understand. I like to think I'm over all that stuff."

"I took it," said Raina. "Over a decade ago. It told me I wasn't a woman and I believed it." She was briefly silent, then said, "What brought you to the COGIATI anyway?"

"There was this long thread of stuff on Twitter with all these girls making fun of it," said Lila. "I didn't know what it was so I Googled it."

"You have a Twitter?" said Raina.

"After Sophie died," said Lila.

"Ah."

"So did you take it?" said Wendy. "Do you know if you're trans or not?"

Lila laughed. "I did, like, five questions."

Aileen showed her phone. "Found it."

"Noooo!" Raina wailed in mock sorrow. "Don't do it!"

"*Describe your relationship with mathematics*—wow, you weren't fucking around."

"Told you."

"*You get a phone call from somebody you met for the first time a few days ago. How easy is it for you to remember who they are by the sound of their voice?* What the ever-loving shit?" said Aileen. "And this was written by a trans woman? And she still has it up?"

"I'd imagine," said Raina, "that she still thinks it helps people. That old guard's still around."

"I guess, hey," said Lila.

"Kinda want to hate-take this," said Aileen, still scrolling.

"Don't," said Raina. "It's not good for you. Even if you know it's silly."

"She's right," said Lila.

"I always think," said Raina, "how desperate this woman probably felt when she was writing it, how much she must have thought she was doing the right thing, how she was helping the rest of us. What her psychiatrists high on John Money must have screwed into her brain. There wasn't anything else for her, either."

"Yeah," said Wendy.

"Still, though. Do you know even Andrea James wrote a hate-on for the COGIATI?"

"Holy shit, you're kidding," said Wendy.

"Who's Andrea James?" said Aileen and all the others immediately screamed.

Hours later, they stumbled home and crossed Portage, the four of them laughing and leaning on one another. A man on the corner grimaced and shook his head, and a spit-fused "fuuuck youu" left Wendy's mouth but no one heard it.

Wendy's brain was a hunk of flesh lurching two seconds in front of her body.

They clattered up the stairs, Raina saying, "Heavens, fuck, I never even swear let alone drink this *fuck*ing much," and Wendy took down a bottle of Raina's whisky and said, "M' dear, may I be so bold?" and Raina said, "Oh, *I would*."

She made expert sours and poured the drinks and toasted everyone home again. They all went up to the living room and put on stupid YouTube clips that Wendy could barely even make out. They laughed and smoked cigarettes with the windows cracked open and The xx playing off somebody's phone, making jokes as Wendy's vision faded and flickered around the edges and their voices test-patterned around her brain. Wendy snuggled under the covers next to Aileen's beautiful warm body as the others chatted, and she drifted in and out of sleep, her cheek a square on the tattoo lines on Aileen's shoulder. She drooled a bit on Aileen's side. Gross.

Wendy lurched up, embarrassed, kissed Aileen goodnight, told her to come down when she was ready. Raina snickered, and Lila said, "Goodnight dykes. Goodnight ... trikes."

"You don't even make sense ... pike!" said Wendy. Lila laughed, and one of Wendy's last thoughts as she moved downstairs was that she felt younger, much younger, like she had in certain fleeting moments when she'd hung out with Sophie, and she let this thought settle and put itself at rest, and she took a nice, long, real, last deep slug of the whisky before changing into her nightgown, laying her body between her blankets, and letting herself drift further.

When she woke, Aileen was sitting beside her with her hoodie on. Wendy moaned and twisted herself in the blankets. She felt cozy and unable to sit up. She stuck a hand out into the cold air to wave. It took effort. *Worthwhile* effort.

"You're up," said Aileen.

"No-o-o-ope." Wendy snuggled her body around the other girl's.

"Cuddly, aren't you."

"Last night," Wendy said into Aileen's ribs, "was fun."

Aileen gave out a short bark. "You don't remember what happened when I came down then, do you."

"H-u-u-uh?"

"Bloody hell."

Wendy realized Aileen hadn't been responding to her touch.

"When I came down," she continued, "you were sitting on the bed with your arms crossed around your knees. You told me to hit you. I didn't do it, of course. You said, 'Hit me, hit me, hit me.' You told me to restrain you. You got up in my face and pushed me and said, 'Come on, hold me back.' You were trying to imitate my accent too, by the way. You looked bloody terrifying. I got a lock on you and you tried to wriggle out. You have a bump on your head?"

Wendy realized an ache on the back of her skull. "Um. I. Think," she said. Her head was literally swimming and it was physically difficult to speak. She was trying very hard to respond in a proper manner.

"Yeah, you bashed your head nasty on your dresser while you were struggling. You almost got away once, you were trying to make a run for the door. Said you were going outside. Let's see what else. You said, 'You think you're so tough, you think you're soooo, so tough. Tough Aileen, tough fucking Aileen.' You were blabbering on bobbins about that for a while. I got you into the bed so you couldn't move. Raina and Lila came down to see what was going on. Raina said—I'll quote her, 'Wendy just gets like that sometimes.' Told me to shout at her if you got out of hand. You struggled and told me to hit you again and you told me I was a cunt. Then you were crying. You said you wanted to die. You said you wanted to die more than a few times. You said you wanted to die in a very scary and repeated manner, Wendy. And I sat and held you while you blubbered until you went to sleep."

Aileen stood up, and it seemed she would say something else. Like she had one more fact that was desperately vital for Wendy to hear out loud.

Wendy tried to form an apology. Her head fell forward and she got out a word that sounded like *Bohh*.

Finally Aileen said, "Been waiting for you to wake up for a while."

Wendy tried to respond again, but it was hard, it was extremely difficult for her to focus, to form words in her brain and look at the other girl and make those words into sounds. Her head bobbed again. All she could see was a mat of her knotted hair.

Aileen shook her head. "I've got things to do." Then she left. Wendy heard the scuffling noises of a jacket and boots downstairs and then the door open and the wind and the door shut.

Hours later, her phone rang and woke her up. She scrabbled to it with a groan. *No, I don't want to, whatever, I don't care if it's my favourite client, and he's got a million dollars—*

It was Michael.

Right. They were doing that today.

"Hey," she rolled over. Her head was still buzzing. "Yeah, I'm still in," she said, her hand mushing her cheek. "I'll be right down. No, I'm ready, for real. Yeah, down in one sec."

She bounced up and threw on a dress then set a timer for five minutes. In front of the bathroom mirror, she scrubbed and brushed and lined until the timer went off. She looked okay. Nice.

"So where we going?" she said in Michael's car, a nice grey sedan with food wrappers on the floor.

"Rae and Jerry's."

"Rae and Jerry's!" she hooted. "Alright."

"You been? We're going to the bar."

"I've never been to the bar. My dad took me a few times when I was in high school. Apparently, he took my mom there on one of their first dates."

"Good man," said Michael.

"Yeah, and it was always such a *big deal*, you know; put on something nice, we're going to *Rae and Jerry's*."

"It's a good spot, man."

"I thought it was so elegant back then, like those waiters, with the bow ties ..."

"Same waiters probably still working there." Michael gunned it down Maryland and turned onto Portage. "They probably don't let them out."

"Live in the basement," said Wendy.

"Feed them cockroaches," said Michael.

"Ew!"

"Oh, sure," he bugged his eyes out and juggled his hands in the air. "Make a joke about eating bugs and *I'm* the asshole. Waiters living in the basement, though, that's just hilarious, good clean fun."

Wendy giggled. "I'll have you know I'm a *very* delicate soul."

When they got out of the parking lot, Wendy took out her ponytail and let her hair spill down over the collar and front of her coat. It was a clear night and the moon was silver and blue against the black.

"That's new, eh?" Michael said. "The coat."

"Yeah," said Wendy, startled. She'd just gotten it last week, telling herself it was to be more pro for work. It was sexy but subdued, black and snug, lined with wool, and tied with a belt.

"Looks good on you. It's pretty," he said, holding open the door.

They entered the restaurant. Wendy hadn't been here for over a decade—well, damn. Since she was a boy. There were the same fake candle lamps, white tablecloths, dark wood panelling, red vinyl chairs and booths, and paintings of mountains on the walls. A waitress in a white shirt and red bow tie went by with a steak. Michael ducked through a wooden door on the left. "In here," he said.

The bar had darker, more pronounced and spaced panelling, swivel chairs of the same red vinyl, round Formica tables with no cloth, jazz on the speakers, the fake candle lamps turned into boxy lights, and a long bar with glass and racks of wine. Michael shrugged off his coat. "I maintain that if the Coen brothers ever shoot a movie in Winnipeg, they'd have to do it here."

Wendy laughed. "You never told me you were funny."

"Oh, fuck off!" He had a horse-y laugh. "See, I'm not your boss much longer, so I can say all sorts of shit to you now. What you want to drink?"

"Rum and Diet Coke."

"You got it. What kinda rum?"

"Oh. Um, I don't know."

"They got everything, just say it."

"Shit."

"Captain? Kraken?"

"I don't know—Kraken. Sure. Kraken's good."

Michael waved the waitress down. She knew him.

"You come here often?" Wendy said.

"I don't live too far."

"Oh yeah, you're in, like, western Wolseley-ish right?"

"Not for long."

"Huh?"

"You know I'm getting divorced."

"No, I didn't know that."

"Fuck me, thought I told everyone. Well, Wendy, I'm getting divorced."

"Son of a bitch," said Wendy steadily. "I'm so sorry."

"Yeah," he said. "Lose the wife, lose a job—pretty cool Christmas, huh?"

"That's awful."

"Eh, the job I'll be fine on. I've already got a promise for some interviews. No one's gonna hire a manager during Christmas season, but I'll find something before the end of winter."

Their drinks came. "Well, I guess we should switch to whisky after this, then," said Wendy.

"A whisky girl," said Michael. "Shoulda known you were a whisky girl. Let's get some appies. Chicken fingers?"

They got in the car around eleven as the bar was closing down. He ran through a close yellow on Portage. "Guess I didn't notice that," he said. "I'm a little bit drunk."

She laughed. "It's cool."

"I had fun with you, Wendy, I had *fun.* You are *cool.* I think you've been holding out on how *cool* you are. We got two more weeks together at least, eh?"

"At least," she said.

Michael's brown eyes were pure and smiling.

"At least, yes."

They were silent for a short while as she sat in his car. Then she leaned over and hugged him. "Goodnight, Michael. I'll see you in a couple days."

He gave her a quick peck on the neck. "Hey ... maybe I should walk you to your door?"

It was so cute. He was a goofball and nearly two decades older than her but he had a good heart, she'd never had reason to doubt. And still didn't.

He really was the nicest, purest guy to be interested in her, in a certain sense. *When was the last time a guy was actually* interested *in me? Let alone had an idea of the person I actually am? Michael may not know all about me, but he knows I'm a transsexual and he knows I'm a drunk and—well—I've spent more hours around him than almost anyone else in the last two years. He's seen me snarling and mouthing off to customers and co-workers alike, seen me slouching in to the store hungover more times than I could count—and Michael has always been good to me, always, when I've deserved good and when I haven't. Always.*

Oh, what am I thinking? He just wants to get laid! Maybe suck the dick he doesn't know I don't have. Nice fantasy, tranny-brain.

"It's cold," she slurred. "But maybe next week we could do this again? Or maybe, I don't know, Christmas!?"

She felt stupid but open and honest, and Michael looked confused but hopeful.

Wendy got out of the car and waved. "I'll see you at work Sunday! I'll pick the bar next time!" Michael laughed then and gave her a thumbs-up. She went up the stairs, turned off her phone, and hopped into bed.

It all made her think again about how the lady pills had made her like boys. Or maybe it wasn't the hormones at all. Or any such mystical thing. She had always loved boys, had tried to make out with boys in high school, but it just didn't work. And maybe that made sense—how could she like their touch when her body was so wrong? Yes, there was a part of Wendy that needed validation from men, always, but millions of cis women needed that too, didn't they?

Did she want to fuck Michael, though? Would that be *fun?* She tried to remember the last time sex with a boy had actually been fun. Did she even like sex any more? With anyone?

It was all a muddle. Boys, work, her dreams, girls, the chopped-up clit buried in her pussy. She had gone into the laundromat the other day. Taj and his dad were both there, and the three of them chatted like pleasant neighbours. *I almost had sex with your son, but he was disgusted by my body* thought Wendy as the dad talked about an upcoming snowstorm, about how he wanted to expand and put a coffee shop next door to the laundromat.

For years now, sex kept changing on her. Her own desire felt milky, like silt, something in a river, something she could see until she tried to hold it and make it function, and it ran through her fingers into nothing.

Well, not just sex even.

What did she want from her life, exactly?

Wendy was thirty years old. Her life had kinda never really changed. Sure, she transitioned at twenty-two, she was on her second stint as a hooker, but—honestly? Her adult life at thirty looked a lot like it had at nineteen. She worked a lot and drank too much and hung out with her dad. As much as her living sitches had varied, she still lived within the same five square miles she'd lived in since birth—never south of Corydon or north of Ellice, save that one disastrous year at U of M.

Now, this morning, smoking in her fluffy slippers and moon-blue nightgown, air snaking into her window, this question turned itself around in her mind.

What *about* the future?

What, she was going to live forever?

Did she know any trans girls older than her, besides Dex and that old lady at the support group? If Wendy made it to sixty, that'd be alright, no?

So, okay, what if her life was half over?

What did that feel like? Why did this thought not bother her?

Wendy wasn't happy, but she was moderately stable, and her life was rich with drinks and roommates and stupid hot boys and girls and her fun dumbass dad. She had so much good; she really was blessed. Should she *want* her life to change? What would that look like? What did life satisfaction look like for someone like her? Was she supposed to look for a retail job again and quit hooking? Ask Michael to help her score a manager gig somewhere? Try school again, disastrous as the first time was?

Go back to church?

Quit drinking?

Move away?

Was any of that going to make her happier?

And if Anna had been a woman Wendy could talk to and be honest with, what would she have said? If Anna could have joined her wisdom to Wendy's truths, what would Anna have to tell her? And what if that trip hadn't hurt Wendy; what if Wendy had left the older woman's house full of warmth and unpoisoned insight? What if, instead of feeling an immediately sealed-off devastation to Anna's anger and bitterness, she could pick up the phone right now and think about Anna's words and repeat them back to her and ask Anna more about what they meant. *It is un-Christian to believe God must be asked in order to give. I don't think unhappiness matters much, in the end.*

And what about Sophie.

Sophie's life had included an infinite whiplash of much bigger changes than Wendy'd ever dealt with. Sophie had moved heaven and earth to improve her life many times—and she was dead.

Wendy wasn't as strong as Sophie. That's how Wendy felt. But there was a difference between strength and resilience. Though Sophie had been resilient too. That was true. It was.

No. She wasn't fucking stupid. She was a pissy, alcoholic tranny hooker, for better and for worse, and probably always would be. She would die too soon or late in life, depending on your point of view. She would probably die alone. When Wendy thought coldly and rationally about her death, she mostly just hoped she'd go after her dad. She felt raw thinking about Ben having to bury her.

What, she thought broodingly now. Her manager's kindness and affection already evaporated into resurgent anger. Like Michael would give a shit about her? Like he was not going to end up like every other fucking asshole who fucked her?

What she knew of Henry, her grandfather, had been peaceful and deep, a pebble rippling in a lake. Had he been miserable? Had his life been bad or unhappy? He would probably say no. Anna would say no. Wendy assumed they were wrong. How old had he been when he died?

67.

Had it not been a blessed thing he'd made it that far?

And Anna.

Anna was doubtless telling the truth. She probably didn't feel cheated, but thought of herself as sick. The way you know that, if you move your leg a certain way, it will hurt. Or if you don't believe in God and follow His Word, you'll go to hell. It wasn't a matter of deserving; it was like how secular people thought about physics: If you fall off a cliff, you'll die, whether you deserve to or not. Wendy didn't feel cheated either.

Except—what would Henry's life have been like had he not chosen isolation? Did he have a choice?

Seven weeks ago, Wendy had said to her friends, "Henry didn't have a choice!" as if she'd been arguing with some imaginary snot-nosed kid on the Internet, as opposed to ranting to the patient, real women in front of her. Henry had choices that Wendy couldn't comprehend, but he did have choices and he believed in them wholeheartedly. All the Mennonites around him likely would have approved. *Maybe our God wasn't the lie*, Wendy suddenly thought about her people. *Maybe our isolation was the lie.*

After her Saturday shift at the store the next day, she had a call to the Ramada by the airport. A guy who wanted her face down with her legs straight out and locked together as he fucked her ass. "I'm a top, but I like shemales, I dunno why," he mused as she took off her boots. He took a long time to come and looked whimpering and childish as she left.

The elevators opened by the front desk; the night clerks glared when they saw her. Wendy smirked at them and readied a smoke.

Ernie'd texted her again: *Giiiirl Bojack Horseman you wanna come over!!*

It was midnight.

She also had a text from Raina: *I might have found a house. Two bedrooms,*

850 a month. Can you come see it with me tomorrow morning?

You bet

Then, waiting for the cab to turn onto Wellington, she saw white glittering lights in the driver's side mirror. It was the downtown skyline! All the way from out here. She could see all the way down to Portage and Main? She could! God! The buildings were bigger and more majestic than she'd ever noticed. They glowed, huge and luminous and gorgeous.

Then her eyes adjusted. They weren't buildings. They were Christmas trees. Lined up on the hotel side of the boulevard. Twinkling.

Back home, she counted up her money and looked in the envelope she kept hidden in her room. She'd pocketed away well over a thou in just a few weeks. And the now-sizable paycheques from the store were going straight into a savings account. She could ride out the rest of the winter. January and February business was always fall-off-a-cliff dead, and March was barely better. The boys didn't really come back until the thaw of April, and she wouldn't be a new thing around anymore by that time.

It was a strange phenomenon, though, the January thing. Business was always fine all through December, even though it was cold then too. Wendy didn't really get it. Although, as Sophie had once observed dryly, "No one makes a New Year's Resolution to see more prostitutes."

Fucking—Sophie—

In her bathroom, sipping the last from a mickey, Wendy stood in front of the mirror in her bra and underwear. It was a few hours till dawn. There was light from the street shining in from the window, the sound of the tap dripping, and the garbage truck beeping some houses away. She'd have only a few hours to sleep before her Sunday shift.

Her hair was almost down to her waist these days. The whites of her eyes were jaundiced and sallow, and her cheeks were mottled and dry. She touched the left side of her jaw, which had begun to hurt recently, a half-stabbing, half-aching pain toward the back. She moved it around and felt the gums through her skin. She knew she shouldn't be smoking again. But.

"Hello! Message for ... Tulip. I thought it was very. Nice to have you out up here. Hope you had a good visit too and that you might want to come again. Sometime." Anna coughed. "I haven't been." She coughed again, multiple times, enough for Wendy to think, *Oh, sweet Lord don't tell me she's*—and then, "*Excuse* me! I haven't been feeling too well lately. Troubles. Well. I'll hear back from you. The number's the same. Goodbye now."

A long silence with no scuffle or a click and then, "Oh, I. There was something I forgot to tell you. Last time you were here. Philippians Chapter 2, verses 12 through 18. Those were also. Meaningful verses to Henry. Thought you'd want to know that too. Anyway. I hope you've been having a. Good week. Tulip. We'll talk to you again soon. As we move closer to Christmas! Christmas is coming soon."

The place Raina found, the two-bedroom for $850 a month, was a tiny aging dollhouse of a building deep in the West End, on a short street between a school and a park by the Arlington Bridge and the rail yards. It had an unfinished basement, two bedrooms upstairs, a cozy kitchen that took up most of the main floor, and a huge backyard where the old man who owned it smoked with a hardened stare into nothing.

Wendy and Raina conferred in the kitchen for only five minutes. "I feel like I'm gonna grow old here," Wendy said. "I don't want to move again for a long time."

"Oh?" Raina said. "This feels permanent to you?"

"That was easy," said Wendy in the cab back.

These choices were happening to her so quickly.

Raina stared out the window. "I'll be glad for the change of environments, Wendy-burger, I cannot lie. *I* am getting old."

"Promise I'll only ask this once, lady. What do you need from me now?"

"Keep me company through this miserable winter," said Raina.

Wendy reached for her hand, and the two women looked out opposite windows. The sun was setting and the houses and snow were turning orange and white-blue.

"Genevieve and I are on the rocks. I don't want to talk about it," Raina added.

"I'm sorry."

They were silent a while, then Wendy said, "What are you doing for Christmas?"

"Putting my worldly possessions in boxes, it seems."

"You're not going to New York?" Raina usually went south for at least a few days during Christmas to a big family thing on her mom's side in the Bronx. She would send Wendy pictures of herself buried under a sea of little cousins.

"Not this time," said Raina. "I don't mean to be bleak, Wendy, but I'm not much up for cavorting around lately. Fun as our night at Cousin's was."

"I understand. Do you want to come out to the country with my dad? I don't know what we're doing this year with my grandma gone, but we'll be out there and you'd be welcome."

"Thanks for that." Raina squeezed Wendy's hand. "Pretty girl." They were quiet, then Raina added, "I might. Ask me later."

"I get it."

"Do you? You always seem to thrive so much on social interaction. Not that I'm a hermit, but you're even less so."

Eventually I gotta tell her I'm ho'ing again, Wendy thought. *If she hasn't figured it out already.* She was very considerately feigning ignorance if so.

Hey! Her dad texted the next day at the store. *Granite Curling Club with the buddies tonight come meet me.*

Wendy walked up to the bar on the second floor and downed a beer as she and her dad watched bozos throw rocks down on the ice.

"The rickshaws are coming in April, girl!" Ben said. "This is happening. Block off your summer."

Something in her stirred and had enough.

"Dad, did anyone ever think Opa was gay?"

"Oh, yeah! Well, there were rumours," said Ben.

"Rumours," said Wendy.

"People always thought he was soft. I dunno why, lotta fuckin' Menno guys in his generation were kind of pantywaists," he said. "Some of them. Me and my brothers, we grew up brawling; it was different for us, I dunno why."

"Mmm."

"My day was just different," he said. "You would have never survived, you don't know how good you have it."

"I guess."

"It's like Louis C.K. says, though, when I was growin' up, the word 'faggot' just meant, you know, being a faggot."

"Huh?" said Wendy. "What are you talking about?"

"I don't fuckin' know," he laughed. "I'm blasted."

"Well, sometimes I wonder if, like, maybe your dad was like me!" she said, dazzling and charming. "Maybe? Is that crazy to think about?"

"Wha, you think my dad was a *girl!*" Ben nearly choked he was laughing so hard. "Well, shit, maybe he was! There's weirder things! I could have a *son* who's a girl! Oh, wait!" He laughed some more, his face getting redder and redder. He punched her in the shoulder with the most loving, happiest face she'd ever seen. "Guess I got you on that one, don't I?" he said. Wendy heard herself giggle in response.

The music changed, and Wendy's face suddenly brightened. "This song!" she said.

"This song?" The lines in Ben's face were deep, but when he didn't know something he suddenly looked worried, younger, like a confused teenage boy. When the singer began, it clicked. "This is Lou Reed!"

"Yeah!" said Wendy. "'Coney Island Baby.' You know it?"

"Sure. That's a great album."

"It's about his girlfriend Rachel," said Wendy. "She was trans. Lou wrote it for her. This whole album is about her."

"Huh," he said. For a second there was some wonder in his eyes, and Wendy allowed herself to drink in the idea that he, too, could feel what it meant to her. "Crazy," he said. "Who knew he was into that shit too? The Velvet Underground was one of the greats, you know, the *greats*."

"I know," said Wendy.

"Nah, you don't know," her dad mused. "You can't try to tell someone what the seventies was like. Some things you just can't understand. Which is fine. *Hey!*" he said jovially, placing his palm over the beer that had just come for Wendy. "How many? You counting?"

"Two," Wendy said instantly.

"Two right now or two all day?" he replied.

"Both," she said. She had a mickey in her bag with two slugs pulled out of it.

"Good man," he said, uncovering his hand. "Aw, shit, sorry—"

"It's fine."

"It's just habit, you know."

"All good, Dad."

There'd been a day ... when Wendy was a teenager. She had short brown hair and wore a yellow T-shirt and loose blue jeans and white Reeboks. She looked like a boy and she called herself a boy and she thought of herself as a boy. She had no words or world that made sense of her as a girl—so she didn't think of herself that way. It was May and the sun was bright and summery and fresh and the wind smelled like grass. She bought a bottle of Diet Coke at the corner store and rode her bike to the Forks, steering with one hand and drinking the Coke with the other. She sat on the curve of a little rise that overlooked the skating rink, where some teenagers were kicking around a ball. Beyond them, the river, slow and gentle and brown. She breathed in and she felt perfect. She had a vision of herself then from behind. With long, long hair, and the line of a bra strap under her shirt. Long, long, long hair, that blocked off her face, went down to her jeans. This vision of herself was pure. She breathed, shut her eyes, and for a brief moment had no self-awareness or worry or shame. When she opened her eyes again, one of the girl teenagers was standing off to the side, looking at the boys who were kicking the ball.

The next day, Wendy bought two king cans and fell asleep at two in the afternoon after a half-shift at work—Michael had said, "You're tired, we're overstaffed, you've been working too hard. Go home. I'll make up your hours some way. Go take care of yourself. I'm telling you to go home, Wendy. I'll check up on you later."

As she slept, she dreamed of a man creaking up the stairs and slowly opening the door to her room and enveloping her in a cloud. She woke up—but couldn't move. She screamed "Help!" with all of her might, but her muscles wouldn't move. She couldn't fucking move! With a whisper of a "help ..." gasping from her lips, she woke up for real. Her bladder was throbbing, and her phone was ringing. Some guy staying at the Fort Garry was about to get back from work and badly wanted her ass.

But before that dream with the man creaking up the stairs, Wendy dreamed of herself and Henry. They were sitting on a couch, and Henry was swaddled in long billowy clothing. Henry had a baby in her arms, and its face leaned against Henry's chest. Her hair was thinning and grey like it'd always been when Wendy was a kid, but her fingers were long and smooth and lotioned. The lawn outside was growing fast, and someone needed to cut it. Everyone else was yelling and there was chaos and smoke everywhere, but Henry just stayed there and smiled at Wendy, and her smile got bigger and bigger with joy pouring out of her face, and as the couch grew scratchy and the air under it whirled and screamed, Henry pulled her feet onto the couch with the baby still in both arms and leaned forward on her knees in her long billowy clothing looking at Wendy, and she laughed with her radiant, pure lit-up smile getting bigger and bigger until both of their faces were almost touching with light light light shining from all of Henry's soft lotioned body, until they were so close, Henry now silent and smiling at Wendy deep and big and light, and neither of them moved. Wendy woke up thrashing and sitting up in the same motion with her eyes scanning every part of the room and her heart beating fast.

It was four o'clock and the sun was streaking its last blues and greens and oranges across the snow and the ice and the darkening sky. Wendy cracked open the second king can as she walked down to the river. If she made this call, she'd be happy. If it was good, she'd turn her phone off for the night and go out and drink. She would shut her fucking phone off and run out into the city and light up the sky. She put on her headphones and listened to that song "Violet" again. She put it on repeat.

But she wished she hadn't bought the king cans. The mickey from yesterday being long gone. Her love, her real true love, was cold hard alcohol mixed with something light, like diet pop or water. There was nothing else that felt so clean in her body.

26

The guy at the Hotel Fort Garry was staying on the sixth floor. Wendy hadn't been in here for some time. She knew friends who partied here, and once there'd been a wedding. The literal Queen had stayed here once, but somehow the rooms just never got that expensive. They weren't cheap either, but regular people still stayed here.

She walked through the quiet hall past an open staircase, past trays of silverware and newspapers in front of doors. She had a long thin hoodie under her coat and under that, a dark-blue, full-length nightie, a thing that, were it summer, could pass as sexy street clothes.

The man at the end of the hall who'd called her opened his door and ushered her into a tiny room with beautiful patterned wallpaper, a window facing an airshaft, and a lush queen bed. The man looked mid-fifties, with intense five o'clock shadow, a T-shirt, boxer shorts, and an Australian accent.

"Holly," he said, like she was greeting him at a job interview.

"Mmm," he said after he kissed her, as if he was sampling food.

The cash was lying on the chair. He picked it up and gave it to her. She stuffed it away in a zippered pocket. He unscrewed a full bottle of white wine and offered her some from a plastic cup. He sipped it twice before undressing her quickly, methodically, kissing her, and grabbing her tits. He turned out to be one of those who didn't really like to have his dick sucked but went along with it for a minute or two before guiding her head up and matter-of-factly saying, "Get a condom." He fucked her ass as she lay on her back, looking at her with wild eyes, with her legs in his arms like a machine. He turned out to be one of those men who wanted to fuck for a while before coming. Wendy studied a spot on the wall and noticed his breathing, focused face.

After he came, she finished the wine in bed as he flushed the condom down the toilet. Unless they were true creeps, sometimes Wendy liked to linger for just a minute after they finished. Especially in hotels. A lot of them liked that kind of thing anyway.

"Oh. Well, would you like more wine?" he laughed, seeing her empty cup. He re-filled it and lay down next to her, naked. He put his free arm around her, and she put her head on his shoulder.

"So," said Wendy. "You're here for work, or ...?"

"Yes, indeed, ma'am! Five days I've been here, and I'm leaving tomorrow. You were my reward for a hard week." He winked at her and squeezed her shoulder. She giggled.

"What do you do? If you want to tell me."

"I work for a tech firm. We're opening a new branch here."

"You're opening your Canadian branch here," Wendy said, deadpan. "Seriously."

"It's our second. We already got one in Toronto," said the man. "We were going to do Vancouver, but, fuck, it's expensive out there."

"Wow." Wendy swirled her wine in the little plastic cup. "A tech firm, hey?"

"This is what everyone's gonna do now," said the man. "It's like how factory jobs used to be," he said. "I trained as a typesetter. I trained before computers. You know what that is?"

"I do," said Wendy. The half hour was almost up. She reached for one more little cup of wine.

What kind of world does the core of your brain expect that you, you personally, get to live in? Wendy wanted to be loved. However easily she might have abandoned or ruined her prospects, Wendy did still believe she would have love.

By the elevators in front of the open staircase, Wendy looked through the window expecting a storm, but it had stopped snowing. Under an arch she could see a parking lot and an old gilded apartment building across the way. The street was pristine and quiet and footprint-less.

She walked through the reflecting marble lobby. The roads outside were empty sheets of blue and white, ice stretching far, far away, looking like outer space. She put on her headphones as she walked through the revolving doors into the night. She felt okay about where her life was headed.

Acknowledgments

Thank you to all the friends who read this story and talked to me about it, full names this time: Torrey Peters, Jeanne Thornton, Marika Prokosh, Maeve Devine, Meredith Russo, Cam Scott, Kate Friggle, Zoey Leigh Peterson, Calvin Gimpelevich, Gwen Benaway, Morgan M Page, John Toews, and Sherri Klassen—special thanks to Cat Fitzpatrick and Daniel Shank Cruz, who gave more of their time to this book than a friend could ever ask for.

To the Arsenal folks: Brian Lam, Cynara Geissler, Susan Safyan (blessings on all your future endeavours with your ever-watchful eye!), Robert Ballantyne, Shirarose Wilensky, and Oliver McPartlin, thank you. I'm humbled and proud, if that's a possible combo, to say I'm published with you.

Thanks to the Winnipeg Arts Council, who provided funding in this book's genesis.

Thanks to Terry Loewen and my mom for Plautdietsch advisories and other insights from inside the house. Thanks to Nic Bravo for a joke or two. An enormous thank you to Shawn Syms, for so many reasons. And the book Wendy remembers in Chapter 20 is Lorrie Moore's *Anagrams*. To every Mennonite who has been good when there are costs. Bless you. To the housemates who shared space as I wrote this, all I can say is thanks for putting up with my silly ass ... Jillian, Kendra, Brittany, Sharla, Kiki, and most of all Sybil, who knows more than anyone.

CASEY PLETT is the author of the short story collection *A Safe Girl to Love* and co-editor of the anthology *Meanwhile, Elsewhere: Science Fiction and Fantasy from Transgender Writers*. She wrote a column on transitioning for *McSweeney's Internet Tendency* and her essays and reviews have appeared in *The New York Times, Maclean's, The Walrus, Plenitude*, the *Winnipeg Free Press*, and other publications. She is the winner of a Lambda Literary Award for Best Transgender Fiction and received an Honour of Distinction from The Writers' Trust of Canada's Dayne Ogilvie Prize for LGBTQ Emerging Writers. She lives in Windsor, Ontario.